BY
CAIO
NANDO
ABREU

Dulce Veiga?

AUSTIN UNIVERSITY OF TEXAS PRESS

Texas Pan American Series

Obra publicada com o apoio do Ministério da Cultura do Brasil/Fundação Biblioteca Nacional/Departamento Nacional do Livro

This book was published with the support of the Ministry of Culture of Brazil/National Library Foundation/National Book Division

Printed in the United States of America

First edition, 2000

∞ The paper used in this book meets the minimum requirements of ANSI/NISO Z39.48-1992 (R1997) (Permanence of Paper).

Library of Congress Cataloging-in-Publication Data

Abreu, Caio Fernando.
[Onde andará Dulce Veiga? English]
Whatever happened to Dulce Veiga? : a B-novel / Caio Fernando Abreu ; translated from the Portuguese with an afterword and glossary by Adria Frizzi.
p. cm. — (Texas Pan American series)
ISBN 0-292-70500-X (cl. : alk. paper) — ISBN 0-292-70501-8 (pbk. : alk. paper)
I. Frizzi, Adria. II. Title. III. Series

PQ9698.1.B68 O5313 2001
869.3'42—dc21 00-037705

Whatever Happened to
Dulce Veiga

Whatever Happened to

A B-NOVEL

Translated

from the Portuguese

with an Afterword and Glossary

by Adria Frizzi

Contents

Whatever Happened to
Dulce Veiga

In Memory of

Nara Leão

For

Odete Lara,

Guilherme de Almeida Prado,

Cida Moreyra,

and all the female vocalists of Brazil.

"I had seventeen dollars in my wallet. Seventeen dollars and the fear of writing. I sat erect before the typewriter and blew on my fingers. Please God, please Knut Hamsun, don't desert me now. I started to write and I wrote:"

John Fante, *Dreams from Bunker Hill*

I

MONDAY

Toothed Vaginas

1

I should have sung.

I should have doubled up with laughter or cried, but I no longer knew how to do those things. Or perhaps I could have lit a candle, rushed to Consolação church, said an Our Father, a Hail Mary, and a Gloria, anything I could remember, after plunking some change, if I had any—and during the past months I never did—in the metal box "For the Souls in Purgatory." Give thanks, ask for light—the way I did in the times I still had faith.

Those were the days, I thought. I lit a cigarette and didn't assume any of those dramatic postures, as if there were a camera in a corner somewhere watching me all the time. Or God. Without a judge or an audience, without close-up or zoom, I just sat there at the beginning of that scorching February afternoon, staring at the phone I had hung up a moment before. I didn't even cross myself or raise my eyes toward heaven. The least one is expected to do in these cases, I guess, even without faith, as if reacting to some mystical, conditioned reflex.

A miracle had occurred. A modest miracle, but essential to someone who, like me, didn't have rich parents, investments, real estate, or inheritance and was just trying to make it on his own in an infernal city like the one throbbing outside my still unopened apartment window. Nothing particularly sensational, like suddenly recovering one's eyesight or rising from a wheelchair with a beatific expression and the lightness of someone who walks on water. Even though my myopia was getting worse all the time and I often felt weak in the knees—whether from chronic hunger or mere sadness I couldn't say—my eyes and legs still worked reasonably well. Other organs, it's true, much less so.

I felt my neck. My brain, for one.

That's enough, I said to myself, naked, paralyzed in the middle of the sticky midday penumbra. Think about this miracle, man. Simple—almost insignificant in its simplicity—the small miracle that might bring some peace to the string of aimless and erratic bumps which I, with a certain complacency and no originality, was in the habit of calling *my life*, had a name. It was called—a job.

I looked at my face in the old scratched mirror, at the marks that belonged to the glass or my skin—I no longer knew which—and nodded in greeting. "Very good, congratulations. Now you're employed." I felt no thrill of pride, no *quiver* of hope light up my bloodshot eyes or push out my sagging chest where—I didn't want to remember but I did—less than a week earlier I had discovered the first gray hair.

I sighed.

It's true that only a complete idiot or someone totally inexperienced would feel, I won't say ecstasy, but some kind of animation for having gotten a little job as a reporter at the *Diário da Cidade*, possibly the worst paper in the world. I don't think I had turned into an idiot yet, not completely anyway. And as for experience—well, that marked face, still puffy from sleep, with a three-day stubble, watching me from among the mirror's scratches, seemed to have plenty of it. All right, said the face in the mirror, since you insist on confusing experience with devastation . . . I sighed again. No, my dear face, filling page after page on the typewriters of that pre-computer-age rag was certainly no reason to jump for joy.

But I *had* to be happy. And when you want to be, you are. I began to be. After all, that day might be the first step toward emerging from the morass of depression and self-pity in which I had been wallowing for nearly a year. I liked the expression *morass-of-depression-&-etc.* so much that I almost looked for a scrap of paper to jot it down. I had lost the paranoid vice of imagining I was always being filmed or appraised by some god with multifaceted eyes, like a fly's, but not that of being written about. If I had been a dancer, would I have imagined perhaps that I was being sculpted constantly, in every movement? Ah, each gesture, a true aesthetic apology of pure form.

It was funny. And pretty schizophrenic. But suddenly reality had become much less rhetorical.

"You start today, pal," Castilhos had said on the phone. In that voice at the bottom of which, to feed the old subliterary habit, I could have detected something I'd call gruff-complicitous-fondness, although it was actually nothing but an excess of nicotine and busted balls. "And see if you can keep from fucking up on the very first day, okay? I swore to the guys you were a hotshot."

Frightening: the night before, I had gone to sleep a nearly forty-year-old unemployed journalist, in debt, bitter, solitary, and disillusioned, to awaken the following day, magically, with that voice from the past informing me on the phone that I was—a *hotshot*. From today on, a life of facts. Action, movement, dynamism. The clappers snap shut. God turns another page of his endless, supremely boring script. The sculptor chips off another piece of marble.

I put on water for coffee. Whitish mushrooms were growing in the dampness of the kitchen. Nice. Sort of bucolic, even. I turned on the radio, got in the shower. The apartment was so small you could practically do all those things at the same time. With one hand I lathered my head, with the other I adjusted the volume of the radio in the living room, stretching out a leg to turn off the burner when the water boiled.

"Giddy-up! Onward ho! Yee-haw!" I yelled under the ice-cold water. "Yippee-hi-yo, Silver!"

Then I heard a familiar tune on the radio. It said something like, "reality doesn't matter, what matters is the illusion," with which I completely agreed. During the last months, anyway, nothing had happened to me besides fantasies. But the song that echoed in the recesses of my memory was old, like a bolero or a fox-trot, and what came out of the radio now was one of those rock songs with a desperate electric bass, mean percussion, and hysterical synthesizers. The female singer's voice sounded like glass ground up in a blender. In any case, I thought, the lyrics are right. And all the things I remembered, or thought I remembered, because in remembering them so intensely I had ended up turning them into sheer—and lousy—literature, no longer mattered.

What was left of the last piece of soap slipped through my fingers. It was so small it disappeared down the drain.

2

"You're kidding," I said. "Does this group really exist?"

Castilhos tapped the ash of one of his cigarettes in the air. He had been smoking three or four cigarettes simultaneously for as long as I'd known him, about twenty years. Some were balanced on the edge of the desk, the metal rim covered with dark burns, others were scattered in the ashtrays lost among piles of papers, photos, clips, folders, envelopes, plastic cups, artificial sweetener, tubes of glue, wads of money, lottery tickets, writing pads, pencils, pens, half-eaten sandwiches, Diet Coke cans, and a clay ox from the Northeast, which I knew from other newsrooms. The fan behind him blew the ashes in my eyes. The temperature in the carpeted room must have approached a gas chamber's.

He set the cigarette in an ashtray shaped like a pair of hands cupped as if awaiting manna from heaven. I thought I knew the ashtray too. Past newsrooms, other times. Actually every one of those knickknacks looked familiar, including him. And that wasn't exactly what I'd call a "pleasant feeling."

Castilhos shuffled through the photos, pulled out a mulatto girl in a thong bikini and white boots, clipped it to a page so furiously scratched out that the corrections had perforated the paper.

"What's so strange, just because of the name? It's the times, what can you do? Now they're called Grunge Rats, Filthy Worms, Disgusting Bugs, stuff like that." He turned to the lower side table, stuck a sheet in the typewriter and pounded away. "Check out this babe, man!"

I looked at him uncomprehendingly. As far as I knew he liked the skinny spiritual type à la Audrey Hepburn. At most, Deborah Kerr. Among the newest, Michelle Pfeiffer, maybe. Never mulatto girls in white boots.

"The caption: 'Check out this babe, man!' Twenty-four characters—without the exclamation mark it fits just right." He tore the sheet out and barked, "Pai Tomás, come over here."

"Perfect," I said. I had forgotten that talking to him was always like that. Two or three intersecting themes interrupted by sighs, coughing, snorts, phone calls, cigarettes, and shouts. Abrupt cuts, retakes, and counter-themes, without any preface, like as-I-was-saying or stuff like that.

"Pai Tomás! Where did that harebrain go?" He distractedly ran his yellowed fingertips over the mulatto girl's thighs. Castilhos' hands always amazed me. Instead of predictable hairy paws, they were small, plump, rosy. Whenever I began to hate him, all I had to do was look at them. I immediately forgave him everything. "Vomit. The other day some kids came up with this group. Not group, band. That's what they say nowadays. There was another one, The Slugs. Beelzebub and the Inverted Cherubs also turned up. It's the times, what can you do?"

The phone rang, he answered. I looked around, but the huge and decadent room, with its floor fans, was nearly empty. Except for a young man, hair bristling with gel, all in black, who was furiously typing, perhaps a scathing review of the Inverted Cherubs.

"We close at eight," Castilhos was barking. "Eight on the dot, dammit. I want it on my desk by seven, at least to have a look at that crap, okay?" He slammed the receiver down, cigarette butts flew in all directions. "Lamebrains, all of them. The other day one of them wrote that some woman won the Academy Award for best *actoress*, is that pathetic or what?"

A black man suddenly materialized next to his desk, young, but with completely white hair, like a *Preto Velho*, an Old Black Spirit of the Umbanda religion. He gave a military salute, serious. Beneath the unbuttoned khaki shirt I saw a ritual necklace of red and black beads. They glistened, shiny with the sweat of the black skin. Castilhos raised the photo of the mulatto girl and waved it in my face.

"Pai Tomás, this is our new Entertainment reporter."

"*Laroiê!*" said Pai Tomás, bowing his white head.

I smiled. That is, I contracted the muscles of my face to show my teeth. I was feeling a little weak, hadn't eaten anything all day. I blinked, and when I opened my eyes again Pai Tomás had vanished.

With Castilhos, you never knew for sure when things stopped looking funny and became pathetic, folkloric, or vaguely menacing. Behind his desk the filthy windows filtered the gray light of Avenida Nove de Julho. The city looked like it was under a bell jar fogged up with steam. Smoke, exhalations, evaporated sweat, carbon monoxide, viruses. I looked at his hands again and, without really trying, I gave it one last shot.

"To be honest, Castilhos, I need the job pretty bad. But I don't know if I'm the right guy for it."

"Sure you do. You know perfectly well. And you're going to do everything just right, okay? So what if the girls' band is called Márcia Fellatio and the Toothed Vaginas? It's a very original name, and they must be groovy girls. It's on the radio all the time."

"I only listen to Gregorian chants," I lied. Then I sighed, "Dykes, sexists, teenage rebels without cause or consequence."

"A good title for a piece. But first go see them, then write it." He lit another cigarette. And repeated, "It's the times."

"What can you do?" I concluded for him. "Give me their number."

He pushed aside a pile of papers, grabbed an address book with more loose sheets in it than all its pages put together. And it's still only February, I thought. He handed me a scrap of paper.

"Talk to Patrícia. Or Vanessa, Mônica, or Cristiane, one of those modern names. What's going on here? There aren't any more Veras, Juçaras, Elviras. And what about Carmens?"

"Castilhos, do you still live in that apartment on São João?"

He opened the drawer with his foot, then slammed it shut loudly, pushed his glasses up on his forehead and caressed the horns of the Northeastern ox. This I remembered: it was the signal that our conversation was over. As I was getting up, I said:

"Beware, warrior, when the fingers of the great master caress the bovine's horns."

He grunted. Maybe it was a smile, I don't know.

I headed for the exit, picking my way through the empty desks. A blonde in her fifties, wearing lots of fake gold and a low-cut imitation leopard-skin dress, bent over her typewriter as I passed. She could have been vulgar, but something about the elongated neck and the square shoulders, thrown back, betrayed a certain aristocracy. Perhaps a recent divorcée trying to get a fresh start, an ex-ballerina from Russia fascinated by the tropics and forced to do sordid translations in order to survive. Behind her a calendar of the Japanese Seicho-No-Ie cult read, "Now is the time to be reborn." I was sitting down beside her to make a call when Castilhos hollered:

"It's Friday's cover," and then, without getting up, but in a perfectly pitched voice and an English so flawless I understood absolutely nothing, he recited: *"'Disable all the benefits of your country, be out of love with your nativity, and almost chide God for making that countenance you are.'"*

The young man in black stopped typing, his hands suspended in midair over the keys.

"John Donne," he ventured.

The ex-ballerina from Russia clapped her hands.

"Fernando Pessoa."

She was completely off base. During the twenty years I had known that game, the only Portuguese author Castilhos admitted was Camões. And on one occasion, to everybody's surprise, Florbela Espanca: "*Always the same strange disease of life, and the heart the same open sore!*" Now everybody was waiting, looking at me. It was as crucial as an initiation test.

I shot out:

"Shakespeare."

Castilhos confirmed:

"*As You Like It.* Act four, scene one."

The others clapped. I bowed in acknowledgment, then I asked the blonde's leave and picked up the phone. Before I could dial the number, she stuck a hand covered with rings and long scarlet nails across the table.

"Nice to meet you," she said, with no Russian accent whatsoever. On the contrary, with its open vowels it sounded slightly Bahian. "I'm Teresinha O'Connor."

"Teresinha what?"

"O'Connor," she repeated, laying the accent on thick. "Of Irish descent, you know. I write the gossip column. When you have anything of interest, will you pass it on to me? People who deal with the arts always have something."

"You can count on me," I said. And I began to dial.

3

An infernal racket was coming from the background. A murder, bullfight, children's party, or rape. *It's only rock 'n' roll,* I thought, they must be rehearsing. We continued to shout back and forth without understanding each other. Then I heard a loud noise, like a door slamming, the racket now muffled, and the voice on the phone.

"Who do you want to talk to?"

"Vanessa," I said.

"Which, Redgrave or Bell?"

"Either one."

"There are no Vanessas here, honey. Try Jane."

I struck back:

"Which, Fonda or Bowles?"

Her surprise was exaggerated. She was from Rio de Janeiro, I figured from her shushing *s*'s and scratchy *r*'s. And she was having fun.

"You said Bowles, Jane *Bowles*? I don't know that one."

"Listen," I said. "If you insist we can go on like this for hours. I can call Marianne Faithfull or Moore, Charlotte Brontë or Rampling. Very cultural and all. But it just so happens that I'm working, sweetheart." The *sweetheart* wasn't part of my vocabulary, but I thought it would help. And in a more formal tone, "Who am I speaking to?"

"Patrícia."

Neal or Highsmith, I thought of asking, maybe Travassos. It was contagious.

"You're the person I want to talk to."

"Talk, then, love."

While I explained that I needed to write a piece about the group and so on—I thought it would be better to say that, *the group*; I didn't feel ready yet to utter in public something like *Márcia Fellatio and the Toothed Vaginas*—Teresinha O'Connor was frantically placing calls from the desk next to me. She was the kind who dials with the tip of her pen, then chews the cap while she's waiting for the call to go through.

"Fine," Patrícia said. "The press is the press, only that's not how it *really* works. You call and act like the interview is already on. First I need your birthdate."

"Huh?"

"Date, place, and time. Like Yoko used to do when all those people wanted to interview John Lennon. Just because we're from Brazil doesn't mean we're not selective, know what I mean?"

"But what do you want it for?"

"To do your astrological chart, of course. I need to see if everything adds up."

Rocker, intellectual, and astrologer. She must wear glasses, I thought. And I pictured the pink surface of Neptune, Miranda, volcanoes of frozen gas. Then the Voyager lost in space, Mick Jagger's voice screaming into infinity *I Can't Get No Satisfaction* on behalf of us all. I had to think to come up with the right date, I almost couldn't remember the year.

"*That* old?" Patrícia seemed disappointed.

"Uh-huh."

"And the time?"

"That I don't know."

"Nothing doing, then. Without the exact time, how can I figure out your rising sign? Isn't it on your birth certificate?"

"No."

"Ask your mother."

"My mother lives abroad," I lied.

"Call her up, it's not that expensive. Call from the paper."

"She doesn't have a phone—'it's a village lost in the Carpathians,'" I fabulated to myself. In the snow, in a cabin with no telephones or newsrooms, gossip columnists or rock bands, only moose. Where the hell were the Carpathians anyway?

"At least tell me whether it was in the morning, afternoon, or night."

"Early morning," I said. It was true, my mother always said she hadn't slept all night. To make me feel guilty, of course. But once she said something like, when I looked out the window the sun was rising and you were coming out. I liked that, at least it was a sunny day.

"Hold on," Patrícia said.

At the other end the infernal racket returned. Little by little the newsroom was becoming more animated. Fat guys from the Sports page, disheveled girls from Entertainment, pimply teenagers from the City Desk. I was getting old. And grumpy. I looked down, began to draw concentric circles on the back of the paper with her number. Slowly rotating my head, which in that heat made me feel even more dazed. Miranda, I enumerated, Carpathians, Passo da Guanxuma. All so far away, all fiction. Below the concentric circles I wrote "everything revolves around it," like a card I'd seen somewhere.

I was filling in the second *o* with ink when the racket returned, then became muffled again.

"Hello," I said.

"Look, darling, today's impossible. We have a recording session.

Besides, Moon days aren't favorable. Very unstable, you know what I mean? Only Friday, Venus' day. And at six in the afternoon, with Leo rising and the sun in the house of the other."

I articulated each syllable so meticulously that anyone, even a toothed vagina, could understand that I was getting mad:

"Patrícia, I have to turn in this article Thursday. To be published on Friday. I can't wait for the stars to be favorable and Uranus to be in the house of whoever the fuck."

She didn't say anything, I wondered if it was the expletive.

"It's the cover," I enticed. It even looked like *Vanity Fair*. "The cover, in color."

Suddenly she gave in.

"All right. We're going to tape a clip in the studio shortly. Come down there. But absolutely no interview. Only after the chart. Here's the address."

When I finished jotting down the endless you know where there's a kinda grungy gas station and there you'll see an underwear billboard with a very sexy guy and right next to a hideous building with green tiles, I put out my cigarette in Teresinha O'Connor's bronze ashtray, very artsy. She offered me her cheek to kiss.

"Three to get married," she demanded.

I gave her one, without touching her skin. Or the layer of makeup between my mouth and her skin. I grabbed a stack of paper and rushed out. At the door, I heard Teresinha's voice:

"Hey, don't forget my news items, okay?"

4

Before finding a cab I passed two dwarves, a hunchback, three blind men, four cripples, a human torso, a man with only one arm, another wrapped in rags like a leper, a black woman bleeding, an old man on crutches, a pair of mongoloid twin sisters, arm in arm, and so many beggars I couldn't even count them. The set consisted of trash bags giving off a sweet stench, flies buzzing, and children hovering around.

At the corner a man in lederhosen and a little green hat was playing a hurdy-gurdy for one of those parakeets that draw lots.

I stopped. The man made the parakeet peck the little folded paper three times before handing it to me. It said:

"Hard work will provide you with all the comforts of life: learn to be happy by living honorably, ask and you will receive an unexpected fortune on which you will live well, this is what the stars tell."

The Japanese driver tried to strike up a conversation, but I answered with a grunt, so he gave up after commenting that it was going to pour. I moved the seat back, stretched out my legs, rolled down the window. He turned on the radio. I prayed he wouldn't tune in to one of those shows with hyper-realistic descriptions of some little old lady's rape, maggoty sandwiches, slaughters in orphanages. Suddenly Cazuza's raspy voice began to sing. He's going to change the station—I was sure of it—but he didn't. That made me like him a little more, so oriental, a Buddhist, maybe, so I asked him to please turn up the volume, leaned my head against the sticky plastic headrest, and, for nearly one second, very briefly, while the car crept along in the congested traffic, over the scorching asphalt, my shirt soaked, the stack of paper turning into a solid lump between my fingers, I closed my eyes, the wind blowing on my face, drying the sweat, and, once again, for nearly one second, like someone who suddenly sighs or blinks and keeps going, swift as a moth flitting across a summer night in search of a light to hover around, like someone turning on or off that same light in an empty room in order to feel the vibrations of the wings still hovering in the air, not the insect itself, already gone, in the murky depths of the mind, I wanted to see through the darkness of the world, without desiring or provoking or taking the lead, for nearly one second, finally, inside the cab heading toward Ibirapuera Park, I thought of Pedro.

5

Before I even saw her, a blast of dry ice hit my face through the door she opened and immediately closed. She stood before me, like the guardian priestess of some treasure. A priestess at least six feet tall, no older than twenty or so, and looking like one of those long-legged birds pausing by the edge of a swamp in some environmental picture. She would have been funny, if she hadn't tried to look so serious.

As I had imagined, Patrícia wore glasses. Not round, huge, to indicate that she read a lot, or with colored frames, to make it very clear that, in spite of reading a lot, she wasn't a nerd. Cat-eye glasses, fifties style, from some fancy curio shop in the Jardins section. Her kinky, almost blond hair hung down in disheveled cascades to the waist of her skin-tight jeans. Tattered, of course. Her feet were shod in the heavy boots of a soldier or mountain climber. She gave the impression of not being the least concerned about looking pretty, nice, or well-mannered. Perhaps because of that—that look of a problematic high-school girl—she had a helpless way about her.

I couldn't take my eyes off her t-shirt. On her chest there was something like a vertical open mouth, a bloody maroon blotch against the white background. Within the purplish outlines of that menacing mouth, two rows of saw-edged teeth, like a shark's, threatened between the lips. It was when I thought *lips*, twisting my head to see better, that I understood. It was a toothed vagina. But I was sure only when she turned and I was able to read the name of the band, written on the back.

She was looking at me with a bored expression. There was nothing special about me. Jeans like hers, but without tears, white t-shirt without a vagina or phallus on it. No earrings, no green streaks in my hair. A war uniform, that of someone who wants to remain invisible. And I had wanted to, for a long time.

She asked:

"Are you the guy from the paper?"

I said yes.

"You look real square."

I said I was.

She peered at me over her glasses.

"Your rising sign must be Pisces."

I continued to stare at the vagina between her breasts, without saying anything. I knew that we could get caught up again in one of those labyrinthine dialogues at any second: Dorothy Parker or Lamour, or Dandridge, maybe?

That's when I began to hear it.

From behind the door came a familiar music. Not just familiar, there was something more disturbing in it, or in the strange feeling it aroused in me. I tried to listen more closely, but it wasn't exactly what I remembered, even though whatever it was that I remembered, or almost remembered, but couldn't quite identify, was there as well, in the music or myself. It gave me a feeling of nostalgia, sorrow. And something else more somber, fear or pain. In my mind blurry figures intertwined, fleeting, like a badly tuned TV, confused as if two or three projectors were simultaneously casting different images on the same screen. Fusion, I thought: pentimento. And I saw again a dark room with a very high ceiling, daylight shut out by the curtains, an old-fashioned ashtray in the shape of a small round box, the kind women in black and white movies from the forties carry in their purses, a strand of pearls on a woman's white neck. It didn't make any sense.

Patrícia was looking at me with curiosity. A reflection made a rhinestone on one of the tips of her glasses sparkle. Perhaps because of that, so clear-cut among those vague images, an armchair took shape in my memory. Or imagination, I didn't know which. It was a classic armchair, a green velvet *bergère*. I looked around in search of a green like that. There was none. Leaves that never see the sun, moss, bottle-ends—a piece of glass I had found once in the sand, so green and polished by salt and water that it looked like it had absorbed the color of the marine depths. It was like that, the green of the armchair.

"I know this music," I said.

Patrícia shrugged.

"Everybody does. It's our big hit, it's number two on the charts."

I pushed past her.

"I need to hear better."

"You can't interrupt—" she began to say.

But I had already gone in. The large room was foggy from the dry ice. Through the mist, I gradually began to make out some men, or parts of them. Torsos, heads. Then, in the back, a painted cardboard set reproducing dilapidated buildings surrounded by huge trash cans nearly the same size. Unexpected objects spilled out of them: a mannequin's leg, a pendulum, a cello split in half, beheaded dolls, plastic flowers, garlic braids. Salvador Dalí in Hollywood, I thought, designing the sets for a Christopher Lee movie.

Against the buildings, three girls dressed in jeans and shirts like Patrícia's were playing drums, electric bass, and keyboards. They were the Toothed Vaginas: a black drummer, hair braided with colored beads, a fat keyboard player with a nearly shaved head, and a huge Japanese chick. In front of them, leaning against a fake lamppost, another girl with bleached hair, dressed in black leather from head to toe, with a guitar. From where I stood I couldn't see her face. Only the contrast between her heavy clothes and her almost white hair, hovering like a halo around the starkly pale face, beneath the bluish spotlights. As unreal as an angel. An angel of darkness, without wings or harp, a fallen angel. It was Márcia Fellatio.

When I entered she stopped singing immediately. At the same time, telepathically, the three Toothed Vaginas also stopped. Patrícia whimpered in my ear.

"I tried to warn you. Márcia hates this."

Out of the fake fog, a man yelled.

"Hey, what the fuck's going on, kids? It was going great, this ain't gonna cut it."

Márcia slammed the guitar against the lamppost. The cardboard pillar shook in the painted Styrofoam base. Hands on her hips, she glared at me and Patrícia. In slow time, the black girl with the cornrows began to beat on one of the cymbals. It seemed intentional: the obvious soundtrack for the crescendo of suspense one second before the burst of rage.

"Patrícia!" Márcia screamed, an overseer ordering a hundred whiplashes, and salt rubbed in the wounds. "Haven't I told you a thousand times I don't want strangers around when we're recording?"

"He's the guy from the paper," Patrícia explained. Her voice sounded childish, strident. Ridiculous, and at the same time consistent with that long-legged bird look. "He barged in, it wasn't my fault."

The post-punk-pre-apocalyptic-prima-donna looked straight at me. Perhaps because of the lights, her eyes shone too brightly. Synthetic, as if they were made of acrylic or emitted laser beams. An accursed beacon, leading seafarers astray. I guessed they might be green.

"Who did you say you work for?"

"The *Diário da Cidade,*" I stammered. I would have liked to say *The New York Times, Le Monde,* or something like that. "I have to write a *cover* story about you. It wasn't Patrícia's fault, it's me who."

Márcia kicked the post again. A man yelled, "Easy, girl, you're gonna fuck up the set that way."

On the drums, the cymbal continued to rattle. The Japanese chick wrenched from the bass a strident chord that rent the air. Leaning against the electronic keyboards, the fat girl was smoking with a cynical little smirk stamped on her face. I could tell they were having a good time.

One of the men clapped his hands. "What's the deal, *boys*?" Nobody laughed. "We ain't got all day. You wanna tape this shit or not?"

Márcia's laser eyes swept across the studio.

"What you call *shit*, I call *art*. You only see as far as your eyes let you see."

"Right," said the invisible man apologetically. "I'm sorry, I didn't mean it. Let's get on with the recording."

Patrícia squeezed my arm.

"Isn't she *awesome*?" she whispered.

All you could hear was the percussion punctuated by the wail of the bass. Márcia hung her head, kicked the crooked post carelessly, and picked up her guitar.

"All right," she said. "Never mind, we'll let it go this time."

"Recording!" shouted the director.

Márcia turned her back and raised her right arm, her forefinger pointing to the ceiling. On her wrist, a spiked bracelet. Márcia looked at the other Toothed Vaginas, then counted, stamping her foot on the floor.

"One, two, three!"

A bloodcurdling guitar chord made me picture one of Teresinha O'Connor's long scarlet nails scratching a blackboard from top to bottom. Márcia began to sing again.

That ground glass voice, harsh and piercing, churning inside a blender, not ugly or off-key, but uncomfortable in the way it took up space in your brain, that voice which, regardless of what it sang, gave the impression of coming from the depths of atomic ruins, not the fake ruins of that cardboard set, but Hiroshima's, Cologne's after the bombing, the rubble of a village near some nuclear plant, after the explosion, a survivor of the end of everything, that radioactive siren voice—was the same I had heard on the radio, while I was taking a shower before going to the paper.

I ran my hand over the back of my neck, the goose bumps didn't go away. Because—I suspected more than knew—it wasn't just that. I knew that music from another place, another time. I paid attention to the lyrics.

Distorted by an arrangement reminiscent of a radioactive wind blowing through a gothic cathedral, accelerated, moaned, and screamed, completely different from the serene tone it had once possessed, polluted by the contaminated wails of the guitar and drums imitating distant explosions, it was an old hit from the forties or fifties. To my surprise, I could remember all the lyrics.

I began to sing along, moving my lips without sound—I couldn't sing:

"Nothing more,
nothing but an illusion.
It's enough,
my heart thrives on delusion.
Believing everything
that love, lying, always says
I go on like this,
happy in the illusion of happiness.
If love only causes us
sadness and pain, the illusion of love
is better, so much better.
To keep my poor heart from confusion
I wish and ask for
nothing but a beautiful illusion."

Nothing, nothing more, Márcia was repeating, almost motionless, stepping away from the post only to lean forward, dramatically holding her hand out and lifting her face, disfigured by the ghastly light filters. Closing my eyes, I saw that green armchair again. And nothing else, nothing more, until I began to remember the same lines sung by another voice. A woman's voice, ancient, thick, heavy.

"Cut!" someone shouted.

Then I remembered, in a flash: Dulce Veiga.

Dulce, Dulce Veiga had recorded the same song too.

Ten, fifteen, how many years ago? The goose bumps traveled from the back of my neck to my arms, strange as a premonition.

Dulce Veiga, I said to the darkness.

What, asked Patrícia.

I didn't answer, the lights came on.

The director shouted:

"Five minutes, we're going to shoot the reverse angles next."

Márcia came out from among the trash cans, walking toward me. From somewhere Patrícia produced a Coke with a straw in it, which she handed to her. Very close to me, Márcia took off her jacket. She wasn't wearing anything underneath. She had small, firm breasts, with hard nipples, as if she were aroused. Between them there was a tattooed butterfly. Transformed into a mammy, Patrícia began to cool her off with a straw fan. I couldn't take my eyes off her breasts.

"Sorry about the scene," she said, her voice a little hoarse. Her eyes were indeed green. "I can't concentrate when there are strangers around."

"It's all right," I said.

"Okay," she said.

"Okay," I repeated.

"*Hunky-dory*," the Japanese chick said behind me, running her hand over my ass.

"That song," I said. "That song you sang."

"It's called 'Nothing More.'"

"I know it."

"So what? Everybody does. It's an old hit by Orlando Silva, we just."

I asked, abruptly:

"Do you know Dulce Veiga's recording?"

Márcia made the straw gurgle with the last sip of Coke.

Without answering, she handed the empty bottle to Patrícia. In a corner, the three Toothed Vaginas were eagerly crowding around a mirror placed on the knees of a short guy. From where we were we could hear the rack-rack of the razor blade hitting the glass. I felt a cold wave in my intestines. Márcia blew the cigarette smoke upwards theatrically, like a third-rate diva. Stretched out like that her long neck had faint blue veins, pulsing. I thought of Lestat the vampire: he'd go crazy.

The Japanese chick called out:

"Don't you want some? Come quick before these sluts snort it all up."

Márcia invited me:

"Wanna do a line?"

The short guy passed the mirror, Patrícia handed Márcia a rolled bill. She leaned forward. When she raised her head, her eyes looked even shinier. She passed me the bill. My share—almost a hand's width, a generous line—consisted of the *i* of her name written on the mirror. Half in the left nostril, half in the right: I snorted, a shiver in my stomach. I raised my head and asked again:

"Do you know Dulce Veiga's recording?"

She brushed her nostrils with the back of her hand. I was afraid she might wound herself with the spiked bracelet. I sniffed, small bitter grains rolled down the back of my throat. It was good stuff.

"Of course I do. Dulce Veiga was my mother."

"What do you mean, *was*? She's dead?"

Márcia gave me a searching glance, then lowered her head.

"No, she didn't die. She disappeared one day, suddenly, many years ago."

"What do you mean, *disappeared*? Nobody vanishes like that, without a reason."

Márcia bit her lip long and hard, staining her teeth with red lipstick. She seemed annoyed.

"She disappeared, dammit," and she shoved her fist in my face. I thought she was going to punch me, like in a movie. But she opened her hand in the air, near the tip of my nose, making a popping sound with her lips. "Poof! Like that, she vanished. Just like that. I was still a baby. It was twenty years ago."

Then, I didn't say. The green armchair, the room with the high ceiling, the round ashtray, the strand of pearls. And a baby. Among the ruins of the buildings, one of the cameramen began to clap his hands.

"Come on, everybody. Take your places."

I said:

"I met your mother."

I don't know if she heard me. She gave me a cold kiss.

"Tomorrow, for sure. Call us at home, we'll set up the interview."

But, I started to say. I needed to talk about Dulce Veiga. About her, about me, about that time. Slowly, in a studied manner, Márcia began to walk back to the set, putting on her jacket at the same time. Halfway, she turned, eyes flashing, violently pulled up the zipper, and screamed loud enough for everybody to hear:

"Hasn't he gotten the fuck out of here yet? I can't work with this guy staring at me."

The short guy who'd held the mirror pushed me outside. I was too dazed to react and yielded. Outside, far away, anywhere, maybe where the green armchair, the bloodstained syringe, the cradle in the dark corner were. I don't know how I could have forgotten it all, but now I didn't know the right way, if there was one, to remember either. So many things, so many years after Dulce Veiga. Before being shoved outside, I turned back and managed to catch one last glimpse of Márcia. She was standing, with her back turned, next to the lamppost, the guitar slung across her body, her right arm raised like a spear, her hand closed in a fist, only the forefinger pointing upwards.

Then, I didn't say after the door closed, then I met you too, *baby*.

6

It was getting late. The clouds were rolling across the sky, torn by flashes of lightning in the distance, near Cantareira. The wind dragged empty cans and newspapers down the street, windows slammed, people hurriedly closed the doors of shops and houses, men were briskly rolling down the metal shutters of the newspaper stands. A clap of thunder struck far away, then another, closer. A dog yelped, then howled. A storm's coming, I thought, and began walking quickly toward Ibirapuera Park, in search of a cab or a bus, before the streets got flooded, impracticable, the city a disaster area, like every summer afternoon.

From a balcony someone cried out:

"Eparrê, eparrê-i, Iansã!"

That's when I saw her.

On a street corner across from the park, in the midst of the strong wind, standing beneath the princess flower tree covered with purple blooms, was Dulce Veiga. All in red, a full-blown white rose pinned to her lapel, a purse the same color hanging from one of her crossed arms, white gloves. Parted exactly in the middle, covering her temples and high cheekbones, her straight blond hair fell in two points in the space between her thin lips and rather proud chin, which she held up, without a smile or a gesture, to see better, her eyes fixed in the direction I was coming from. Blown by the wind, the only thing that moved in her body was her hair. It covered and uncovered her face, blew around it, so straight that it always fell back in place when the wind subsided. She stood there, indifferent to the strong wind and the first drops of rain. Watchful, patient. As if she were waiting for me after all those years.

When I reached the opposite corner I waited for the light to turn green, so close I could see the strand of pearls around her neck. On the other side of the street she raised her right arm, her forefinger pointing to the sky, in a gesture identical to Márcia's before she began singing. At the same time, a silver flash of lightning fell among the trees in the park. I closed my eyes, blinded. When I reopened them, searching through the spaces between the passing cars and the first cold rain pelting my face, Dulce Veiga was no longer there.

Maybe she'd gotten into a car, maybe she'd gone into the park. I ran across the street and went into the park after her. The rain was getting heavier and colder, and I thought I saw her disappearing around the curve of the tree-lined walk, among the bamboo, the high heels of her red shoes sinking in the wet ground. I called out her name, inaudible even to me, muffled by the noise of the passing cars, of the rain turned into hail incessantly pounding on the warm ground. My clothes were soaked, I'm going to catch a cold, I thought—and no, I couldn't, the paper, the interview, the fever in the empty apartment again, my fingertips searching for the ominous signs on my throat, the back of my neck, in my groin. I took shelter under a tree, sat on the ground, put my arms around my knees. I huddled like a dog afraid of thunder, watching the granules of ice falling diagonally. The wet earth gave off a penetrating, secret, intimate scent, like sex or sleep. I leaned my cold forehead against my legs and closed my eyes again.

7

The first time I saw Dulce Veiga, and there were only two times, she was sitting in a green velvet armchair. A bergère, *although in those days I didn't even know that was what they were called. I knew so little of anything in those days that, later, when I tried to describe it in my mind and on paper, I said that it was one of those classic armchairs, with a high back and something like two wings jutting out at the height of the head of the person sitting. For some reason, even today, when I think of it, I also inevitably think of a black and white movie from the forties or early fifties.*

Dulce's head was thrown back, sunk between those wings. As if she couldn't see me, as if I weren't there. Standing under the arch that divided in two the high-ceilinged living room, I could only see her very white neck, a strand of pearls gleaming against her skin. In the dim room—it was probably almost night and, besides, the curtains always remained closed, I would find out later, without anyone telling me—the shadows falling upon the armchair and her blond hair prevented me from seeing her face. I could only see her long, thin hands, with red lacquered nails, standing out like moving silhouettes in the bluish afternoon penumbra. In one hand she was slowly swirling a glass of cognac. In the other she held a cigarette.

Dulce Veiga only drank cognac—to soften her voice, she said. But since she smoked constantly, especially when she drank cognac, which was very often, I no longer think that was the reason. In those days, when I met her, I believed everything I was told. I was very young, twenty, and I possessed the absolute certainty of eternal youth, like a little vampire or demigod.

I'm not absolutely certain if it was the first notes of Billie Holiday's rendition of "Crazy, He Calls Me" that came from somewhere inside the apartment, it could also have been "Glad to Be Unhappy," "Sophisticated Lady," or any other of those husky, moaning songs. In those days I didn't know them, but I'm sure that either on that occasion or the other I asked who it was and she said Billie, and I made a note of it, ever so diligent. All this that now seems a banal cliché, in those days—I repeat without ever tiring of it because it's beautiful and magical in its melancholy: in those days—everything was new, I didn't even suspect the difficulties that lay ahead. I say there was music, without fear of lying, since even if there was none and the silence of the apartment was only broken by the sound of the cars down on Avenida São João—even if there was not, any, ever, I repeat: it would be so perfect if it were exactly as I think I remember it, so many years later, that it's become the same as if it had been.

I didn't see her at first when I entered the room. But I must have felt somebody's presence, something like a heavy breathing, a sweetish perfume of jasmine, moonflower, manaca, or another of those old-fashioned, overly scented flowers. I stood still in the dark until I began to perceive more definite shapes in the corners. Behind the armchair, the cradle covered with the Indian cloth, then the coffee table with the round marble top and some objects to which, that first moment, on that first day, I paid no attention. I was only looking at her.

When my eyes had adjusted to the scarce light I was able to see all of her, sitting in that green velvet armchair, legs crossed, dressed completely in black. She never used more than two colors, but this, like many other things, I would only learn later. The ember of her cigarette moved up and down in the dark, at times brighter, when she inhaled. I must—and I say must *because I can't remember exactly the gestures I made, the things I said or thought—I must have reached to turn on the light in the high-ceilinged room. Because, of this I am certain, suddenly a thick voice, a voice that only countless cognacs, cigarettes, and coffees could have made that way, a voice of green velvet, as thick as the armchair's, arose in the midst of the shadows to ask querulously:*

"Don't turn it on, please. It's fine like this."

I think I pressed the tape recorder against my chest. I was very skinny, I don't think I was even twenty, and filled with so many illusions. I think I asked if we could begin the interview, and she said yes, or maybe she didn't say anything for a while, I don't remember. But I'm sure that, before raising her face, she reached out to put the glass of cognac down on the marble table, then she picked up a little black round box, opened the top with a sharp snap, and balanced her cigarette on it. Only then did Dulce Veiga raise toward me her face with high cheekbones, her green eyes, and I was able to see her straight blond hair, parted in the middle with millimetric precision, falling in two points in the space between her thin lips and her rather proud chin. I don't know if that was the time the baby cried, and she got up, leaning on the worn arm of the chair to slowly rock the cradle. But that wasn't in character, and I know that I don't know for sure because my memory has retained an image of her completely motionless, looking straight into my eyes the moment she said with a sigh:

"All right, we can begin."

8

It was almost night when it stopped raining. Near Pinheiros the sky had crimson tones higher up which gradually dissolved into orange and then more intense and luminous, golden near that horizon you never saw. I slowly crossed the empty park, hearing in the distance the sirens of ambulances, police cars, and fire trucks, and went around the lake, where a solitary boat made me think, once again, of that word whose meaning I didn't know for sure. Pentimento, I repeated: pentimento, a sentiment with pain. The wet clothes were drying against my skin, water from rain and sweat.

Near Avenida Brasil I suddenly turned, as if someone were calling my name, but there was no one else in the park, and then, looking up at the sky, near Interlagos, I saw a rainbow. A faint rainbow, barely visible. I had to strain, squint a little to see better the lilac and blue almost lost in the night beginning to fall, only the green and the yellow clearer, like the Brazilian flag. I could make a wish, I remembered, but I no longer believed in that. I turned and went on.

I looked up at the patches of sunset, turning more and more golden all the time, and then I saw it, blazing silver, slightly above the violet strip over the tallest buildings, the first star, it must be Venus. *First star I see tonight,* I remembered, *I wish I may, I wish I might, have this wish I wish tonight,* we used to play hopscotch scratched with pieces of brick on the sidewalks of Passo da Guanxuma, I always stepped out of bounds in the sky block when it was time to turn around, with a hop, eyes closed, repeat it seven times, eyes open and fixed on the star until the last wish, then never look up again. Standing at the intersection of four corners, the first star on my left, the rainbow on my right, the city ahead, the park behind me, I took a deep breath of air washed clean by the rain and made a wish. I repeated my wish aloud seven times, there was nobody around to stare and maybe laugh, a man not so young, soaking wet, talking to himself, asking for who knows what.

Strength and faith, which I had lost, were what I asked for.

There were no b
splashing mudd
portation. I deci
ordered a cogna
favelas, cars was
building evacua

A man on c
me the butterfl
not the lucky ty
got to take a ris
took the opaq
tents. It hit my
strung them t
spread to my a

I rubbed my hands briskly. ...
of *The Voice of Brazil*, announcing the government news broadcast. Someone swore, the guy at the cash register turned it off. I paid, lit a cigarette, and began to walk across town.

10

It was a sick, contaminated building, almost terminal. But it was still in its place, it hadn't collapsed yet. Even though, judging from the cracks in the concrete, by the ever-widening gaps in the indefinably colored tile facing, like wounds spreading little by little on the skin, it was only a matter of months.

Beloved old hovel, I thought with some fondness, the kind of fondness you feel for a blind, mangy old dog, as I ran my hand over the perpetual *under repare* sign hung on the door of the broken elevator by the Northeastern doormen.

Once again I went up the semi-flooded stairs, which always reminded me of some hospital I'd never been to. A hospital under quarantine, isolated by some unknown and deadly pestilence, in the heart of Rhodesia: Karen Blixen would bring food and vaccines. I had done it so many times that, even with my eyes closed, without counting the steps, I could identify each floor just by the smells

t—fried onions, beans, cat
ntical in their black dresses and
e how many of them there were—
ose dialogues from the soaps they

*ght to do this to me. After all, it's been seven
votion, more than love!"*

*k of . . . love? Only if you're speaking for yourself,
s I'm concerned it's been seven years of bitterness and
t."*

*st know the truth, Leda. As unbearable as it may be. Look me
eyes and answer me, if you still have any dignity left. Is there . . . is
re another man?"*

I didn't hear Leda's answer. The awful truth. Or the freeze-frame of an impenetrable face, flaring nostrils: scenes from the next episode.

On the second floor I was submerged in that smell of gyms, cheap cologne, and used rubbers. The apartment of the two Argentinean guys who did body-building, weights, and—I suspected—also hustled through the newspaper. From my apartment I could always hear one of them rushing out right after the phone rang, on the exact days—I had been watching the paper—the massage section of the classifieds offered the pleasures of "Argentinean stud, athletic superendowed for insatiable men and women." On Sundays, when they must have felt homesick for Calle Florida and there were no clients, you could hear Carlos Gardel's voice from the open window, *nostalgias de sentir junto a mi boca como un fuego tu respiración*. Gardel was silent now, replaced by the moanings of some porn video interrupted by nearly unintelligible exclamations, except for a *coño* or *mira que conchuda, hombre*.

For over a year, since Lidia had left me her apartment after fleeing to the interior of Minas Gerais, none of it had been a surprise. Depending on the mood each day, it might sound folkloric, bizarre, sordid, depressing. Sometimes Pedro Almodóvar, other times Manuel Puig. But that night I was too exhausted to think anything.

It seemed worse, it seemed real.

My floor always smelled like incense. Not those Indian sticks bought at natural food stores, but a different kind, thicker and cheaper, colored cones from the shops of Praça da Sé. In any case, scented. Church smell. Mystical, nauseating. From the vents of the apartment next door gray columns of sweet smoke escaped, mainly on Fridays, transforming the hallway into a hazy, liturgical tunnel. It was my neighbor Jandira's apartment. I tried to step lightly, so that she wouldn't open the door and start a conversation. But it was useless.

I was putting the key in the lock when I heard her voice.

"Have you seen Jacyr around?"

Jacyr—she liked to tell people how her son had been named that because, in an act of love, she had fused her own name with that of her ex-husband-Moacyr-that-scumbag—was a skinny kid of about thirteen with a high-pitched voice who occasionally cleaned my house, went to the post office or the bank for me, or stood on the corner of Rua Augusta handing out flyers advertising "the awesome telluric powers of Jandira de Xangô." Ever since, at Lidia's insistence, I had written the text of those flyers, Jandira had decided I was a-gem-of-a-guy and was always trying to help me out.

I said I hadn't seen anyone and turned to face her. She was a light-skinned mulatto, a little over thirty, very slender waist, huge ass, magnificent teeth. She was wearing a silver turban, enormous earrings. She didn't seem too worried.

"He went out before the rain, Iansã is raging. And he hasn't returned." She looked at me more carefully, and kind of cross-eyed, the way she always did when she began seeing things. "You look different, what happened?"

"I found a job," I said.

She clapped and raised her hands in praise.

"*Kaô kabiesile*, father! Thank God, I prayed so much to Xangô. Now you'll see how justice is on your side, son. From now on, Xangô will take care of all your needs."

I thought that if the job at the *Diário da Cidade* was just, then Xangô must have been drinking. But I didn't say anything. I turned the key, started to open the door. Under it, on the floor, was a letter, with its green-and-yellow bordered envelope. Maybe—I felt nostalgia, hope, and doubt—maybe it was from Pedro. I was anxious to pick it up, but Jandira wouldn't quit talking, she wanted to know everything about the job.

"It was a long day," I lied. "I'm tired."

I started to go in, the letter lay quivering on the floor. She stopped me.

"Come see me tomorrow. You need to throw the divination shells, Oxum is calling for it."

I said alright, but had no intention of going. There had been a time when Lidia didn't even go to the supermarket without consulting Jandira, the oracle next door. I had become disillusioned, she hardly mentioned any of that stuff about future wonders—you will be invited to a party, you will meet someone who. She just told me to bathe with certain herbs, which I didn't do, the markets were closed by the time I woke up. Cards, saints, numbers, stars: I wanted to get those things completely out of my life. I wanted reality, a reality with nothing behind it but itself. Only a little deeper, more undisguisable, with no other meaning besides what you could see, touch, and smell, like the smells, nauseating but real, of the building's hallways. I was sick of the invisible.

Before going in I asked:

"What about Jacyr?"

Jandira shrugged.

"When Oxumaré is willing, he'll show up."

If you need anything—I said—if you need anything, call me.

I picked up the letter from the floor, looked at the sender's name. It was Lidia, probably going on as usual about all those colonial churches, white walls, blue doors and windows, mountains, and cows in Diamantina, Sabará, or Mariana. About how she had finally found peace & harmony & how happy she was to have gotten the hell out of São Paulo & just what was I still looking for in this polluted, malignant, & damned city? Reality, I mentally replied. I left the envelope on the table without opening it. Those letters were bad for me.

Everything was bad for me. I looked around.

On the walls I had stripped of all Lidia's vestiges—Che Guevara, John Lennon, Charlie Chaplin—there was only a huge poster, almost six feet wide. Within a black frame full of white holes, like a contact print, was a strip of yellow sand dipping into an almost green sea. In the distance, on the other side of what was probably a bay, some bare mountains. Completely arid, not at all tropical. In the foreground, against the mountains and the sea, standing in the sand, a woman in an old-fashioned two-piece bathing suit with her hands crossed behind her head. The woman was a little pudgy, with a thick waist and short legs. She was wearing cat-eye Ray-Bans, like Patrícia's. Beneath her, on the lower edge of the contact print, was written, *Ist es nicht aufregend, dieses Leben?* Which someone in Berlin had told me meant "isn't this life exciting?" or something like that. It was absolutely silly, it almost always made me feel like laughing. And that was so rare that I repeated: "Isn't life exciting?"

I still hadn't gotten used to the absence of the answering machine, so I looked at the telephone without any machine under it, no little red light blinking at me. It was always the same, since I had sold it: I walked in, looked at the opulent German and felt like laughing, then I looked at the telephone and felt like crying. Someone had thought about me, and I wasn't there, what a shame, leave your message after the beep. The bookcase sagging under the weight of books, nearly all poetry, the dusty typewriter, the stove in the kitchenette, the empty refrigerator. No microwave, computer, washing machine, freezer, fax, floor buffer, VCR, vacuum cleaner, CD player, clothes dryer.

I was a manual laborer, pre-electronic: broke. I was thinking about going out into that muddy city to get something to eat when there was a knock at the door. It was Jandira, with a glass of milk and a piece of cake on a plate. Over them an immaculate white napkin, very clean. I reached out, asking:

"Any news of Jacyr?"

"Don't worry about him. Jacyr can take care of himself. Eat that, you're looking very skinny, son."

I gave her a kiss. She always smelled of rue.

"God be with you," she said.

Amen, I should have said. But I didn't say anything.

I closed the door. I took off all my clothes, tossed them in the middle of the room, then lay down on the sofa under the window. I thought about turning on the radio—but I couldn't bear hearing Márcia's voice, and there was always some risk of that—about turning on the TV or opening a book, but I knew I wouldn't have been able to concentrate on anything—Rogério's and Leda's trials, holes in the ozone layer, volcanoes in Java, earthquakes in Mongolia. I thought about going to the movies, but I had already seen everything that was playing in the city, including the summer blockbusters, in which schizoid teenagers suddenly become the school's idols and win over the homecoming queen, about drinking another cognac, ten cognacs, but there was nothing to drink at home, about calling somebody up, I wondered what had happened to Regina, but I'd disappeared for such a long time that I would have had to give explanations and say and listen to things like where have you been and what are you doing, and no—I really wanted nothing but to stay there, naked and worn out, collapsed on the sofa wet from the rain.

I felt my neck, on the right side. Inconspicuous, they rolled beneath my fingertips.

I turned off the light, and as I was eating Jandira's cake, in the darkness barely illuminated by the reflections of the neon light from the funeral home across the street, without wanting to think about anything that had happened, I vaguely remembered that there was someone else in the apartment on São João that day, when I saw Dulce Veiga for the first time, and shortly after, or at the same time, slightly aroused, balancing the glass of milk on my belly, I remembered the butterfly between Márcia's small breasts as well, but her breasts became confused with the muscular chest of the Argentinean I had seen in the hall one day, and while the shouts of the transvestites down in the street came in through the open window together with clouds of mosquitoes, before falling asleep, for the third time that day, drifting in and out of trifling matters, I thought about Pedro once again.

TUESDAY

The Hard Core of Beauty

11

Through the dark lenses of my glasses, against the brightness of the two o'clock sun, framed by the rectangle of the building's entrance, cut by the reflection on the cars outside, from the back of the hall where I stood, I thought at first it was the silhouette of a woman. Some customer for Jandira's divination shells—Tuesday was the day they were cast—trying to catch a husband. Or a client of the guys on the second floor, although too young to pay for a man. I was wrong.

Knee-high white boots, leather miniskirt, hair pinned on top of the head, tinkling bracelets, the makeup of a prostitute smudged as if she had slept without washing her face or had put it on without a mirror—it was Jacyr.

"Hi," he greeted me. And then, aggressive, "What's the matter, breeder, you've never seen me before?"

I said:

"Your mother's worried. You disappeared, Jacyr."

He threw his head back. He had a purple hickey on his neck.

"Screw her. And don't call me Jacyr, my name is Jacyra now."

Instead of sighing I took out a cigarette.

"Give me one."

"You're only thirteen."

I tried to put the pack away, but he snatched it out of my hand. When he leaned over for a light, which I gave him, one of the little old ladies, loaded down with bags from the market, passed behind him without saying hello.

"Fourteen," Jacyr corrected me. He lifted his head—his pupils dilated, lids caked with blue eye shadow—blew a cloud of smoke in my face, beer and dope breath, handed me back the cigarette pack and yelled after the little old lady, "Bitch! Mind your own business, you old scarecrow!"

A little respect, I was going to say. They're old ladies, after all. A car alarm went off outside. I didn't want to start the day with another headache.

"I've got to get going. I'm running late."

I was almost at the door of the building when Jacyr called after me. I looked at him, her.

He was standing at the turn of the stairs, one hand on his hip, the other holding the cigarette level with his fake breasts. He looked like Jodie Foster in *Taxi Driver*, mulatto version. He yelled, his voice sounding shriller than ever:

"Don't you want any house cleaning today? I need to raise some dough."

"Tomorrow," I said without thinking.

When I thought better of it, it was too late. Jacyr had already disappeared up the stairs. Before stepping into the street, I stood at the door for a moment. Even with the car alarm gone mad you could distinctly hear the heels of the white boots determinedly pounding up the concrete steps.

12

In the nearly deserted newsroom, before he had a chance to ask for the piece, I said:

"Castilhos, do you remember Dulce Veiga?"

"Dulce who?" he was frantically scribbling across a page in red ink.

I repeated:

"Veiga. Dulce Veiga, the singer."

Castilhos put the pen in his mouth as if it were a cigarette. And only after distractedly sucking on the cap while peering at me over the glasses that had slipped down his nose did he seem to understand. Then he put the pen down next to the ashtray shaped like cupped hands, took out a cigarette and stuck it between his lips. He tried to light it but nothing was happening. He grimaced, I alerted him:

"The filter."

"Huh?"

"The filter, you're lighting the wrong end of your cigarette."

That had never happened before. Even in the dark, blindfolded and with his hands tied, Castilhos could always find his cigarettes in the chaos of that desk, put one in his mouth without looking away from what he was doing and light it quickly, dead center. He was kind of a black belt of tobaccoism. The telephone rang, but instead of answering he took it off the hook and remained like that, the cigarette lit at the wrong end in one hand, the telephone in the other, staring at me as if I had just said that I wanted to cover the landing of the extraterrestrials on Avenida Paulista.

I called to him:

"Castilhos."

Without putting down the telephone or the cigarette, in a soft, slow voice, he recited:

"'The most marvelous is not
the beauty, deep as that is,
but the classic attempt
at beauty,
at the swamp's center.'"

He was gazing past me so fixedly that I turned around. But there was nobody else in the newsroom besides us and Teresinha O'Connor, glued to the telephone. I didn't have the faintest idea who the author of those lines could be. And this time it didn't seem like a test. It sounded more like an epigraph. Or epitaph.

I insisted:

"Do you remember Dulce Veiga?"

"Say it again," he said—he was acting weird. "Say it again, real slow."

"Dulce Veiga, Castilhos, do you remember? That girl Márcia Fellatio, of the Toothed Vaginas, is Dulce Veiga's daughter."

He crushed out the cigarette and didn't light another.

"Whatever happened to her?"

I hung my head sheepishly.

"Rehearsing, recording, that kind of thing. Record promotion, you know. We agreed that I would call today. The Toothed Vaginas ain't easy. I'll definitely have the piece tomorrow."

Castilhos slammed the phone down with such force that a couple of cigarette butts flew off the edge of the desk and landed on the floor. I stamped them out.

"No, you idiot. Dulce, where is Dulce Veiga?"

"How the hell would I know? According to her daughter she vanished about twenty years ago."

"Twenty, twenty years," he sighed fitfully, as if it hurt. He ran his fingers through his thinning, almost completely gray hair, which fell below his ears in tight curls and coiled over the not-so-clean collar of his white shirt. His voice was disconsolate:

"Twenty, twenty years."

I was annoyed at that slow camera & close-up of the reminiscing eyes type of scene.

"Do you remember her?"

He stretched his open hands across the desk toward me, like someone trying to grab at something in the air. The rosy palms turned up, immobile, as if waiting for a butterfly—I thought of Márcia's breasts, of the lottery ticket seller—to alight on them before closing quickly and carefully, one on top of the other, the butterfly trapped in the hollow of the closed hands. They were sweaty, the rosy palms of Castilhos' fragile hands.

He took off his glasses. In the same monotone in which he recited poems, he said:

"Do you think I could ever forget her? Dulce Veiga, of all people, the best of them all. The most elegant, the most dramatic, the most mysterious, and blessed with that husky voice which could give form to any feeling, as long as it was deep. And painful, Dulce sang the pain of being alive without a cure. And she was lovely, so lovely. Not just her voice, but the way she leaned over the piano with a dry Martini in one hand, leisurely swirling the olive around while she slowly took the microphone with the other. No, please, don't think anything vulgar. As if she were picking a rose to place at the altar of a cruel god, that's how she took the microphone to sing. Like someone accepting a gift that involves her in others' misfortunes, that's how she sang. There was no overt sensuality in Dulce Veiga, but something like a lament for the existence of that sensuality. She sang everything as if she were asking forgiveness for having feelings and desires. A part of her existed in the middle of this, wallowing in the mire of passion. The other was a cold goddess, removed from the wretched muck of humanity, searching for pleasure. That face looked as if it were sculpted in white marble, so distant . . . You may think I'm exaggerating, but all of us who saw her even once, and there was a time when, although there weren't many of us, we were an exclusive circle, a legion, a sect of fanatics at Dulce Veiga's feet. There was never anyone like her, and there never will be. You may think I'm exaggerating, but those who had the privilege of seeing her for a day, an hour, or even five minutes know very well, that—"

"I did," I interrupted.

His eyes sparkled. He must have been a handsome man, I suddenly realized, the kind who recites poetry after the third whiskey. Castilhos fixed his moist eyes on me, his long lashes caressed the bags swollen with alcohol, cigarettes, and time.

"You're very young, buddy."

"Not as young as you think. Or I'd like."

He put his glasses on again.

"You met her?"

Remembering, such a dangerous thing. But I gave it a shot.

"I wasn't even twenty. I think it was the first interview I did in my life. For *Bonita*."

He laughed. Stained teeth, but his own.

"*Bonita*," he repeated, "the magazine for the pretty woman. It was so long ago, that was fun."

I said:

"I went to her apartment twice."

He groaned:

"Whatever happened to Dulce Veiga?"

And clapped his hands together hard. The butterfly, I thought, he crushed the butterfly.

"The interview," I stammered.

Castilhos caressed the horns of the clay ox. But it wasn't what I thought. He lit a cigarette, at the right end.

"Forget the interview, you'll do it tomorrow. Later, whenever, it doesn't matter. Now sit down and write."

"But what?"

"A memoir. You're gonna write a memoir, okay?" He raised his hand, traced the letters in the air with the cigarette smoke. "'*Whatever Happened to Dulce Veiga?*' That's your title. I want it on my desk at six P.M. without fail."

He buried his head in his papers and began again to scribble across the page in red ink. From the back of the newsroom came Teresinha's shrill voice, "You don't say, she of all people, that old bag!" Castilhos was busy circling the last paragraph in red, moving it with an arrow to the top of the page.

"Imbeciles," he growled. "They always put the lead at the end of the piece, what can you do?" And in the same tone, looking at me crossly, "Sixty full lines."

I glanced forlornly toward Teresinha's desk. She waved without putting the telephone down.

"Ask Pai Tomás for the file from the archive. There must be pictures of her."

I began dragging myself toward Teresinha's desk.

Damn, damn the minute I'd spoken Dulce Veiga's name and awakened the editor-in-chief's mystical-artistic-libidinal memories. I'd never written a memoir in my entire life, and there was still that shady area I hadn't managed to shed light on: somebody, there was somebody else in Dulce's apartment that day, or the other, I couldn't remember. Lost in the midst of the newsroom I raised my head toward one of the fans. Air, I thought. Earth—there was none under my feet, that horrible carpet blackened by time, fire only in the embers of Castilhos' cigarettes, and sticky water oozing from the palms of my hands.

When I managed to move again, he called me back and handed me a record.

"It came for you," he said. He winked, and added, "Beauty in the middle of the swamp, the poem. William Carlos Williams: 'The Hard Core of Beauty.'"

I took the record. That, at least, made sense: *hard, hard core.*

13

The record was called *Armageddon.* It didn't surprise me, or the fact that it had been sent so quickly. After all, astrology aside, Patrícia must be an excellent manager. What I wasn't expecting was the dedication on the cover, written over Márcia's face. A pale, androgynous, mutant face in a close-up, with only the green eyes in color, and the rest of the group sprawled on a desert-like stretch of sand, in black and white.

In purple ink and a tiny handwriting that didn't seem like her at all, it read, "*Where is the way where light dwelleth? And as for darkness, where is the place thereof?* (Job 38:19)." And underneath, "For our encounter." It was signed *Márcia F.* F as in ferocious, I thought, as in fuck, felicity, falsity—and many other things. I was reading the titles of the songs on the back of the cover, almost all of them written by her, some lyrics by Patrícia—it must be the same, one Patrícia Woolf—others by a certain Ícaro, with titles like "Final Battle," "Atomic Love," or "Cesium 90," when Teresinha called out, "Your second day and already getting presents, eh? For me to get anything I have to promise a thousand items in return."

"A sincere wish is always fulfilled," I read on the Seicho-No-Ie calendar behind her.

"It's for a piece I'm writing."

She stole a glance at the record.

"Márcia Fellatio and the Toothed Vaginas. I heard it on the radio. Interesting, but too noisy. I prefer Charles Aznavour, you know?" She crooned in a lousy accent, "'*Que c'est triste Venice, les temps des amours morts*.' I have so few items for my column today, it's awful. There's nothing going on in the summer. The only news is Lilian Lara's latest plastic surgery. Some news: that old bag must have had over thirty already."

Lilian Lara was a famous soap opera actress, one of those blondes of an indefinite age between thirty and sixty. Every once in a while I'd see her picture on the cover of one of those magazines I'd never buy, or hear her saccharine voice coming from the TV of the little old ladies on the first floor. I stuck a sheet in the typewriter, an old Facit as heavy as a tractor. My mind was blank, but I needed to pretend to be busy so Teresinha would leave me alone.

"Don't you have any tidbits for me?"

I was going to say no, but I remembered:

"Have you ever heard of Dulce Veiga?"

She squinted. Her lashes spattered tiny dots of black mascara around her eyes.

"You mean *Edith* Veiga?"

"No: Dulce, Dulce Veiga. A singer, more or less from the same time."

As she strained to remember, time seemed to collapse over her face. The wrinkles spread from her forehead to the darker roots of her bleached hair. From his desk, Castilhos shot us a scrutinizing glance. I needed to work.

"Of course," she suddenly said. "My, it's been so long. She was so stylish, whatever happened to her?"

"Nobody knows. That singer, Márcia, is her daughter."

Teresinha slapped her forehead.

"How *fabulous*. I already have a sensational title: 'Like mother' and ellipses. Tell me more."

I told her what I knew, that is, close to nothing. It was enough. The phone rang, she answered, and I remained alone with the blank page and the typewriter.

Write, but what? I had only decided not to reveal that Márcia was Dulce Veiga's daughter, that was Teresinha's department. And all I remembered was so vague, almost impossible to tell. I typed an inevitable *qwertyuiop*. I crumpled the sheet and threw it in the trash. I lit a cigarette. I ran the tips of my fingers over Márcia's face on the record cover, where was that way where light dwelleth? She was wearing a spiked black leather choker. The photograph was cropped at her chest, a little above one of the butterfly's wings.

It was after three P.M., the newspaper staff were beginning to trickle in. The young guy in black, hair spiked with gel, nodded from afar. I tightened my facial muscles & etc. Pai Tomás wasn't around for me to ask him for the file; I didn't dare call out his name, everyone would stare at me, my palms were sweaty, I wanted to be invisible. I lit another cigarette. Le-thar-gic, that's how I felt, ap-a-thet-ic, co-le-op-ter-ous. Out the windows clouds were building in the gray sky, it was going to rain again. I got up to get some coffee. Too weak, plastic cup, too much sugar.

"More than you," I thought, "more than you, I remember your yellow shoes." That line—was it a line?—had been turning over in my head for over ten years. That was it, I never knew what came after. Was there actually something after? Man, was I bored. I glanced at the paper, a new movie by David Cronenberg—I loved *The Fly*, had even written an article comparing it to Kafka: the-same-damned-genesis-of-all-outsiders-that-had-produced-*The Metamorphosis*, something pretentious like that. Of course, I identified a little, I had put in my years of therapy, after all. Flies, roaches, insects. I was doing everything in my power to get depressed, and I couldn't stop myself.

Back then, I ruminated, before life had turned into a string of mornings identical to Gregor Samsa's, back then I at least knew how to write. Writing, I mused idiotically, was not like riding a bicycle or having sex, darling. You forget how, get rusty, grow numb. General crisis.

Dull afternoon, time was passing. Outside a sudden wind blew through the leaves of the only visible palm tree. To lie under a palm tree just like that, postcard, a green coconut in my hand. Then go into the crystal clear sea, past the white foam of the surf, float in the water, your face turned toward the sky, drift in any direction. Islands, algae, coral, dreambeaches. Far from the typewriter.

Then I closed my eyes and began to distance myself from the phones ringing, typewriters clacking, voices fragmented into bits of conversation, to listen only to my own heartbeat. Both hands over the keyboard, in a posture that retains a little of silent prayer and a lot of quiet madness, desperately wanting to give form through words to something that only exists without a face or name, in that remote region of the brain where imagination meets memory and blind intuition. Alone and compliant, lost in the center of this confused crossover, in the midst of the terror of no longer being able, without anything or anyone to come to my rescue, besides the thing itself, and itself treacherous, maybe murderous, slippery like a snake, still and perhaps forever formless, because I, the only one capable of grasping it, might let it get away—that was the biggest fear—I suddenly opened my eyes, rubbed my hands together, put a sheet in the typewriter and wrote:

"The first time I saw Dulce Veiga she was sitting in a green velvet armchair."

14

It was a quarter to six.

I read, reread, cut, added. It felt good, it felt alive. My hands were shaking a little. Taming imprecision, hammering in periods at the end of each sentence. Straitjackets, an attempt to impose a certain order and some clarity on something that was sheer, vague, unchecked nostalgia. I lit a cigarette, then realized there was another already lit in the ashtray. I put out the one I'd just started and, while I smoked the first, I stared at the dusty files Pai Tomás had left on top of my desk. There was very little, but that wasn't the fault of the *Diário da Cidade*, so old this was probably the only good thing in the newspaper: the memory of better times, preserved in the yellowed pages of the archives.

Actually, Dulce Veiga had never been a very popular singer. The kid critics of today's arts sections, undecided whether to call her *obsolete* or *passé*, now would perhaps say she was—*cult*. But this word, which had the irresistible power of reminding me of Isabella Rossellini's heavily accented drawl as she moaned "Blue Velvet," would have sounded ridiculous in those times, almost incomprehensible. Dulce Veiga sang in small, more or less elegant downtown clubs, had made one or two records, had small roles in films—where, before or after singing a sentimental samba, she spoke a few lines, invariably leaning against the piano or smoking at a table on the dance floor, framed by the lamp in the center and the bucket with a sweating bottle of champagne—and had vanished on the opening day of what would have been her first big show: "Deliciously Dulce."

A full house, critics in the audience, friends and admirers: all ready to love her and definitively consecrate her as the best. One hour, two, closed curtain. Behind it, some restlessness among the musicians, a chord on the piano, a sigh from the saxophone piercing the red velvet and spreading like an uncomfortable cape over the audience as well. Coughs, chairs creaking, nervous clapping. Then the first timid boo. Director Alberto Veiga, her husband—I didn't remember this name, could he be the other person in the apartment on São João, that afternoon?—lying, saying that Dulce had had an accident. The following day the official denial and the cancellation of the show: Dulce Veiga had completely vanished.

For more or less a month, in that fated and inevitable rhythm of sensational news, the papers followed the investigations. The front page, later pieces each time shorter in the inside pages, then the police blotter, three columns with picture, half a column without picture. Finally, a short notice two, three months later: "The mystery remains unsolved. Still no news on the whereabouts of singer Dulce Veiga, who disappeared without leaving a trace when."

I looked at the date and tried to remember where I was at the time.

Delivering papers in Paris, washing dishes in Sweden, cleaning houses in London, serving drinks in New York, dropping acid in Bahia, chewing coca leaves in Machu Picchu, swimming in the crystal clear reservoirs of Passo da Guanxuma. My life was made up of loose pieces, like a puzzle without a final shape. I arranged pieces at random. Some came close to forming a story which stopped abruptly, sometimes continuing in another three or four pieces, connected to other pieces that had nothing to do with the first ones. Others remained isolated, disconnected from anything around them. As time went by, I kept running, never a year in the same city. I traveled to avoid ties—sentimental, sticky—to never go back, and always ended up returning to cities that were no longer the same, to people with linear, orderly lives, in whose well-charted course there was no longer room for me.

Tiling a wall with disparate mosaic pieces, that's how it was. The right half of a wreath didn't continue or was completed in the left half of another wreath, but in an unexpected Greek or baroque frieze, which in turn didn't extend to the next tile as a square or a rectangle, but gave way to a lopped off concentric circle.

I underlined some of Dulce Veiga's statements in the longest interview, probably the last one before she disappeared, published on the eve of the show's opening night:

"I sing because singing gives me meaning."
"But I always think there's no point in singing."
"I don't want any of the material things singing could bring me."
"I want to find something else."
"Something I don't even know the name of, larger than me or any song."
"I'd like to disappear some day."
"The way trolleys have disappeared from streets and bandstands from plazas."

Ambiguous, poetic, or confused, there were other sentences like these. I couldn't focus on them. While the hands of the big yellow clock on the back wall moved closer to six, the newsroom sounded more and more like a buzzing hive. Everybody was running from one side to the other, turning in their daily quota of honey—was it really *honey*? Let's just say so, I thought, I was in a good mood. From time to time queen-bee Castilhos checked everything with a glance. I needed to choose a picture and turn my piece in.

I chose: against a light, infinite background, her shoulders bare, Dulce Veiga was tossing her blond hair back, like Rita Hayworth in *Gilda*, smiling. But there were others—seductive, artificial, somber, extravagant. Dulce in a dress made of shiny material, possibly taffeta, with a black tulle rose in her cleavage; in a black shirt, with only her eyes made-up, balancing on a stool like Silvia Telles, trying perhaps to get in the good graces of the bossa nova crowd; a beret hiding her hair, a false mole at the corner of her mouth, that certain air of a militant in the French resistance; her cheek pressed against the back of an armchair, long fingers running through her hair, pearl necklace, her gaze fixed on something beyond the photographer. Almost all beautiful, but none with the lighting of the one I had chosen. Irrationally, I decided that in any case it was necessary to publish a happy image of Dulce Veiga.

There were also photographs with other people: leaning on the shoulder of Pepito Moraes, her favorite piano player; with her husband Alberto Veiga striking a dramatic pose like the leading man of a Mexican movie from the sixties, coat with padded shoulders, cigarette in a holder held between lacquered nails; in a group, around a club table, holding hands with a vaguely familiar powerful-looking man with a thick mustache and a Turkish appearance; receiving a prize from Leniza Maia and giving another one to Maysa, smiling between them. To my surprise, various pictures with Lilian Lara—her best friend, as some clippings from the magazine *Intervalo* stated. In the middle of Praça da República, leaning against the fence around the pond, both in white suits and pregnant. One of Dulce's arms was around Lilian's shoulders, the other placed on her own seven-, eight-month belly. Caressing Márcia, I thought. I looked for Teresinha at the desk next to mine—I had forgotten about her the whole afternoon—she'd like this picture. She had already left, her column was the first one to close.

The dust from the clippings was getting in my nostrils. I sneezed, blew my nose. On the contact print from the opening day of the show I drew a circle in red pencil around the picture I had chosen, making sure the mark didn't interfere with that sort of serene aura around Dulce Veiga's face. *"I want to find something else,"* I wrote in the caption. I closed the files, folded the sheets with the pictures between them, and walked across the office to give them to Castilhos. I thought he was going to read it immediately, but he didn't even look up when he dismissed me.

"Good, you can go for today, okay?"

15

Before he even touched me, I felt his presence like a tingling, a growing warmth in my shoulder. He must have stood like that for a long time, his hand suspended as if he were blessing me, since it was only after the people at the bar began to stare that I turned. Even so, it took me a while to make out his face, slightly above his outstretched hand. He wore a silver ring with the image of Jesus on the cross in relief. Perhaps because of that, because of the silver on the white finger, I felt certain the hand would be cold.

I shook it, when he held it out to me. And confirmed: cold as ice.

"Good to meet you," I said.

He bowed.

All dressed in black, hair spiked with gel on top of his head, shaved around his ears, a cross, also silver, in his left ear, very pale, it was the young man I'd seen earlier in the newsroom.

It wasn't a sick paleness, like people who, out of fear of light, any kind of light, refuse to go out in the sun, and it didn't have the emaciated look of intellectuals who drink until late into the night. It was a sophisticated, aristocratic pallor, like someone who'd lived in Europe for a long time and found tanned skin, a flowered shirt, or any other color besides the black of his clothes and the white of his skin vulgar.

"My name is Filemon," he said. "Forgive the intrusion, but I read your book. I don't remember the title exactly. *Visions*, or something like that."

"*Mirage*," I corrected him. And almost choked on my sandwich. Nobody had read it, I myself had done all I could to forget those lousy poems.

"Nice title. Rather symbolist, isn't it?"

I gulped down the rest of the sandwich. He was smiling with his very black eyes, not with his unexpectedly red mouth. It was nice, his mouth. Moist, large, alive. I felt an irrational desire to kiss that mouth, as he said:

"Nothing against the end of the nineteenth century, especially now, at the end of the twentieth. After all, the basic questions and trials of humankind remain, and always will, the same as ever."

He was too pedantic. I silently nodded in agreement. He kept talking.

"But what I find most curious is that in spite of your subjective, spiritual, and decidedly metaphorical vision of the world, you've tried to incorporate into your verses a language typical of marginal poetry which paradoxically has in turn little or nothing at all that is spiritual and subjective and much less metaphorical in the way it seeks a concrete identification of that reality which after all, you will agree, always ends up evading any attempt at recognition, be it of a literary, scientific, or psychological nature."

He looked as if he had memorized the text, it sounded completely out of place there, in the stale air of the newspaper bar, in front of those round glass cases crammed with eggs with blue shells, the platters of fried fish, chicken and beef turnovers, the smell of onion and fatty ham. There was nowhere for him to sit, so he remained standing, against the large glass window overlooking the street. In order to hear him, I turned the back of the stool covered with torn plastic against the counter. But I couldn't understand what he was saying, even though I didn't take my eyes off his mouth.

From time to time I looked away to catch a glimpse of the night falling behind him, the lights beginning to come on, reflected on the wet asphalt at the intersection of Consolação and São Luís.

I began to hear again only when he lightly touched my shoulder.

"The only thing I don't understand," he was saying, looking right into my eyes, and very softly, so the people around us wouldn't hear, "the only thing I don't understand is the absolute absence of Jesus in your poetry and, probably, in your life."

Beyond the glass pane, down in the street, some people still had their umbrellas open even though it had stopped raining. Coming from Xavier de Toledo, a woman in an old-fashioned ultramarine blue suit, with a tight skirt below the knee, stopped for a few moments in front of the steps of the Mário de Andrade Library. I could only see the lower half of her body beneath the open umbrella. Her tight skirt, her high heels.

"Absence of who?"

Filemon tightened his grip on my shoulder and brought his face so close to mine that his head blocked my view of the street. He was looking right into my eyes, as if he were trying to hypnotize me. Perhaps he was succeeding, because I kept looking, fascinated, at his mouth, which was turning redder and redder, and more animated. Everybody must be looking at us.

"Of Jesus, I said. I spoke the name of Jesus. You know who I'm talking about. I was sent to you to talk about Jesus, the Christ. The man who died for us on the cross. To save us, bleeding and crying, he gave his own life, his own blood, the sacred blood of God Our Lord and of the Holy Virgin Mary. It's in the name of Jesus that I'm here, doing something I don't usually do. Because it's not up to me to try to awaken the name of Jesus in the heart of someone who's lost in the darkness of the devil and his subtle deceits."

"Thanks," I said idiotically. I didn't know what to say. I tried to push him away to look at the street again, at the woman standing in front of the library.

He seemed to understand. Or perhaps it was just a dramatic, studied move when he straightened up and announced:

"You have the light. You have Jesus within you, you always did. That's why I talked to you. Jesus is only asleep within your deceived body, your captive soul. Not even you know this. But I can help you awaken him, that's what I'm here for."

Beyond the glass pane, precisely at the height of Filemon's heart, the woman in the old-fashioned suit closed her white umbrella, slowly shook it in the air, as if she wanted to rid it of the last raindrops. Then she raised her head, her straight blond hair, cut at the height of her chin, and looked up in our direction. I began to suspect it was her. And became certain when, light and deliberate as if she were dancing, she switched the closed umbrella to her left hand and raised her arm, her forefinger pointing to the sky, in the same gesture and at the same time as the previous afternoon. Even from the third floor, even through the fogged glass and among all the people who were walking by, hiding her for a few seconds from my eyes, even with Filemon's hypnotic voice ceaselessly repeating words like salvation, path, truth, glory, and sin, I knew without a doubt that the woman standing down there could only be Dulce Veiga.

I took out my wallet, threw a bill on the counter, picked up Márcia's record and got up to leave.

Filemon looked at me, astonished. I touched his shoulder, as he had touched me earlier, through the black silk of his shirt. He was staring at me with his mouth agape. Before running down the stairs I leaned close to his face and, without thinking about the others looking at us or anything else, not even about what I was doing, I quickly kissed him on the lips. They were hot, unlike his hands, and as soft as the silk of his shirt.

As I stepped out of the bar into the grimy tiled hallway, I still had time to glance up, behind the counter, and see the image of St. George in a niche with fluorescent lights, his spear pinning the dragon beneath the legs of his white horse, with a lit candle, a glass of cachaça, and an overblown red rose at its feet.

I ran into Pai Tomás. He saluted:

"Ogum iê!"

16

As I stepped out into the street I began to worry I wouldn't see her. Because she would disappear like the afternoon before, like twenty years ago, and also because at that hour, undecided between night and day, the neon lights still hadn't come on and the lilac of the sunset hidden by the buildings wouldn't be enough to make her visible. But, nearly in the shadows, the dark blue of her clothes increasingly blending with the falling night, Dulce Veiga was still there. On the other side of the street, waiting for me.

Against a red light, without paying attention to the cars, the screeching brakes, and the shouts, I started to cross toward her. When she saw me, and I was sure she could, everyone could see the solitary dazed man that I was in the middle of the intersection, Dulce turned and began to walk rapidly. Her heels hammered down the sidewalk, they had already reached the corner by the time I made it to the front of the library. And maybe because of the recent glut of news from Eastern Europe, maybe because of the austere clothes she was wearing, for some reason or none at all, mere delirium, I decided to turn left, pass the Metrópole arcade and enter the Lufthansa agency. I pictured her disembarking in East Berlin, like a spy in a movie of the cold war era, and then going on to Budapest, Prague, or Warsaw.

I called out her name, she didn't turn.

Dulce Veiga crossed the street, disappeared somewhere behind the newsstand, and then I thought she might enter the Eldorado Hotel and sit at the bar with glass walls through which, if you watch closely, you can see furtive homosexuals on the prowl across the street, among the trees of the square, more numerous as the night draws on, order a cognac or a cup of tea and sit there, waiting for someone or no one, or maybe just smoking alone, nearly motionless, watching the street or not, maybe thinking about nothing in particular, the face with the proud chin remaining expressionless as time passed, the drink and the cigarette came to an end, and night fell over the city.

I called out again, she kept going.

Then, who knows, I fantasized as she walked down the opposite sidewalk and I waited, once again, for the lights to change, I too could walk into the bar—nearly empty at that hour—sit in the vacant chair in front of her and. I wouldn't know what to do, maybe show her Márcia's album, or what to say, and before I could choose from a bunch of dumb formulas like *do you remember me?* or *I've been thinking about you* or *may I keep you company?* the light turned green, and to keep from losing her I was forced to cross without having made up my mind about what I might do or say, if indeed I would say anything, if she were really there and I, maybe, went in as well.

But none of that was going to happen, because she didn't stop, she was already well past the bar's entrance without having gone in. I followed her as far as the corner of Avenida Ipiranga, where I thought she'd cross again to Praça da República, and when I thought that I imagined the square would be different, the old one, not the dilapidated one of today. But if she had already crossed before, I thought as I began to run, it wouldn't make any sense for her to cross again now, in the heavy late afternoon traffic, and I continued to think things like that, of no importance or logic or clarity, until she disappeared down the little arcade inside the Itália building.

I entered the arcade. And came out again, scanning the street-corners that fled from or plunged into the damned center of the city. I went in again.

There was no sign of her in the few shops still open, or in the six or seven corridors that meet at that point. Only a cold wind came through the passages, perhaps the first that summer. I thought of leaving, but glancing at the elevator panel I realized someone had just gone up and maybe, I immediately thought, maybe she—as I always did every time I came back to town—had gone up to the terrace on the top floor, from where, with some effort, in the remnants of light still in the air, she could see or at least imagine the greens of Praça da República, the shady streets that slope down toward Bexiga and the outline of those hills far beyond Barra Funda.

My hands perspiring, I pressed the elevator button.

17

I counted each of the forty-one floors. Getting off at the top to take the other elevator that went on up to the restaurant I heard the sound of a piano. Single notes, apparently unconnected, so far apart that at first they didn't seem part of any melody. Only after a while, putting together the scattered notes in my head, did I recognize "Manhã de Carnaval." I felt like singing along, but I could only remember the part that says there's a new song in life, or something like that.

Other than the waiter leisurely wiping the counter with a rag and the man with long gray hair leaning over the piano, the bar was empty. The waiter barely glanced at me, I began wandering among the tables, watching the piano player's hunched shoulders and his hands on the keyboard. When he turned to reach for the glass of whiskey on top of the piano, I recognized Pepito Moraes, Dulce Veiga's pianist.

I stopped next to him. And asked.

"Where is she?"

He continued to play with his left hand while drinking with the right, and looked me up and down without showing any surprise. After he set the glass back on the piano, he answered:

"She who?"

"Dulce Veiga," I said.

"I wish I knew," he smiled, turning to play with both hands. And he accelerated the tempo. "I wish she'd show up again someday."

I leaned over the piano, so my face would be at the same level as his creased face.

"I saw her come up here."

Pepito half-closed his eyelids, curious. The lines spread to the corners of his eyes and down his cheeks to join the creases at the sides of his mouth. His voice was very calm, as if he were talking to a child. Or a lunatic.

"You must be seeing things, buddy. Dulce Veiga disappeared twenty years ago. Nobody's seen her since."

And, of course, it could very well be that both the woman of the previous afternoon and today were not Dulce Veiga, but someone else, who I had imagined and embellished; and it could be that she was nothing but a projection of my mind; it could also be that it really was her, but that she'd kept going, down other streets, and that I had lost her once again. But, finally, it could also be that Pepito and Márcia and Castilhos were lying.

"Tell me about her," I asked.

He accelerated the tempo even more, so that if before the tune had to be pieced together between the spaces that separated each note, now it would have to be discovered within those same notes, which piled up and transformed it into a sort of nervous, neurotic march. Suddenly he stopped, turned toward me, and lit a cigarette.

"It's not an exciting story, buddy. It was a long time ago."

I insisted, he repeated everything I already knew. The opening night, the theater packed, Alberto Veiga lying and saying that Dulce had had an accident. On stage, Pepito and the other musicians still trying to play something. But the audience left, they wanted Dulce and nothing else.

His eyes were gleaming, it must be the whiskey.

"I don't want to remember. It hurts to remember things that went away and won't come back. At first I felt angry, I felt that she wasn't thinking about anyone else when she disappeared. Just herself. But you can't judge what's going on inside another person. She wanted something else."

"What?"

"She didn't know herself. She repeated it all day long: 'I want something else, I want to find something else.' During rehearsals, when she stopped singing, between songs. And everything was great, it was going to be a terrific show. The best of the year. I'm over it now, I don't feel angry, I don't feel anything. Just a pang of nostalgia, from time to time. When I think that it could have been different."

"How so?"

He finished his drink, raised his hand. The waiter came and filled his glass. "Would you like one?" Pepito asked. "I'm buying. I won the animal lottery today."

I declined, he continued.

"Different, that's all. Can things actually be different from what they are? I don't know if there isn't a pre-ordained plan, like a destiny, a script. There was a time, the time of the show, when she could have become the biggest singer in Brazil. And I would have gone with her. Rome, Paris, New York. It didn't happen, that's all. It didn't go that way, she didn't want it to. And she didn't care if others did. She left, I stayed here and there, playing the piano while people eat, drink, and flirt. Without listening to what I play."

"But where did she go?"

"Nobody knows, buddy. She kept everybody waiting that night at the theater and didn't show up. Never again, to this day."

I showed him Márcia's album.

"Did you know this girl was her daughter?"

"So I've heard, they say she's very talented. Just think, who would have guessed. I held that kid in my arms, she peed all over me, too. Dulce didn't have the slightest instinct for mothering. And after Saul she got even worse."

Saul: that name stirred something in me. Something that had remained hidden that afternoon, in the apartment on Avenida São João, in front of the green armchair.

"Who's Saul?" I asked. And didn't want to know the answer.

Pepito took a large slug of whiskey. Beyond the glass panes it had gotten completely dark. The wet asphalt of Ipiranga was a web of reflected lights, mirroring the upside-down image of the buildings. Some couples began to fill the bar. Almost all well-dressed men in their fifties, accompanied by younger girls, heavily made-up. The lights in the room got dimmer, Pepito smiled mischievously:

"Oh, one of Dulce's loves. She had many, not even I escaped."

I wanted to ask more, but the waiter came back, looked at me askance and whispered something in Pepito's ear.

"I have to play," he said apologetically. "After all, these guys pay me for that. I have to give these gentlemen a hard-on so they can fuck their secretaries. 'Night and Day,' 'Love is a Many Splendored Thing,' that kind of stuff. Come some other time, if you like, you seem alright. But come before midnight, because after that, buddy, I'm always plastered."

I insisted:

"I want to know where she is."

"Give up," he said before beginning to play. "You're not gonna get anywhere."

I clutched the album in my hands. And asked again:

"Which animal came out?"

Pepito turned without understanding.

"What?"

"The animal, the animal lottery you won."

He laughed:

"Ah, it was the butterfly. The thirteen came out, the butterfly hit the jackpot."

He began to play again, a cigarette dangling from his lips.

As I walked out of the bar, I thought I recognized the tune. It wasn't one of those old American hits. Mixed up with the memory of the butterfly tattooed between Márcia's breasts and the lottery ticket seller at the other bar, the other day, in a fox-trot, fast, almost like a bouncy joke, Pepito was playing "Nothing More," Dulce Veiga's last hit.

And Márcia's first, I thought, counting in reverse order each of the forty-one floors of the Itália building, down to the street level.

18

I don't know how exactly, but I managed to get to my place without running into any of the little old ladies, the Argentinean hustlers, Jandira and Jacyr—or Jacyra. No letters today. Behind the door, only dust, scattered clothes, open food cans, stacks of books, records without covers, brimming ashtrays, newspapers strewn about. I put Márcia's album down on the table, next to Lidia's letter, which I hadn't opened. And, as I did every day, I asked no one and nothing, standing in the middle of the small living room:

"Isn't this life exciting?"

The poster pin-up didn't smile.

My intention was to go to sleep immediately, without putting any order into that mess, without thinking about anything. I took a Lexotan, Lidia's bequest—it was the last box. Then two, then three. I was beginning to feel numb when I remembered I hadn't called Márcia to set up the interview. I went through the pockets of the pants thrown on the floor, until I found the paper Castilhos had given me. I unfolded it slowly—each movement an eternity—still damp from the rain of the day before. And as I remembered old cocktails of crummy drugs—Romilar, Artane, Tenuate—I stared at the concentric circles drawn over the sentence "everything revolves around it," and everything was indeed revolving, slowly revolving, the Lexotan was beginning to kick in. It took me a while to remember that the number was written on the back of the paper.

Oh, right, the call.

At the other end an answering machine came on, the kind with music recorded before the message. Not a heavy rock tune, but, unexpectedly gentle and sweet, Nara Leão's voice singing "It's Wonderful." When she said *it's marvelous that you should care for me*, the music stopped and Patrícia's voice came on, saying that it was an answering machine, & etc. It felt good to hear Nara right then, I wanted to hear more, but it would be impossible to find my copy of the album in that mess, in that state. So I called again, just to hear Nara singing those wonderful, soothing words: our story is never going to end.

I took off my clothes and threw them on the floor. One more pair of pants and a shirt. Another pair of underwear, another day, it didn't make any difference. It was all just more dirt piling up.

Saul: Pepito had said. He pronounced it *Sá-ul*, stressing the *a* of the first syllable, dividing the name in two stages, two starts. The first, a truncated sigh; the second, an abrupt leap. Sleeping, a leap in the dark. I thought of crossing myself, there's no Jesus in your life, Filemon was repeating, but in the middle of the Son's name I began to remember a childhood prayer that ended with something like *if death pursues me the angels shall protect me amen*, I had always liked the angel part, I liked angels, fallen, cursed, or pure and virginal, I also remembered a picture of the guardian angel, hands outstretched—the way Filemon had stretched his over my shoulder—over the heads of two children playing on the brink of the abyss. A bow in the boy's hand, a ball with colored sections at the girl's feet, at the brink of the black precipice, one step from the fall.

The concentric circles were revolving in my head, the beginning or end nailed to a vortex in the center of my forehead, but the worst, the worst would never be real death, nothingness and never, the worst was not remembering, not being able or even wanting to remember, the way I didn't remember the second and last time I had seen Dulce Veiga, like someone trying to kill undesirable memories, supposedly to clean up his act.

Everything I forgot or denied, I vaguely realized in the middle of falling, was what I was the most. I turned on my stomach, naked.

He wore a tank top, like the Argentinean downstairs I had seen in the hall one day. One afternoon, in another time. I nestled in those arms belonging to a body whose face or physique, torso or head, I couldn't see, while the concentric circles continued to revolve, mushrooms grew monstrous in the dampness of the kitchen, the sweet smell of the incense seeped in under the door, the light slowly faded, like the end of a play, until the last visible object, a table or chair, was so enveloped by darkness, barely discernible in the increasingly faint light, a tabletop, a leg, two arms, and while common, these objects, perfectly recognizable in full light, if seen like this for the first time, as the light gradually fades and you begin to guess them for what they are in reality or mentally transform them into the myriad others they could be, you begin to invent them more than actually see them, their outlines gradually blurring in such slow darkness that nobody could determine the exact point of transition between the beginning of this darkness and the end of the light, and at this exact point—pentimento—neither I nor anyone else could say for sure what they really are. Those objects, these memories. Whether two legs of a chair, a table, or a woman. Whether two arms of an armchair, a man, or a beast.

WEDNESDAY

The Moslem Beast

19

I'm standing in the middle of the dilapidated church.

The slanted light enters through the broken stained glass windows, falls in colored wedges over the collapsing pews. From the window to the floor, my eyes follow a sunbeam, half green, filtered through a shard of stained glass, half the color of the sun. And at the exact point where this light beam falls on the cold mosaic floor, a snake slithers—half green, half the color of the sun. I think of turning back, but continue to stare at the floor in front of and around me without moving. It's covered with snakes. They wind around my feet, coil in the broken pews, climb the empty altars, like a living carpet. When they escape into the shadows from the wedges of light, colored by what's left of the stained glass, I can see that their scales are a light, almost chestnut, brown. Something in me isn't afraid, even though I feel revulsion for these bodies I imagine to be as icy as the mosaic under my feet.

I look for the statues of the saints, but there aren't any on the empty altars, covered only with snakes among stubs of melted candles. Like real people, as tall as me, but immobile as statues, the saints are scattered around the interior of the church, among the dust, the snakes, the wedges of light. It must be Holy Week, I think. Lent, because they're all covered with sheer purple cloth. Gauze, lace, tulle. Through the sheerness I vaguely make out a familiar silhouette, some forms, and little by little I guess, aided by childhood memories. That one, holding the child, must be St. Anthony; the other, with his hands tied behind his back and three arrows stuck in his bare torso, St. Sebastian; the one among white roses, with the crucifix in her arms, St. Theresa of Lisieux; further back I barely discern the large wings of St. Michael the Archangel, brandishing his sword around which a live snake coils.

I walk slowly among the statues and stop in front of an effigy with its back turned, which I can't identify. Flowers, harp, or lamb—there's nothing in the arms hanging at its sides. Somewhere a harpsichord begins to play Handel. I touch the head of the statue to push aside the purple veils of mourning for the murder of Jesus of Nazareth, the cloth slips off the immobile body. She turns toward me, the bare face of a blond woman. From within her skull, from the empty eye sockets, from the orifices of the nostrils and ears, through her gaping toothless mouth snakes slither—brown, slow, alive. I follow the snakes' movements down her shoulders, through her clothes, between her bare breasts. Farther down, I can see the hair around her parted sex and, inside it, two rows of pointy, serrated teeth. I quickly drop my eyes to the ground. With her bare left foot, she's crushing the head of a snake of a different color.

I wake up screaming before I have a chance to determine what color it is or identify the woman. But I don't need to remember her name, I know very well who she is.

20

That real sound, piercing the morning. Too coarse for a harpsichord, too vulgar for Handel.

I leapt off of the couch, bumped into something hard with my ankle. *Fuck!* I cried. And hopped around in circles on one foot in the middle of that mess, trying not to step on something that was no longer there. I knew I had been dreaming, but I couldn't remember anything except a mounting sense of fear and the harpsichord music.

The doorbell rang again. Nobody ever came to see me at that time, nobody came to see me without calling first, nobody came to see me. I yelled, *coming!*, pulled on one of the pairs of pants strewn on the floor and opened the door.

It was Jacyr, not Jacyra. In shorts and very clean white sneakers, a red t-shirt with a picture of Prince on it, not a drop of makeup on his small monkey face, he had turned once again into the lanky mulatto kid, the son of Jandira and Moacyr-that-scumbucket. He pushed me aside and barged in unceremoniously.

"It's almost noon, I've been ringing for hours. I'm not going to be on call all day, breeder."

I remembered too late, as I tried to place him in that fading morning, the house-cleaning agreed upon with Jodie Foster in the hall downstairs. Jodie was gone, leaving in her place a kind of shorter and lighter-skinned Grace Jones, disguised as an urchin, all arms and legs. I tried to organize in my memory the remains of the previous day, and what I needed to do today, the interview with

Márcia—I need a date book—and then forgot again. Behind the fragments of the sentences I had written in the newspaper, memories like Filemon's spiked hair or Pepito Moraes' glass of whiskey on top of the piano and all the rest, were other images.

Perseus held Medusa's severed head by her serpent-like hair in one hand, brandishing in the other a sword with a snake coiled around it. How does it manage to slither along the sharp edge like that without being cut in two, I thought and, in a quick cut, as if the director were changing the shot and it were all a still frame, Perseus, Medusa, and the snake were on an altar, in a slowly dimming cone of light.

Between those images and the apartment, which seemed to have survived an earthquake, Jacyr bustled about tirelessly, picking up books, clothes, cans, looking at me in an odd way.

"What's the matter, you've never seen me before?"

"You've changed," I said.

He shrugged, as if adjusting an invisible shawl.

"It was the rainbow after the rain. It happens all the time. Mother says it's Oxumaré, who I carry within me. Six months a man, six months a woman. I turn into such a crazy girl when he descends upon me, then it passes—" suddenly he crossed himself and raised his hand heavenward in salutation, "*Aroboboi*, mother!"

"The snake," I said. I didn't know why.

Agile as a ballerina, Jacyr twirled around. He shook a dirty sheet in the air.

"You look like you've been drinking, man. I bet you got smashed yesterday. What did you do, smoke, snort? I even thought you were getting laid." He glanced at the empty couch scornfully, suggestively. "But everybody knows you're not that kind of guy."

I ran my hand over my head, as if I were smoothing down disheveled thoughts, and took a cigarette from the table. Jacyr snatched it from my hands.

"No sir. It's very bad to smoke on an empty stomach."

He was solicitous, like his mother, only in an insolent way. He began to push me toward the bathroom. His soft voice, his hands on my bare shoulders. It was good to have someone alive in that apartment.

"Take a shower while I make some coffee."

I closed the door of the tiny bathroom. From behind it and the ridiculous sticker of a penguin drying itself with a yellow towel—Lidia had probably put it there—I heard Jacyr buzzing and crackling around the living room, like an insect with feverish wings.

I turned on the shower, but the cold water couldn't wash away those remnants and reflections of lost, distorted images. Among the black hairs on my chest, I inadvertently discovered two completely white ones. Tomorrow there will be three, I thought. Then ten, a hundred. A thousand, then what? One of those fifty-year-old gentlemen I would shortly become, with tufts of gray hair escaping from the open collar, a gold chain gleaming among them. Dignified, only a little pathetic. That was the best way to be depressed the rest of the day. Then I felt like singing that everything, everything was all right, I repeated, scrubbing my head—but I couldn't remember any song, I couldn't sing—as I sailed along in the small miracle that had begun two days before. A job: wake up, shower, shave, drink coffee—and have somewhere to go.

Jacyr had flung open the window overlooking Rua Augusta, in front of the funeral home across the street. Was *Happy Days* a funny name for a funeral home, or an appropriate one? Without filters or disguises, in the midday light, the apartment looked even smaller, dirtier, more crowded. It, as well as myself, fared better in the dark, like some plants and animals. Away from the morning sun.

I sat on the edge of the table with the towel wrapped around my waist. Jacyr set before me a cup with a broken handle, filled with coffee. He put his hands on his hips.

"You could do a little weight lifting. Some pecs would be great. Why don't you start exercising and put some pecs on that body? We girls are crazy about big-chested men."

I tasted the coffee. Too sweet.

"I think a man's chest is much nicer than a woman's. Even better if it's hairy, very hairy. You know the kind of chest where the hair blends with the beard? Then the guy shaves his beard and kinda looks like he's wearing a turtleneck. Just seeing that makes me feel like dropping to my knees and sucking him off."

I lit a cigarette, Jacyr snatched it away. I lit another.

"That big black guy, you know the big black guy with dreadlocks who's always hanging out at the Kenya Bar? The one who sells dope, he says he's got one that's *ten inches* long, can you imagine? That's not a banger, it's a boa constrictor."

I tried to focus on something else. There was nothing besides the disorder and Jacyr's voice, occupying all the space inside my brain, preventing me from thinking. Loud, lewd.

"I can handle eight all the way, no problem. I don't know about ten, I'm kinda scared. It could mess you up inside, I don't know. One of these days I'm gonna try it, don't you want me to buy you some dope from him? All you have to do is give me the dough, I've tried it, it's good stuff."

I remembered Lidia's letter, lying on the table two days now. I pushed away the books, papers, brimming ashtrays, Márcia's face on the album cover, and picked up the envelope. I opened it with deliberate slowness, as if it were something so important that Jacyr would feel compelled to shut up just from the atmosphere. But he wasn't looking at me, too busy smoking and dancing around.

"He looks like he'd like to fuck me standing up in the Kenya's bathroom. A hotel is out, I'm a minor. When there's no other choice, I'll put out. But it doesn't go in well, it's better on all fours. Then it goes in all the way."

It wasn't a letter, it was a poem by Cecília Meireles, Lidia was in the habit of doing that. Instead of letters, those letters talking about the delights of the whitewashed walls, sea-blue doors and windows & etc., poems. Jacyr kept talking about chests, chest hair, cocks and cum, the sound of car horns was coming in through the open window. With a quick step Jacyr turned on the radio, which was playing Laurie Anderson, *strange angels sing just for me,* something like that, the open letter, against the vase of dying violets, I read *This is the salt boy,*

the salt boy that weighs down my heart, and at the same time, unexpectedly, after more than twenty-four hours without thinking about it—and I realized only now that all this time I had done nothing but remain aware of my being unaware of him in my mind—in the transition of the blank space between those lines of poetry and the rest that said *look into the depths of my eyes,*
through this prism of tears,
look, look, and you shall see, with a shiver rising from the base of my spine to the wet hair on the back of my neck,

my eyes blurry with sunlight, water from the shower, or tears, who knows which, a sudden emptiness that not even all the obscenities Jacyr kept mouthing could fill, make funny or lighter, within that longing that wouldn't leave me no matter how much time passed, and within it, even without remembering, just carrying on, I woke up every day, took a shower, brushed my teeth and did all those routine things, like someone who, by fits and starts, mechanically, goes on living even after losing a leg or an arm which, even though it's missing, still hurts—without being able to avoid it, unexpectedly, without wanting to avoid it, I remembered Pedro once again.

"What about that guy who was always coming here?"

Huh, I said, who.

"That handsome guy, the one who looked kind of golden. The one with light-colored eyes. He doesn't come around anymore."

Abruptly I said it was very late, I was running behind, I had a hellish day ahead of me, and I got up, pushing Jacyr aside a little too brusquely. He bumped into the table, spilled the remains of the coffee on the dying violets, on Lidia's letter, on Cecília's poem, and as if my eyes blurry with who knows what had zoomed to the paper, before stepping away, I read the lines, now stained, speaking of that boy *on whom I so longed to nail*

wings of Love and Angel. I could have stood there, watching the coffee stain slowly spread over the poem, remembering everything I didn't want to remember, and that way, standing forever in the middle of the apartment, as the lives of other people unfolded beyond the window, outside and far away from me, perhaps I would just feel sorrow, nostalgia, and the kind of bitter surprise nobody can cure—I could have. But I repeated that it was late, I had a hellish day ahead of me, I didn't have time and I'm sorry, you know, this city, this life, this morning.

I put on my pants, shirt, rummaged around in search of money, I was going to be up the creek if I didn't get an advance at the paper, Castilhos would put in a good word, paid Jacyr and left. Without allowing any indiscreet questions, cheap complicity, slimy consolation.

As I was closing the door I glanced back and saw Jacyr leaning over the table. Smiling like a child who just got a present, he waved the cover of Márcia's album in the air, shouting:

"You didn't tell me you had this, breeder. She's a woman, but she's a goddess. Can I put it on?"

Outside the two little old ladies' door, as I was heading for the street, I heard the rock 'n' roll shaking the walls of the building in the voice of Márcia Fellatio and the Toothed Vaginas:

"The past is just a pitfall,
there's no present, nothing at all,
the future is demented:
we've all been tainted."

21

Leaning over the counter of the Kenya Bar in front of a glass of beer, the black guy was humming what I figured must be a reggae tune. Long wiry hair, carefully separated in rows, like flower beds in a plowed field, falling just below his shoulders in thin dreadlocks braided with red and white beads. It must be him.

When he realized I was watching him, he turned, facing the street, his face raised defiantly. I lowered my eyes. Then he spread his legs in the skintight white pants. He wasn't wearing underwear, at least there was no visible line beneath the pants. It could only be him. He tossed his dreadlocks back, the beads sparkled in the sun. I blinked and looked down again. He thrust his crotch forward and stroked it with his hand covered with bracelets. It was definitely him.

I hurriedly crossed the street and disappeared into the phone booth.

After three rings I heard the coin drop at the other end and the recording with Nara Leão come on. I was going to hang up without leaving a message when someone turned the answering machine off and a familiar, irritable, sleepy voice mumbled a hello.

"Patrícia? I'm calling to set up the interview."

"Set up what?"

"The interview. With Márcia, for the *Diário da Cidade,* it's gotta be today."

"No way, only if it was."

Her voice was drowned out by the exhaust of a motorcycle.

"Speak louder, I can't hear you."

Patrícia shouted:

"At six o'clock, with the sun on the cusp of the seventh house."

"Too late, I'll be there at four."

"With the sun in the eighth house—no way."

Maybe at noon, she suggested, with the sun in the tenth house, but noon had already passed. Then perhaps at eight, with the sun in the sixth, but that was when they rehearsed. And several more of those combinations, all incomprehensible to me. The black man's gaze was burning a hole in my back. I began to sweat, I had to get out of there.

I urged her:

"The coin's about to drop."

"It could be tomorrow, then. Because of the moon in Gemini, you know."

Before we got cut off, I managed to yell:

"Today at four, without fail. Give me the address."

Patrícia seemed paralyzed by my firmness. She gave me the address without arguing. I memorized the street, the number—it was a house. I was good at that type of thing, at times I remembered a number for years. But I couldn't identify the neighborhood by the street name or the phone number. Possibly Morumbi, artistic delusions of terminally bored rich girls.

Jackhammers vibrated at the construction site across from the Kenya Bar, next to the funeral home. Nearly naked Northeasterners, wheelbarrows, rocks, suspended on the scaffolding, ants bustling in a long line, from Cariri to the Luz train station, they reminded me of *Metropolis*. The city was going to blow up someday, but that had nothing to do with me. Or did it? I hung up. With a nail, someone had scratched on the red enamel, *I wanna suck youre big dick*. The black guy was now leaning against the bar door, glass in hand, watching the street. From above, like a king. From the back of the bar came a song with primitive percussion, drums in the jungle, repeating something like Bob Marley will always live in the heart of the black people. It made you feel like dancing, but nobody had time for that. Only he, the strong black man with the dreadlocks, was sinuously swaying his body in the white skintight pants and a flowered shirt tied at the waist.

A bus stopped, I squeezed in among the office boys piling up at the exit. Holding on to the door to keep my balance, between the hot breath of damp flesh within and the hot breath of the dry sunbaked asphalt without, I looked back. One hand slowly stroking his warrior's spear, teeth, beads, and skin gleaming in the early afternoon light, the black man was raising a glass of golden beer.

Like a toast, to me.

22

The fan blades were silently turning. No sound of telephone or typewriter. In black and white, the newsroom was a still frame projected into space. In the rear, his back to the window through which filtered a light always dim because of the dirty panes, Castilhos was floating amid clouds of cigarette smoke. On the left, dressed in gray, facing the wall and completely still, Teresinha O'Connor was gazing at another page of the Seicho-No-Ie calendar which she must have just turned. I looked around for Filemon, but there was no one else in the room besides those two statues. Which weren't made of salt, but papier maché from countless newspapers.

Drums in the jungle, I remembered, turn on a radio and let the Afro music shake up that still life. Or walk in calling out *good afternoon!* in a loud voice, so loud they'd be forced to move, if only to look at me sullenly, without a word. But standing at the door—if the camera had changed angles and substituted my eyes for Castilhos', or those of someone positioned behind him, above his hunched shoulders—I was part of that scene, too. The slightest movement and the cameras would roll.

I went in. So stealthily that Teresinha started when I read aloud the sentence on the calendar.

"'Be the leading character in any circumstance.'"

She smiled sadly, she looked like she'd been crying.

"Poor me, I'm just a bit player." And added, pointing to my desk, "The star today is you, darling. Those just came."

On top of the desk, among stacks of papers and newsprint, was a dozen red and white roses. The kind you buy at a florist's, mixed with ferns and other tiny white flowers that looked like stars. Pinned to the pale blue ribbon, a card. I couldn't recall having met anyone likely to send me roses in my entire life. I took the card, Teresinha was watching me. It wasn't a common, store-bought card. The sepia linen paper bore the initials 'A.V.' embossed in gold on the right-hand side. I read aloud, so Teresinha wouldn't think—I didn't know what she might think, and whatever it was it didn't matter in the least.

"'Thank you—I was touched. Only a special sensibility like yours could remember the unforgettable Dulce Veiga with such tenderness. Come see me, I might be able to tell you more.'"

Unforgettable, tenderness, sensibility, touched: I didn't like those words in the least. Below, before Alberto Veiga's baroque signature, was a telephone number. I thought of a Parker 51, gold cap, I'd never seen another one. And it took me a while to remember the picture of the Mexican B-movie Lothario: Dulce's husband and, as far as I knew, Márcia's father.

"Congratulations, they're well-deserved," Teresinha said. "I was touched too. Beautiful text, very spiritual."

"Thanks," I said. And only then did I remember to open that Wednesday's *Diário da Cidade.*

On the front page of the arts section, the blocks of text framed within four columns, the photograph of Dulce Veiga tossing back her blond hair hollowed out the words. The quality of the newspaper's print was abysmal, apt to make Scandinavian blondes look like African goddesses with unusually straight hair. But thanks to some miracle, that day, in that picture, the serene aura surrounding her face had been preserved. Dulce was gazing at some point above the observer's head so intently it made you feel like looking too, and she was almost smiling. Her pale face with high cheekbones showed no contractions or lines. As if that were its natural state, almost smiling, gazing at some place far away. Where things were different, good, worth living. But even though everything in the picture gave the impression of life and joy, the bouquet of roses over it suddenly transformed it into a tombstone gnawed by time.

Teresinha whispered:

"Whatever happened to Dulce Veiga?"

Perhaps she's dead, I thought for the first time.

Castilhos called from the back of the newsroom. He handed me half a dozen telegrams without a word. I tore open the slips, fumbling with the staples. And death, I thought again, telegrams always brought a foreboding of death, come immediately stop father is sick stop, perhaps not in a cemetery, but anonymous, without any tombstone or roses, on the side of a road, in the corner of some vacant lot, under a heap of garbage, some place far from everything, without ever having been found, because nobody had noticed the smell of decay. Twenty years later, only bones, remains of clothes. Intact, besides hair and nails, the pearls, maybe. A strand of pearls as white as the bare vertebrae of her neck.

I pushed the thought away. The telegrams were all from people I knew, praising the memoir, wanting to know more about Dulce Veiga. No clue, no lead. I passed them to Castilhos.

"Very good," he growled. And with the ember of the cigarette he began to burn a hole in one of the telegrams. "So your memoir was a hit."

"I didn't think anyone would remember her."

Castilhos burned another hole next to the first and stared at it. I stared too. The burning edges sparked for a moment, until they found the extinguished edges of the other hole. Then they went out as well, to form a single orifice that looked like a horizontal eight, like this: ∞.

"Writing has such mysteries. Suddenly, without expecting it, one day you manage to awaken something that's alive inside many people." His voice was a little bitter, perhaps he had never attained something like that himself. He burned another hole under the first two. And before the three holes came together, forming a triangle with rounded points, he said with a certain irony, "I just hope you don't plan to rest on your laurels. Or Lauras. What about that piece?"

"I've already set up the interview. I'll definitely have it tomorrow, is that OK?"

"That's fine. But there's another problem. Rafic called, he wants to talk to you in person."

The happiness—was it happiness?—I had begun to feel with the roses, the telegrams and all that, suddenly vanished. Rafic was the owner of the paper, of buildings, islands, yachts. Now he wanted a TV channel and, it was rumored, he'd gotten involved in politics. Nobody ever uttered his name, they just whispered *He*, menacing omnipresence. He never came to the paper, but, like a sort of Moslem Big Brother, he knew about everything that happened there.

"What does he want?"

"Invite you on a cruise of the Greek islands, maybe. Andros, Tenos, Mykonos, Delos, Naros, Thera, Crete," Castilhos rattled off. And caressed the clay ox. For a moment the cigarette remained poised between the yellow horns, like a third smoking horn. He held out a card. "The man's address. He wants you to go see him today, at six sharp and without fail. Don't be late, the boss hates to wait, what can you do?"

With the sun in the seventh house, I thought incongruously. In order to do the interview with Márcia I would have to arrive under an unfavorable sun. Fuck Patrícia and her stars, I thought. I better get moving.

Teresinha was gazing at the roses with her arms crossed. She looked more O'Connor than ever. Maybe she was thinking about Dublin, some long lost love, with the same expression as Anjelica Huston standing on the stairs as she listens to "The Lass of Aughrim" in *The Dead*. Absent and without sorrow, and precisely because of that even more sorrowful. But it wasn't snowing outside, over all of Ireland, over Dulce Veiga's grave. Beyond the windows of Castilhos' desk, São Paulo was sizzling in that February's torrid 100-degree heat. Teresinha was sighing, now a prisoner in the Martello tower from where, on exceptionally clear days, and perhaps today was one of them, you could see Bray Head.

I thought about taking the roses to Márcia, maybe they'd pacify her. But toothed vaginas must hate flowers. Unless they were cacti, anthuriums. Phallic, pointed. I put Alberto Veiga's card and Rafic's address in my pocket, took a white rose from the bouquet and, in my most elegant inflection lifted from a British movie dubbed by Herbert Richers, I bowed and offered the others to Teresinha.

"Lady O'Connor, even though you may not realize *it*, you will always be the leading character."

Oh, she raised her hand to her mouth.

But I was already gone. Without anyone noticing, on my way out, as I let the film frame revert once again to its stillness, I put the white rose on top of Filemon's typewriter, grabbed the tape recorder and split.

23

The house wasn't in Morumbi, Jardins, or any other of those exclusive neighborhoods. After wandering all over the place, consulting a tattered city map in which the streets invariably continued on the pages that were missing, asking at streetcorners and getting answers like, count three traffic lights, but there were only two, then turn left, but there was no street on the left, the cab driver managed to find a small two-story house in the upper section of the Freguesia do Ó neighborhood. I paid the fare without complaining, it was the newspaper's money.

It looked like a town in the interior. A fig tree in the middle of the square in front of the church, children playing ball. Even stranger, it looked like a house in the interior. Provided, of course, I didn't look past the low roofs and smack into the reeking sludge of the Tietê River, a thread of pus underscoring the city's skyline. There was almost no pollution that day, the transparent gray over the city and the sky scattered with clouds so white and round that, had I still dared to write bad poems, I couldn't have resisted comparing them to flocks of sheep. Greek ones, of course. Possibly Armenian. Maybe because of those faraway lands, who knows, I remembered Teresinha O'Connor—yes, it was definitely one of those rare days when you could see Bray Head on the other side—and regretted not having brought the roses.

In the six feet of yard between the door and the low wall, which the ivy was beginning to cover, there were no anthuriums, cacti, or catclaws. In the freshly mowed lawn grew azaleas not yet in bloom, daisies drooping from the heat, and a jasmine bush. Someone seemed to be taking good care of them, but it was difficult to imagine a toothed vagina doing something like that. Maybe a maid, maybe it was the parents' house. Patrícia's parents, of course.

Patrícia opened the door. She had replaced the cat-eye glasses with another, heavier, pair, a piece of tape holding the broken stem together, she was wearing cutoffs and had a book in her hand. She no longer looked so modern. On the contrary, she reminded me of one of those girls who already look like old maids when they're twelve. The only contemporary thing in that setting was the motorcycle parked on the sidewalk.

I tried to read the book's title, without looking at her. And when I looked, even though it wasn't even three in the afternoon, I realized she wasn't mad.

"I had to come earlier. I have an appointment at six."

"It doesn't matter. I had forgotten we're on daylight savings time. With the sun in the ninth house it might even work out. Suddenly you two are traveling together."

She stepped aside to let me in, there was a vague smell of condensed milk about her. The living room also looked like a living room from the interior, modest and clean, a rather worn print sofa, matching armchairs, crocheted doilies on the back and arms. So where's the rock 'n' roll, I thought, looking at the wall with reproductions of English prints from the beginning of the century.

A white and light gray cat was sprawled on one of the armchairs. Patrícia introduced her.

"This is Vita Sackville-West."

She sat in the armchair, put the cat in her lap and closed the book. It was Virginia Woolf, *The Voyage Out*. On the pale green cover, inside a room overlooking a bay full of ships, there was a girl lying on a sofa with a print almost identical to the armchairs in the living room. If the girl on the cover had worn jeans, or if Patrícia had been wearing one of those white dresses full of ruffles, they'd be practically identical. I lit a cigarette.

"Want one?"

"I don't smoke."

I pointed to the book.

"She looks like you."

"That's why I bought this edition," Patrícia said. Then she studiedly turned sideways, took off her glasses, put her hair up in a bun, lowering her face a little. "I'm absolutely certain I'm Virginia Woolf's reincarnation. Don't you think I'm her spitting image?"

It was true, or nearly so. She still lacked a certain anguish. I tried to joke:

"Too bad this time Vita reincarnated as a cat."

"On the other hand, I'm certain Márcia is the reincarnation of Katherine Mansfield. This time around we've settled that business."

Well, now the afternoon will get colder and colder, and as the mist rises from the river Ouse, she'll light the fireplace and make tea, Earl Grey perhaps, in porcelain pots and cups with delicate wildflower wreaths, and wait for Roger and Lytton. Then, when we're already on our second or third cup of tea, poor Leonard will arrive, loaded with the proofs of Hogarth's new editions. And later at night, without paying much attention to the bulletin of the bombings broadcast by the BBC, we'll read aloud Eliot's new poems, enraptured. Or badmouth Joyce, that boor, interrupted only by the arrival of little Quentin and Vanessa—but who would be Vanessa? Hardly likely that it'd be the keyboard player with the shaved head or the huge Japanese chick on the electric bass—and me? Maybe E. M. Forster, back from India to meet Alec Scudder.

I began to feel so comfortable I stretched out my feet toward some invisible damasked velvet stool.

"Careful," I warned. "Don't go filling your pockets with stones and walk into the Tietê River."

Patrícia was about to reply something. Intelligent, good-humored, maybe a little pedantic, but in keeping with the new Patrícia who, besides making me feel very good, had nice legs, tanned by a sun Virginia Woolf had seen very few times, if ever. She began to open her mouth, stroking the cat.

But all of a sudden—guitar solo—rock 'n' roll entered the scene.

Standing on the wooden stairs, in her panties and without a bra, completely out of place in that suave British ambiance, a copy of the *Diário da Cidade* in her hands, Márcia was screaming, "Who let this guy in? Patrícia, you're gonna pay for this. Who does this idiot think he is, using me as an excuse to exploit the story of a poor missing woman in some sleazy scandalmongering rag? And on top of that this O'Connor bitch writes that I'm Dulce Veiga's daughter. I've said it before and I'll say it again: I know nothing about this goddamn story. I'm not gonna say a fucking thing about it because I don't know anything myself."

Meowing loudly, Vita jumped off Patrícia's lap and disappeared in the back. Márcia threw the paper across the living room.

"I want to be recognized for my own talent. I refuse to fuel all this bummer necrophilia about my mother."

She stormed up the stairs, a door slammed.

Patrícia threw the book on the armchair.

"That's the way she is. She's a Leo, a star. You're Aquarius, the opposite. You know all that stuff about attraction and repulsion?" She began to climb the stairs. Suddenly she stopped, turned, and said, in a voice that sounded inexplicably sad, "Everything's gonna be alright. After all, you two have moons in conjunction, in Virgo. You must have had some incarnation together already."

Alone in the living room, I smiled at Dulce Veiga's smile, lying on the floor. "I want to find something else," said the caption. Me too, I sighed.

The cat came back and installed herself on top of the paper. Perhaps she wasn't Vita's reincarnation, but she was undoubtedly very British, even though Burmese, with her reserved manner, the small dark spot on her face that gave her a permanent air of aristocratic disdain. I held out my hand to pet her, but she shied away and walked toward a screen in the corner of the room, so slowly that she seemed to be inviting me to follow her.

Behind the screen there was a small desk and a bookcase with two rows of books. On the top shelf all of Virginia Woolf's works, including diaries, letters, plus Leonard Woolf's, Quentin Bell's, and John Lehmann's biographies. Well-thumbed, marked up, in disarray—they certainly weren't hidden there to impress visitors. Who, out of the way as this place was, must be rare anyway. Below, besides the *I Ching*, just astrology books, most of them in English. I read the names of some of the authors at random—Liz Greene, Robert Hand, Stephen Arroyo, Dane Rudhyar—they didn't mean anything to me.

The cat rubbed against my legs, then jumped on the desk. And there, among packages of Indian incense, crystals, stones, and countless little boxes of every size and shape, was what I figured must be my astrological chart, my name was at the top of the sheet, anyway. I'd seen them before in magazines, but I didn't understand the marks inside the circle of the zodiac, connected by straight lines, blue or red. I ran my hand over Vita Sackville-West's back. She raised her thick tail, then let it drop lightly on the drawing of what seemed to be a planet shaped like a trident, covered with red marks connecting it to other planets.

"I've never seen such a tortured Neptune in my entire life," Patrícia said behind me.

"I was just taking a look, I don't understand any of it."

The cat jumped into her arms. And the two of them peered at me with the same slightly cross-eyed look, as Jandira de Xangô did when she saw in me things I myself couldn't see.

"You must have such frail feet," she said.

It was true. My feet were skinny, weak, too small, they stumbled and hurt all the time. I thought Patrícia was going to ask me to take off my shoes, but she nodded toward the upper floor.

"The superstar is calmer. You can go up now."

As I was going up I began to understand. Downstairs, England, beginning of the century, faded flowers in the prints, tea, and sympathy. Upstairs, New York or Berlin, the poisoned end of this century. The division was so radical you couldn't even call it crazy. On the contrary, it seemed perfectly balanced. Even more so when through the window next to the stairs I saw the pitanga tree outside: Brazil had been relegated to the yard.

Like an exclusively female pop gallery, on the walls I recognized posters of Janis Joplin, Patti Smith, Tina Turner, Laurie Anderson, Suzanne Vega, Sinéad O'Connor, Madonna, Annie Lennox, and others I didn't know. Among the Brazilians only Wanderléa, Marina, and Rita Lee, dressed like a fairy. I winked at Rita. God willing, I remembered, I want to be an Indian some day. The slight scent of incense and Mu tea downstairs gave way to the heavy smell of pot and cigarettes.

The door of Márcia's room was open. She was still in her panties, but she'd put on that awful Toothed Vaginas t-shirt. She was sitting cross-legged on a bright yellow bedspread on top of a mattress placed directly on the floor, in front of an ashtray filled with cigarette butts. I hesitated at the door, exaggerating my respectful attitude. The male's fear, a toothed vagina must love that kind of thing.

"Come in already, let's get this thing over with once and for all."

I sat on the floor, the recorder between us.

"I'm not going to say anything about my mother."

"That's fine," I said. She lit a joint.

"I'm only going to give this fucking interview because Patrícia talked me into it. She says it's good for the band. Fuck that shit—the media, those head hunters."

Uh-huh, I said.

With all the sun out there the window was still closed. In the semi-darkness, besides the bed and the scattered clothes, almost all black, was a TV with the sound turned all the way down, a VCR, a tape deck, a guitar standing in a corner, and just one poster. Illuminated by the TV's flickering colors, a face frail and hard at the same time, with pronounced jaws, a square chin and feminine lips, the young man—to my surprise it was a young man—looked a little like Pedro, but even more like Jim Morrison. A Jim Morrison who hadn't died, been buried in that cemetery in Paris, or grown old if he'd still been alive or, as they say, crazy and hiding in some remote city in the United States. A rejuvenated Jim Morrison who, in keeping with the times, had also bleached his hair, and kept singing the interminable end of an eternally postponed *apocalypse now*. I was going to ask if it was really him, some photomontage—was it possible to cut and bleach the hair of a photograph?

Márcia passed me the joint.

"Shall we start?"

I crossed my legs and inhaled. She spiked up her hair with her fingertips. I felt like I was in a squatter house in Kreutzberg before the fall of the wall. And pressed the recorder's button.

24

Márcia Francisca da Veiga Prado wasn't a star's name. But there was history in those four names. Márcia, late sixties modernities, legacies of President Juscelino Kubitschek; Francisca, an homage to the Goianian grandmother, her mother's mother, who was said to have Indian and German blood, strange green eyes; Veiga came from Dulce, and Prado from her father Alberto. Alberto had met Dulce when he was only a drama stu-

"Tell me your life story," I asked kind of awkwardly. I'd never been and would never be a good reporter, the kind that goads and provokes, I was afraid of hurting people. Márcia spoke almost without looking at me, with her head low, lighting cigarettes, biting her nails or glancing at the TV screen from time to time. I glanced too, following her eyes, but couldn't figure out whether the afternoon movie was *Imitation of Life*, *Susan Slade*,

dent and she a well-known singer. So he'd chosen Veiga over Prado as a stage name—more dramatic. When her mother disappeared, Márcia wasn't even two. Her father, an only child, sent her first to her paternal grandmother, in Rio de Janeiro, a well-off Portuguese widow who lived in an apartment in Copacabana. Márcia was seven or eight when her grandmother was killed by a car, due to her overindulgence in Port wine. Her father, by then a reasonably well-known actor and director, sent her to the other grandmother, Francisca Veiga, in a place called Alto Paraíso de Goiás. The happier memories were there, like swimming in the river, cotton frocks, thatched roofs, bare feet, and incredible starry nights. She had pictures, if I cared to see them. Márcia sang along the roads trying to capture the sound of butterflies' wings when they stop flying and quiver briefly over the open flowers, and the sound of those flowers, huge red hibiscus, when the wild wind blows in their petals, and that of rocks thrown into the rapids when they tumble under water, hitting other rocks, and that of dry gravel crackling in the sun at noon, and falling stars that turn into sparks when they disappear on the three hundred and sixty degree horizon, in the or *Rome Adventure*. When I asked, she said it was all the same, one of those ridiculous romantic square melodramas from twenty years ago, which she loved. I'm crazy about Troy Donahue, she confessed, and I thought that if it actually was *Imitation of Life* she must find her mother Dulce the spitting image of Lana Turner as Lora Meredith. But I didn't say anything about Dulce, we had agreed on that, I only asked what-else or something like that, avoiding any mention of the roses her father had sent, and continued to listen to her stories, framing in my mind those tropical scenes that seemed to be made to order for a future biopic of the artist as a young woman. She sounded false when she talked about those things, but that falsity, I began to realize, was only a way to mask her emotions, because deep down, behind all the glamorous filters, some things in that lush story had to be actually true. In any case her voice, at times, really sounded as if she wanted it to be. I lit cigarettes, she lit cigarettes, I thought she shouldn't smoke so much if she really wanted to keep those sunny notes in her throat. At the same time, I remembered

heart of Brazil. All very poetic and bucolic and folkloric, while her grandmother Francisca, a sort of medicine woman, prepared tisanes and ointments for the yokels. Being honorable, Francisca tried each of her potions before using them. And as in an ironic fable, one day she mysteriously died, poisoned by one of her own remedies. There were no autopsies or paranoias out there: just a cheap casket, covered with red dirt. And the anguishing certainty: there was nobody left in the world besides Alberto Veiga. An artist father, that is, not stable, capable of every baseness and greatness in the twinkling of an eye. At fifteen Márcia was sent to London, to "complete her education." According to Alberto, that was a dream of her mother's, Dulce Veiga, whose whereabouts remained unknown. That's where she met Patrícia, in the boarding school where she studied and, a little later, Ícaro, who wanted to be a musician. Together they began to play in subway stations and pubs, and she sighed as she talked about Notting Hill Gate, Covent Garden, "I remember you in Ladbroke Grove," the canals of Camden Town, gray afternoons, black clothes, lots of rings. Patrícia collected the scarce pennies and shillings, Ícaro played her radioactive voice and mentally composed titles like contaminated-angel-of-the-delirious-apocalypse-inside-us-all, and the cracks and breaks in her voice were on target and were right that way, completely wrong: she was a nightingale glowing with Goianian cesium. No sound came from downstairs or outside, only some children shouting in the distance, in the street reminiscent of a town in the interior, and when I turned over the tape and said good, let's go on to the second part of your life, she suddenly shivered as if she were cold. She reached somewhere and grabbed her leather jacket, wrapped herself in it as if it were a blanket. I thought that this way—skinny, pale, her wide green eyes, that white hair—she looked like the ad, negative of course, for some anti-drug campaign. The departures, the deaths, the exiles, and I felt a crazy urge to adopt her, make sure she'd get enough milk, honey, wheat germ, vitamins, mineral salts. But I wasn't sure whether that contemporary tremor, that sickly air, that cosmopolitan frailty, were nothing but a sham pure and simple. Little Márcia's thousand faces: the frail one, the crazed drug fiend, the damned and rebel-

something or other electronic, Márcia sang "Guantanamera" in a poncho, "Let it Be" with glitter on her face, "Tico-tico no fubá" with her mouth painted à la Carmen Miranda, as well as Ícaro's first songs, with lyrics by her or Patrícia, who read and wrote all the time in a little room in Bloomsbury. There was a photo in *Time Out* and everything, if I wanted to see it. One day she quit school and fled to New York with Ícaro. They immediately got hooked on heroin, somebody blabbed on them, her father sent for her. He was getting old, felt nostalgia and remorse for not having taken charge of her, he sent for her to have her near in his old age so they could piece together their lives. Márcia went back against her will, she was eighteen, one month in a clinic, Ícaro came shortly after. And Patrícia around the same time. Then she had a falling out with her father, who she called Alberto, a repressive square, met the girls of the band, they thought of something real heavy, very hard, but now she wanted to leave all that, move on to something more Zen, but the record company wouldn't hear of it, you know how that is, the rest I already knew, right? lious orphan. Only I couldn't avoid feeling terribly sad as she continued to reminisce about all those scenes lost in the foggy streets of London, London, glancing from time to time at the poster of the Jim Morrison with a Sid Vicious face, opening folders to show photos, nose pierced with safety pins. The film on TV came to an end, a commercial for yogurt or cookies came on, she clicked the remote and the image faded. Without the light from the TV the room was even darker, with a kind of heaviness hanging in the air. Her voice began to trail off as I tried to ask her some questions, but she seemed exhausted. Huddling tighter and tighter on the yellow bedspread she got quiet, and I did too, because it was so difficult, I knew, to come back here and finally begin to grow or die, it doesn't matter which, it's all the same. Thus, little by little, as we fell silent, the room got darker and darker, and I looked around, Jim Morrison's face on the wall, three rings in his ear, and of course I understood, I understood everything, I asked if she wanted to stop, she said yes, and I turned the recorder off.

25

Lost, because that's how the behavior of someone who doesn't know where she's headed or what she's doing is defined, Márcia was lost in contemplation of the young man's picture. Who wasn't Jim Morrison, or Pedro, or anyone I knew. I followed her gaze. For the first time that afternoon, she shifted her eyes to meet mine, which were following hers, intercepted mid-gaze. Night was falling in the nearly dark room.

We just sat looking at each other like that, without knowing where to go from there. Her eyes: acrylic green, dilated pupils. Mine: circles, fatigue, progressive myopia. Someone needs to take care of you, kid, I thought. I don't know what she thought. Simultaneously we looked away, both seeking, once again, the picture of the young man who resembled Jim Morrison.

She said:

"That was Ícaro."

"Why *was*, he died?"

"Yes, a year ago."

"Overdose?"

"Let's just say so."

In the middle of the silence, and maybe precisely because of that, in the middle of the silence suddenly reigning in my head, the name that Pepito had mentioned emerged, and I asked:

"Who's Saul?"

Márcia gave a start:

"Who?"

"Saul," I repeated, and then again, separating the syllables, "*Sá-ul*, who is he?"

She slapped her bare thigh with her hand.

"I haven't the faintest idea."

And suddenly, screaming that she didn't have time, that it all was beginning to sound like a police interrogation, a pointless and idiotic absurdity, that she had to rehearse and it was already very late, that all she needed was for me to ask her favorite color, her favorite sexual position, that she'd had it, she stood up on the mattress, her strong legs, the legs of someone who's walked a lot, flung open the window, letting in a golden light, then sprang to the middle of the room, pushed a button on the tape deck and, at the sound of Lou Reed singing "Walk on the Wild Side," threw her jacket in a corner and pushed me outside.

As I plunged once again into the pop gallery in the hallway I caught one last glimpse of her on her knees, bending over as she laid out a line of coke on the glossy surface of the guitar.

26

Lying in the armchair, between the Virginia Woolf book and the picture of Dulce Veiga in the paper, the cat was licking her white paws. "Vita," I called to her in a whisper, "Vita Sackville-West." She didn't move. She seemed to be absently contemplating pyramids in the depths of her own eyes, Persian carpets, during the long nights without Virginia, or the lawns of Long Barn. There was nobody in the living room. In the open book Patrícia had underlined this sentence in purple ink: *"As usual in the evening, single cries and single bells became audible rising from beneath."*

Single cries, I repeated, that was nice, *single bells*. In the church square a bell began to peal.

Suddenly I realized with horror it must be six o'clock. I had to meet Rafic, the boss who hated to wait. I would have needed a helicopter to get across the city to Morumbi in less than five minutes: dynamic reporter overcomes another obstacle in the hard struggle for survival. I started for the door, but as I did a completely paranoid thing also began to happen: I became convinced that Márcia must be watching me from some corner, and the other three too, the fat one with the shaved head, the huge Japanese chick, the black drummer with cornrows. All hiding, in their toothed vagina t-shirts, laughing at me. I peeked behind the screen, everything was still the same. Except for a stick of incense on the table, almost burned down to the end, the ash about to fall onto the tip of a crystal pyramid.

Upstairs, Márcia had cranked up the volume to the max. Lou Reed was inviting, "Hey baby, take a walk on the wild side." Indifferent to the bells, the rock song, and my paranoia, Vita remained immobile, as if she were painted there.

I opened the door and walked through the garden where the jasmine was beginning to give off its scent. Nauseating, funereal. The motorcycle was still parked on the sidewalk. I reached the square. Among children and lovers, no cab in sight. I thought about going back to the house, asking if I could make a call, but the insidious toothed vaginas lying in wait would have gotten a kick out of such a scene of male distress.

Suddenly I saw her across the street.

It happened very fast. Dulce Veiga was standing at the church door, wearing a light summer dress. When she saw me, she raised her arm up, toward the sky, as she always did, then let it drop and disappeared inside the church. I went around the blond angel holding the silver fish in the middle of the fountain, but the mouth of the fish was completely dry, no jet of water came out of it to fill the round tank clogged with plastic cups, shreds of newspaper, used rubbers, cigarette butts, a cherub among the garbage.

I should have gone back to call or walked down the hill to find a cab, crossed the city as fast as I could, faced Rafic, the Moslem beast ready to make kebabs of my balls. But irrationally, irresponsibly, I crossed the street in pursuit of her.

A motorcycle braked, the tape recorder fell to the pavement. A guy with a shaved head yelled:

"Are you tired of living, faggot?"

I picked up the busted recorder, the tape falling out of it. If it had been a camera the film would have been exposed and Márcia F.'s moving confessions lost forever. In the square everybody was staring. I kept walking without looking back. Márcia Fellatio and the Toothed Vaginas must be watching it all from the window. As I went up the steps of the church, the guy yelled again:

"My-oh-my, don't tell me she's a good Catholic girl."

I didn't turn, my ears were burning. Chicken, I whined to myself, wuss. I walked into the church, it looked empty, no other door was open except the one through which I had entered. And Dulce Veiga wasn't there. The only person in the church, kneeling next to the main altar, was Patrícia. With her eyes closed, she was praying at the foot of the statue of a black saint placed on top of a glass shrine. I touched her shoulder, she looked up.

"Where's Dulce Veiga?"

"I don't know," she said. "I'm not a detective."

"I saw her enter the church."

"You're crazy, I've been here half an hour, nobody came in." Patrícia pointed to the statue of the saint, put her finger to her mouth, asking for silence, and whispered, "Ask for something. Go ahead, he'll listen."

On the shrine there was a card with the story of a certain blessed Antonio de Categeró, a slave who had become a Franciscan monk, then a hermit, and had died in Italy five hundred years ago. My God, I thought. Pero Vaz de Caminha had just sent his famous letter. Inside the shrine, arranged in an open case, two bones from the Blessed's forearm. It was kind of gross, and I couldn't understand how those small, fine bones had ended up on the upper side of the Freguesia da Nossa Senhora do Ó, or whether the saint was Italian, African, or Brazilian. Patrícia tugged at my pants cuff.

"Ask for something," she insisted.

I did: I asked for help in finding Dulce Veiga. I rapidly crossed myself, without kneeling. I had to rush to goddamn Rafic's place.

"I'm late, I've got to go all the way to Morumbi."

Patrícia crossed herself. She kissed the tip of her fingers, pressed them against the shrine with the bones, then lightly touched her forehead. Even with her new air of the precocious old maid she didn't fit into that scene. Neither did I. Her face seemed very serene when she got up.

"I'll take you on my bike," she said.

Maybe I should have begun to believe in miracles after all. In prayers, dreams, deliriums.

27

The wind whipped against E. M. Forster's face as he balanced on the saddle of Virginia Woolf's motorcycle. His face was tanned by the sun of Calcutta, New Delhi, Poona, maybe. She looked magnificent in her astronaut helmet, black leather jacket, and boots. She dodged buses, zigzagged around cars, took curves like someone defying gravity in the wheel of death, nearly scraping the pavement, slipped beneath trucks' side mirrors. People shouted at them when they passed, they didn't hear. Her long hair escaped from under the helmet and whipped the unprotected eyes of Edward Morgan Forster, holding on to Virginia Stephen Woolf's waist, sixty or seventy years later, back from India.

To see Alec Scudder again, I thought. And as we crisscrossed freeways, among clouds of smog, I remembered exactly, this time without fear, how I had met Pedro.

28

Pedro was so fair that when he was naked I'd stare at him in the dark, expecting his skin to glow like white clothes under a black light. Perhaps because of that, and other things too, the first time I saw him I felt a golden sensation. I say sensation *because, in the beginning, I didn't see his face, his body, the dimension he occupied in space. Wind, dust. All that, which came from him and blew over me, was golden.*

I was almost asleep when he got on at one of those subway stations that are always semi-deserted after ten or eleven at night. Ponte Pequena, Tiradentes, Luz, I'll never know which, I'll never know where he came from, that time and all the others. There was just me sitting in a corner of the empty car, backpack between my legs, dead tired after another one of those bus trips to Rio de Janeiro, he could have sat down. That's what I thought when the doors opened and someone I still didn't know was him got on, and I didn't open my eyes, because it wasn't worth it, I wasn't looking for anyone, back then. Pedro didn't sit, even though all the seats, except mine, were vacant. He stood in front of me, his backpack placed right between his spread feet. And his feet, facing, almost glued to mine, ridiculous, crazy. As if we were dancing, two strange and lonely men riding in a car on the last metro.

At that moment the sensation began to happen. I can still remember how, just before seeing him standing in front of me, I slowly opened my eyes. As if I were waking while someone opened a window, seized by the same golden sensation at daybreak or dusk on a clear day, and the sun, a moment before rising or setting, projects all its presages onto the horizon and if you know how to look, the way animals and peasants seem to know, you can accurately predict what the day or night that's beginning or ending will be like, and the following day and night too, and many more. The entire season—if you know how to look, you can. In the same way, like an animal or a peasant, even though I was neither, perhaps because I was suspended on the edge of sleep, and because of other things too, I foresaw him before seeing him.

I anticipated day after day, in that clear beginning, and all of Pedro's seasons one by one. Then, like those clouds, gold around the edges and purple in the center, which, as the sun rises or sets, is born or dies, slowly spill the darkness of the purple from their core while the gold dissolves so quickly that, if you blink, it's gone in a second, and while you ask yourself what happened? or, where did it go? because the nearly black purple has taken over the entire surface of the cloud, and the cloud itself, beside the new color, has already assumed another shape, unexpected and completely different. That's how he'd become. But for the time being, no, for the time being I just had a golden sensation.

Raising my eyes to the face of that young man who I still didn't know was Pedro, with the jolting of the train, opposite the painted yellow stripe plunging into the tunnel, overtaken by those feelings and all the others I'm trying to describe now, some nameless, like the deliciously paralyzing shudder on the roller coaster one second before toppling into the abyss, I stumbled across a white face swaying from one side to the other, whether from the movement of the train or because I was a little drunk I didn't know.

It must have been a Saturday, it was after midnight.

He smiled at me. And asked:

"Are you going to Liberdade?"

"No, I'm going to Paraíso."

He sat down next to me. And said:

"Then I'm going with you."

29

It wasn't difficult to find Rafic's house. It would have been impossible to ignore that pink neon 58 glowing in the dusk around the curve of Avenida das Magnólias. The lush ferns cascading from the terraced garden above couldn't hide the graffiti on the wall of that concrete cake covered with satellite dishes. Somebody had sprayed in red paint *Turk-off* right next to a huge phallus spurting hundred dollar bills. Rich as he was, I couldn't understand why he didn't have that thing scraped off or painted over. Maybe, I thought, maybe he found that phallus, those dollars, exciting.

As I got off the bike I stepped on a playing card lying on the ground. Before I could see what it was, Patrícia picked it up. It was the King of Spades.

"Beware of that man," she said. And disappeared around the curve, behind the island of banana trees.

The gate opened, I looked up at the camera of the closed circuit TV and had to restrain myself from waving bye-bye. At least my appearance wasn't suspicious, I think, even though I felt a bit dirty. My jeans gave off that wet dog smell, of clothes dried in the shade and ironed when still damp. That smell, mixed with sweat, soot from the streets, must have created a pestilent aura around me. To make things worse, the scent of the moonflowers wafting across the garden made me feel like throwing up.

I had to steady myself against the concrete wall. At the top of the stairs, among impeccable, plump yellow chrysanthemums, a clay dwarf was watching. He looked like Grumpy. In the midst of the orgy of banana trees, dwarf date palms, sansevierias, and other plants with pointed, lustrous leaves that looked like they were made of plastic in that excess of lushness, a butler suddenly materialized. Not at all British, in spite of the uniform and white gloves. I remembered the Filipino butler from *Reflections in a Golden Eye*, it wasn't difficult to picture the soldier stripping down on those lawns, while Marlon Brando watched. The Ceará accent put an end to my fantasy.

"You're the man from the newspaper, ain't you, Mister?"

I said yes and followed him up the steps—he was wearing flipflops. He held his hand out toward the glass wall, then disappeared. Huge like a ship, the room was all white. The rugs, the walls, sofas and armchairs, the table with a glass top covered with Bahian silver. The only colors were in the paintings above the sofas. Primitive, tropical, loud oranges and greens and blues, little paper flags from the São João festival, steep cobblestone streets, little churches atop hills, jungles with macaws and toucans with shiny beaks and feathers, palm trees, and solitary full moons floating over whitecapped tides. All this surrounding what must have been the centerpiece: the portrait of an erect blond woman with an eagle in her hands, in a gold frame.

I wandered around in the middle of it all, my smell stinking up the surroundings. From the speakers placed near the ceiling came a tune so familiar it took me a while to realize it was Ray Conniff. Without daring to soil the whiteness of the sofas, I moved closer to a painting that reminded me of Cavalcanti. I really needed glasses: it looked a lot like the mulatto woman in the photo Castilhos had published.

"Very good, very good. Beautiful, I see you have good taste," a voice said.

I turned, the recorder fell, the tape spilled out again, it took me a while to get it back in, smile, and hold out my hand to Rafic. He was a big, strong man in his fifties, with wide shoulders and completely gray hair, in deliberate contrast with his bushy eyebrows and black mustache. He was wearing a white linen suit, the open red shirt revealing three gold chains among the abundant black chest hair. He smelled like Paco Rabanne *pour homme*, and that reminded me of my own smell. I tried to keep as far away as possible for his own good, but Rafic insisted on coming close and patting me on the back.

"I already know you're a great art lover. Castilhos told me everything about you."

I tried to imagine what kinds of things Castilhos might have told him. Rafic's polished nails pointed to the painting of the mulatto girl.

"Isn't it a true masterpiece? My latest acquisition—I'm a discriminating collector, you know. A young guy, but very original. The girl is a model, actress, singer. One hell of a talent, one hell of a woman. I even asked Castilhos to give her a little plug in the paper."

"Very expressive," I said. The nausea was coming back, stronger.

Rafic pulled me by the arm to a bar, also white, in a corner of the room. The qualities of the mulatto, of the artist, of Castilhos, of the paper—and my own, I feared. He pushed me toward a white stool, went behind the bar and leaned close to my face. Omar Sharif in the role of the Greek magnate, Érico Veríssimo's Mr. Ambassador. He pointed to the glass case filled with bottles.

"What would you like? It's all foreign, all legit."

I had thought of plain mineral water. But before that vision of paradise—glowing Cutty Sarks, translucent Gordon's, golden Fundadores—I succumbed to the temptation.

"Jack Daniel's, straight."

"You sonofabitch," he laughed, gold teeth flashing beneath the black mustache. "Didn't I say you have good taste?"

He filled my glass first, then his, JB on the rocks. During that minute of silence, as the liquid splashed into the crystal, I tried to remember if that song was "Aquellos ojos verdes"—or were they black? I took the first swallow, it smelled like scented wood. "Be like the sandalwood," I remembered—from where?—"be like the sandalwood, which perfumes the ax that wounds it," it sounded like a sentence from Teresinha O'Connor's Seicho-No-Ie calendar. On a panel next to the bottles were several poster-size front pages from the *Diário da Cidade*, from '64 or '68. On one of them I read, "Communism finally extirpated from the country."

"Mr. Rafic, Castilhos said you wanted."

The gold ring gleamed on the countertop. It bore an eagle in relief.

"Don't *Mr.* me, ferchrissake. I'm still a spring chicken."

"Castilhos said *you* wanted to talk to me."

The ring sparkled beneath the crystals of the chandelier.

"Beau-ti-ful, really beautiful what you wrote about Dulce Veiga. My wife Silvinha even cried, she's so sensitive, poor thing. Such talent, such sensitivity, such—such bittersweet emotions, my dear boy."

My shoulders relaxed: I still had a job.

Rafic came around the bar and sat in front of me with his legs spread apart. He must have a big dick, I thought in spite of myself. Fine leather moccasins, but the red socks matching the shirt looked polyester, with a fretted pattern on the side. Then I remembered—I'd seen him before. He was the man holding hands with Dulce Veiga at a club table in the archive photo. I didn't know if it was at the party for the prize awarded to Leniza Maia or with Lilian Lara, I thought of mentioning it, since he was so interested he might know, after all. But the Jack Daniel's, the scent of the moonflowers pouring in through the open doors, the Paco Rabanne and my own smell were slowing down my reflexes. Besides, he didn't seem interested in listening.

"All day long, a success. Since early morning—crazy. Advertising agencies, TV stations, record labels. Everybody wants to know what happened to Dulce Veiga. A publisher wants to bring out a biography, there's a producer already putting together some special, I don't know what. People reminiscing, they even invited me. There's only one thing missing."

He took a swig of whiskey and fixed his eyes on me. I was busy reading another newspaper headline: "Military moralize the country." He moved his face closer, blackheads on the tip of his hooknose, the ruddy complexion of someone who's been drinking a lot for a long time. As if revealing a secret, he announced:

"*Her*: finding Dulce Veiga. That's the only thing missing."

"Right," I said. And took out a cigarette.

He lit it, the gold lighter had an eagle engraved on top, like the one on his ring. He filled our glasses again.

"Therefore, my dear and most talented boy, from now on you are released from your duties at the paper. From now on, babe, your job is going to be exclusively this. A delightful job, finding our beloved Dulce Veiga."

"But she might be dead in some vacant lot, on the side of the road," I continued, "without a tombstone or flowers." Everything was feeling kind of dizzy. And smelling worse than me.

"I'm sure she isn't. It's true that she got mixed up with the wrong crowd. At the time of the blessed revolution. Guerrillas, subversives, people of that sort. An artist's whims, you know. Unfortunately, ferchrissake. That must be why she ran away. And we are going to find her, cost what it may."

"But I don't know if."

"Whatever it takes. Research, interviews, travel. All you need to do is call and I'll okay it, carte blanche. From the airport, at a moment's notice, anything."

The thing is—I tried to say.

"You even solve a problem I have at the paper. Which is precisely *how* to take advantage of someone of your talent. Lack of jobs, recession, unfortunately you know about that. This way you become a special reporter and even take a weight off my conscience for not being able to take advantage of someone of your caliber, you see?"

I saw. It was fairly objective.

"The scoop of the year, babe. The name of the *Diário da Cidade* on top again. And your own, my dear boy. You can even write a book, there's no lack of publishers willing to pay lotsa dough. In U.S. dollars: *Whatever Happened to Dulce Veiga?* Just think of it. A success, as you know I'm very well connected. And just between me and you, don't tell anyone ferchrissake, I've been thinking about running for office. Representative, senator, the invitations aren't lacking. You seem like you're on the ball, you could even work with me, babe. What about a nice little job as press secretary?"

I was getting drunk. A ship on the high seas, on a stormy day, the white room was spinning around me. I pictured Márcia sitting on the floor in her panties and toothed vagina t-shirt, snorting up a line from the glass table, among the Bahian silver. White like the room, the cocaine glistening among silver cashews. And Jim Morrison on the wall, three rings in his ear. *This is the end*, I belched, he didn't notice.

Rafic held his hand out.

"Deal?"

It was take it or leave it. I shook his hand, there was no choice.

I was about to launch into some rigmarole about how I was no detective or anything, and how not even Dulce's daughter herself knew where she was, when a woman walked into the room. Blond, dressed in green, heavy gold necklaces, she shone in the middle of all that whiteness. It was the woman in the portrait, minus the eagle between her hands. Her heels tapped nervously on the wooden floor between the rugs.

"Silvinha, honey, this is the young author of the memoir about Dulce Veiga."

She held out her cold hand, covered with bracelets. She was at least twenty years younger than him, but her eyes, mouth and breasts were beginning to sag, already in the waiting room of her first plastic surgery. Wily black eyes, the slow movements of someone who takes barbiturates. I'd seen her before, too. Of course: she was "the dazzling Silvinha Rafic," always mentioned with photos in Teresinha O'Connor's column, ever present in the Saturday morning TV interviews.

"How do you do," she drawled. "You write superwell."

Rafic put his arm around her waist and pulled her onto his lap. She sank her scarlet nails into his chest hairs, among the gold chains. Under the red shirt, she pinched a hairy nipple. They must have good sex, I thought. Anal, oral, nothing orthodox.

He groaned:

"Silvinha is a poet too. She's published two books, you must read them, I insist. Give him a copy, honey, give him *Sighs of Autumn*, illustrated by Ubirajara Trindade and published by Massao."

She yawned, glanced at her Cartier.

"Some other time, Rá. We're superlate, Joyce is waiting at the Rodeio."

I sighed with relief, and so did Rafic.

"This way he'll come see us again. I like to have young people around. Maybe one of those real artistic *soirées,* it's been a long time. I could invite Valdomiro Jorge, do you know Mirinho?"

"By sight," I said. He was a sixth-rate director turned politician.

"And Salete de Souza, Betinho Simpson, Selma Jaguaraçu, Luizito Barroso, Lazinha Mello e Silva, Nenê de Vasconcelos, Aurore Jordan," the fake gold of the names glittered in the middle of the white room.

Silvinha took a sip from his whiskey, then poured herself a Campari. She wrinkled her nose, maybe she'd gotten a whiff of my stench, then walked to the sofa, stopped midway, pushed a few buttons. Ray Conniff fell silent, Simone's voice came pouring over the room. She sat down, crossed her legs, and began to leaf through a foreign edition of *Vogue*. The only thing missing was a pink poodle at her feet. And the credits of *Dallas* rolling over the freeze frame.

Rafic pushed me toward the exit. It wasn't difficult, I was completely out of commission. Outside, the Northeastern butler materialized once again. The nausea was coming back, I had to control myself at least as far as Avenida das Magnólias. Silvinha waved from the other side of the glass.

"Drop by sometime," she said in a bored voice. "Our parties are fabulous, they're the talk of every gossip column."

Rafic pulled me to a darker corner. Far from Silvinha's eyes, close to another clay dwarf. Judging from the glasses, this one must be Doc.

"Be honest with me, son, are you hard up?"

I squeezed the recorder.

"Excuse me?"

"Hard up, broke, down and out, penniless. I'm a man who came from nothing and made it on his own, ferchrissake. No one understands better than me."

Before I could refuse, though I doubt if I could have, he put his hand in his pocket, pulled out a genuine leather wallet with another eagle engraved on it, opened it and took out a wad of money. He stuck it in my shirt pocket without counting it.

"For the first steps of Operation Dulce."

I started down the tropical miniforest, following the butler's flipflops. At the gate, I looked back and saw Rafic again. Completely white in the midst of the green, with his hand raised, he looked like an admiral on the high seas. The open fingers formed the 'V' for victory. Or vice, vendetta, vileness, vortex, vertigo—I'm drunk, I thought.

"Whatever it takes," he yelled. "Anything, anything to find Dulce Veiga. Our lost nightingale, babe."

I stumbled outside. A viscous, sour-smelling wind was blowing from the Pinheiros River.

"God be with you, Mister," the butler said, and closed the gate.

30

I hadn't eaten out for such a long time. It was like going to the movies. Corner table, pitted black olives, bread with sesame seeds, eggplant paté, Bloody Mary. One, two cigarettes. Across from the young man who was a dead ringer for Rupert Everett in *Dance with a Stranger*, and the couple in crisis, Rita Tushingam and Tom Selleck, pizza, Guaraná, barbed silence. Elis Regina on a soothing FM station, I get sentimental when I sit at a table in a bar, I'm a tired, needy wolf. Filet in Madeira sauce, medium done, juicy mushrooms, fries, risotto Piemontese. The blonde with the Grace Kelly profile, too bad the sweatsuit, a bunch of office buddies singing happy birthday to Antonio Moreno, Riesling or Cabernet? Beer goes down better, but wine hits you harder, *que venga el toro*. A bite, a swig. Lime pie, mineral water. Another cigarette, coffee with crème chantilly, Strega liqueur flambé. At the table next to mine Paula Prentiss and Daryl Hannah stare at the blue flame excitedly, Mel Gibson and Alan Ladd feign indifference. Another three, four cigarettes, Humphrey Bogart look, if you want to know if I still love you—Naná Caymmi on the FM station—try to understand my infinite sorrow. Another coffee, another liqueur, I'm so-and-so's friend, linen napkin, Belmondo and Carmen Maura holding hands on the left. Five, six cigarettes. Check paid, exaggerated tip, come back and see us, I wish. On the way out, the greedy eyes of Shelley Duvall next to Woody Allen. And the thick, still air of Rua Oscar Freire in the February night. Kim Novak goes by in a gray Monza and gets off at L'Arnaque.

I still had a lot of Rafic's money left. First step of Operation Dulce: stuff my face. I should have felt ashamed, but, without feeling anything, only a persistent sense of nausea, I walked up and then down Rua Augusta, calm as a time bomb. This isn't right, I thought, but everything was right, a full moon behind the TV tower on Avenida Paulista. Lust in the air, a prey behind the corner.

She intercepted me just outside the Longchamps Bar. In the classic fashion, asking for a light. She was a redhead, frizzy hair to her shoulders, skintight turquoise leggings. She wasn't wearing boots, but green eyeshadow on her lids. Almost a year without getting laid—I enumerated: you're not taking anything from anyone, life is meant to be lived & etc. An aging James Dean and a Paraiban Kim Basinger, face to face on an island in South America. The birds flew over our heads crying *here and now! here and now!*

I played the game of playing the game, à la Dalton Trevisan.

"Looking for a good time?"

"Maybe, what's your price?"

"A song, real cheap."

"How much, sweetheart?"

"Five hundred for a quickie, a thousand an hour."

"And what about a nice blow job?"

"How does six hundred sound?"

"Good, but."

"At the hotel on Peixoto you have to pay for the room."

"How about at home, better vibes. And cheaper."

"You live alone, big boy?"

"Except for God."

"Then the coast is clear. This way?"

"On the side, right before Praça Roosevelt."

"Okay. Do you know you look just like the shy guy in the Brillo pads commercial?"

"I'll make you shine, alright."

"I-ay oubt-day it-ay."

"What's your name?"

"Viviane on the street. My real name's Dora."

"Queen of the *frevo* and the *maracatu*?"

"I may be a queen, Mister. But I don't take it up the ass."

31

The elevator was still broken, nobody in the hallways. Under the door only the electric bill, which I didn't even look at. After Jacyr's clean-up the apartment smelled of Pine-Sol, as in country-fresh. He was good at that kind of thing. At others too, I guessed. I put the recorder down on the table. On Márcia's album, a note from Jacyr: *"Its awesum, your her friend, get one for me to breeder."* And the poem, the poem was still there, stained with coffee. The only blemish in the apartment, it looked intentional. I had the impulse to put it away immediately, together with all my mementos of Pedro, which I had gathered and hidden from myself. Dora-Viviane was waiting, I ain't got all night, loverboy.

She pushed me down on the couch and for a second I wished she'd go away. It would be complicated to evict her, more complicated than just lying back against the cushions, spreading my legs while she sat on the floor. She unzipped my jeans, didn't seem to mind the wet dog smell. She must have seen worse, years in the trade. The shouting from the street was coming in through the open window, together with the mortuary light of Happy Days, Elba Ramalho on a car tape player and Jacyr at the Kenya Bar, drinking beer with the Rasta, pride of the Nagô race, ten inches. Dora pulled my pants down to my ankles, I kicked off my shoes. She stroked my cock through my underwear, slipped her hand underneath, I closed my eyes, I could see whoever I wanted in her place, I was crazy about Diane Keaton, Debora Bloch, always redheads, I sank deeper into the cushions. Let's play a few licks of lambada, pet, she said, and pulled my underwear down as well, her accent was spoiling everything, I tried to concentrate again, she weighed my balls in her sweaty hand, then grasped the base of my cock, licked the tip like someone tasting orange ice cream, passion fruit ice cream, Patrícia Pillar maybe, not Woolf, it quivered against the roof of her mouth. She slid her hand under my shirt, pinched one of my nipples, Silvinha's fuchsia nails in Rafic's chest hair, sonofabitch, I moaned, and Dora began to suck it gently, from the base to the tip, pulling the foreskin away. I crossed my hands behind my head to keep from touching her dyed hair, her green lids, Nora Barnacle, pull off my pants, I asked, and she did, like a slave, Lou Andreas-

Salomé, take off my underwear, my socks, too, Frida Kahlo, and she did. I opened my legs wide, she knelt between them, moving her tongue in circles, small strokes, then she plunged it deep into her throat, one hand on my nipple, the other grabbing my balls, deeper, I said, lights off, Marilyn Monroe going down *the river of no return*. It was getting harder and harder, stiffer, just the sounds of the street in the distance, loudness, baseness, I thrust my body forward, she backed off, frightened, then understood and adjusted to the rhythm. I pushed forward, she backed off, I backed, she advanced, all of it in her mouth, quicksands, swamp. A few times she took it out to take a breath, don't stop I pleaded, come back, come now, and she did, give it to your pistolera good, she moaned. You white devil, queen of the *frevo*, oh Dora, you southern trash, cocky gaucho, Dadá Corisco, fucking the rural Northeast of Brazil. And deep down in her throat, almost coming and laughing, my eyes closed to see far away from there, with no other part of her body but her mouth touching any part of my body but my cock, this time deliberately, with all the details, as I filled her mouth with cum, I went on remembering Pedro.

32

We got off in Paraíso together.

We bar-hopped until closing time, Pedro and I, drinking beer with Steinheger, then cognac, as the night got colder.

We were talking as if we had known each other for years. For lives, maybe.

When all the bars had closed and the new day was beginning to be born near Aclimação, I invited him to see the apartment I had been living in for less than a month, since Lidia had left.

There was almost nothing there. A mattress, scattered clothes, records, books, half a bottle of vodka or whiskey.

We sat on the floor drinking, smoking, listening to an old Bola de Nieve tape he had in his pocket, who knows why.

Increasingly brighter, the morning light was piercing the sheets of newspaper I had glued to the windows. Like curtains of crime, vice, and misery.

We were almost the same age, no money, women, or children. We laughed about our lives and everybody else's the entire time.

Bola de Nieve was singing yo era como una barca solitaria en el mar y surgiste en mi vida—I was like a solitary boat at sea and you came into my life. *We were getting drunker and drunker.*

I tried to get up to make coffee, but Pedro filled the glasses again. And drew me near him, telling me that he lived far away, that he didn't want to go back home that night, that he'd quarreled with his brother, sister-in-law, nephews.

Pedro's voice was slow and hoarse. Slower and hoarser because of the booze, the cigarettes, the many words, the day rising.

I began to doze off as he asked if he could stay, if he could stay with me. Of course, it was so simple.

I nearly fell asleep, I don't remember. When I awoke he was kissing me.

Pedro's kiss wasn't the drunk buddy kind, drenched in booze and male solidarity, alcoholic need, or complicitous despair.

Pedro's tongue inside my mouth was the tongue of a man feeling desire for another man.

He was handsome. So fair, almost golden.

I tried to push him away, repeating that I'd never done it. I liked women, I was afraid. All the fears of all the risks and transgressions.

He was kissing my lips, my face, my eyes, my hair, my hands, my belly.

I was acting like a frightened damsel.

The morning beards grazing one against the other were too rough, the hard muscles of our arms and legs, the shaved hair on the back of our heads, our chest hair. The smell, the touching, everything else: entirely different from the love of a woman, which is what I knew.

Little and poorly, and with hardly any pleasure, but it was the way I'd been taught it should be. That's how I knew the love of women.

Pedro was repeating in my ear that we couldn't escape it, that we were predestined, that it had been a magic encounter, that he needed me not to die of loneliness and neglect and sadness. I let him repeat all those things that sounded like a soap opera, a melodrama, like Latin America, I let him go on kissing me.

We slept together with our clothes on, in each other's arms.

When I woke there was no trace of him in the apartment besides the ashtray overflowing with the white filters of the cigarettes he smoked.

I didn't know if I'd see him again, I didn't know if I wanted him to come back. I was terrified at the thought of liking another man.

He came back, days later.

When Pedro came back the night was falling. And it was as if all the lights of the house had come on at the same time.

And we had dinner together, went to the movies, to the theater, listened to music, sat around in bars, lit each other's cigarettes and filled each other's glasses. For weeks we did all the things people do when they want to be together, living one another's lives.

Then we went back home and he always started kissing me again, insisting on going to bed together.

Tú no sospechas cuando me estás mirando—You don't imagine when you look at me, *he sang along with Bola de Nieve.*

The two of us standing, our hard cocks pressed one against the other at the door, for months. In the wee hours of the morning I'd manage to send him back to Luz, Tiradentes, Ponte Pequena, I never knew where.

I'd lie down alone, without washing my hands or face, to keep his smell with me. And masturbated night after night, until my skin was raw, thinking about Pedro's face and body, about all the ways of penetrating and being penetrated by him.

But I didn't give in, I was afraid.

One night, perhaps we'd had too much to drink, or nothing at all, perhaps we were, Pedro and I, exhausted by this game, which wasn't a game, he lay on my bed and pulled me down next to him. I rolled on top, on the side, under him, laughing like a maniac.

He took off my clothes, licked my entire body, turned me on my stomach and took me the way a man takes another man.

At first I felt pain, then fear, then pleasure. The way a man penetrated for the first time by another man feels. But not disgust, or contempt, or shame.

With Pedro I only felt joy. A joy that was the flip side of the one they had trained me to feel.

The following morning we stayed in bed all day, listening to Bola de Nieve, ordering pizzas and cigarettes and drinks on the phone.

When it got dark, and it began to rain, I licked his entire body, turned him on his stomach and penetrated him, too. The way I had never had any real woman, not even Lidia, or any fantasy being, in the palm of my hand.

He had small freckles on his back, flecks of gold. A salty taste, the scent of earth dampened by the first rain, a triangle of hair on his back, right below his waist.

I bit the back of his neck, he moaned.

We spent days like this, Pedro and I, one inside the other. The smell, the fluids, the sounds of our guts. Whose was what, inside and out, we no longer knew.

The secretions, the depths.

Days ended when he left. They began again only the moment he came back.

I don't know how long it lasted. I only began to count the days from the day he didn't return.

Since that day I've lost my name. I've lost the way of being I had before Pedro and haven't found another.

I wanted him to return, I couldn't go back to living a life like that, without Pedro.

The following months there was no sign of him in the streets, hospitals, bus stops, subway stations, one after the other, late into the night, until the first light of day in the bakeries.

At times, on the street, someone looked like him from behind. I stopped working. I stopped being and doing anything other than waiting for him to come back.

But Pedro didn't come back, I didn't come back.

The lights of the house never came on again upon his arrival.

IV

THURSDAY

Green Armchair

33

Dulce Veiga, I had to find Dulce Veiga.

I looked at my watch, not even eight A.M. I hadn't gotten up at such an ungodly hour in at least ten years. Maybe twenty, possibly even thirty. Out of the blue, a memory flashed through my mind.

When we went to the border, at the beginning of the summer, my mother spent two days making bread, frying turnovers, killing and cooking chickens. Sensing abandonment, the dog yelped feebly from under the bed. Then father took out of the garage the old Chevy that looked like a bat while I stood there staring at the washed-out morning light in Passo da Guanxuma. The trip took an entire day, all the way to the Uruguay River. A little after noon, father found some shade by the side of the road, near a reservoir, mother spread a checkered tablecloth on the grass and opened the white napkins with the chickens, the turnovers, the bread. Coral vines, she'd say, maybe there are coral vines here.

As if I were starting out again on one of those journeys early in the morning, I placed my right foot on the floor and squeezed shut my eyes, full of sand. Now mother would come with the pot of nearly sugarless coffee, a piece of homemade sweetbread, hurry up, child, we're waiting on you.

Now, now.

Nothing happened. Nothing besides a growing terror, when I remembered Rafic, the money, and what, I didn't know how exactly, I had promised him: to find Dulce Veiga. She could be dead, living in Cristiana, Salt Lake City, Alcântara, or Jaguari, in an asylum, far away from everything. I didn't want to think about it, I didn't want to think about a lot of things, about anything at all.

I needed to know about Pedro so badly.

I took Lidia's letter from the table, opened a drawer and put it away with the other mementos of him. They had been there for almost a year. Very little, almost nothing. The Bola de Nieve tape, a t-shirt with Sal Mineo's face, some poems by Ginsberg and that postcard in sepia tones with the picture of a man huddling by the riverbank. I didn't have to turn it over to remember what was written on the back, right beneath the caption *Pont Neuf sur la Seine: Mélancolie*. I closed the drawer, I couldn't afford to remember. I had to find Dulce Veiga, keep that job, go on living. Even if I didn't find her, even if Pedro never came back.

Life can't be turned off, I thought. And you can't rewind it either. The time machine hasn't been invented yet. Nobody's coming to my rescue. I've been inventing my own days for such a long time. I have to start somewhere.

I sat there repeating aloud these useless, obvious, mournful things. I wanted my mother, I wanted to learn how to get up early again, leave for the Argentinean border and never return. But I washed my face, brushed my teeth, lathered my cock for the hundredth time to eliminate the last vestiges of Dora, queen of *frevo* and oral sex. I brewed some coffee, sat down, put a sheet of paper in the typewriter. It was the best I could do.

I pushed the button of the mangled recorder. Hoarser than I remembered, a little breathy, as if she had just run up the stairs, Márcia's voice filled the apartment.

"Obviously Márcia Fellatio is just a stage name, mostly to match the band's name, the Toothed Vaginas. Our purpose is to give the traditional male, in a state of decadence, lacking the least bit of self-knowledge, first a suggestion of pleasure, and immediately after that another, of complete terror. We want to sound as frightening as a threat of castration, impotence, mutilation. But my real name is Márcia Francisca da Veiga Prado. Márcia F. to my friends."

Besides cigarettes, coffee, and pauses to turn the tape, I stopped a few times to listen to the record. Jacyr had loved it, after all. And Filemon was quite capable of finding in it something like the Rimbaudian-echoes-of-a-generation-filtering-its-disillusions-among-the-ruins-of-all-ideologies-through-shrill-cries-and-distorted-chords-in-the-dissonance-typical-of-the-agony-of-the-end-of-this-millennium. Devoid of Christ, of course.

Not that *Armageddon* was that bad. It could even be called insightful, intriguing, indefinable, or any other of those journalistic adjectives beginning with *in*. The problem was that it made me feel like listening to Mozart. I started looking for the allegro of that Concerto no. 23, which always made me feel like opening windows, taking a shower, shaving, and rushing down the stairs, as if I were twenty and had a limousine always waiting for me, down in the drive.

Suddenly, inspired perhaps by the spirit of Wolfgang Amadeus, I remembered that I had Alberto Veiga's phone number. Maybe he knew something. I took out the card and dialed. Just six digits, probably Higienópolis. He must live a comfortable life. After all, he had supported Márcia's post-graduate studies in rock through the junkie underground of the first world for years. The voice of a man answered, thick with sleep, cranky.

"May I speak with Alberto Veiga?"

"Who is this?"

"He doesn't know me."

"If it's about the play, you can forget it, pal. The audition is over. *I* am going to play Arandir."

I interrupted him:

"I'm not an actor, just a journalist."

His mood improved instantly.

"At your service."

"Tell him it's the guy who wrote about Dulce Veiga."

The voice moved away from the telephone. It murmured something I couldn't hear to someone nearby. Then, before I could even turn Mozart down, another male voice came on. He sounded comatose too. Maybe they slept together, I thought, Arandir and Alberto Veiga.

I began to identify myself.

"You don't have to say anything else. I know very well who you are."

"Thanks for the flowers."

"Thank *you*. It's the least I could do for someone with such beautiful memories of my unforgettable Dulce Veiga."

"Thanks," I said. "Could we talk in person?"

"Whenever you like."

The time to take a shower, stop by the paper, turn in Márcia's interview, preferably before Castilhos came in, I thought. He'd already be apprised of Rafic's maneuvers and armed with some poetic irony in English.

"How about this afternoon?"

"Absolutely, your wish is my command. Come on down to the rehearsal. That way you can check out some scenes from our play. You also must meet Marco Antonio, the best new artist in recent years. He's going to take the Brazilian stage by storm. Who knows, maybe you'll be inspired to interview him."

Maybe, I sighed.

"My most ambitious, most revolutionary work. I need the support of the press more than ever. You know, an artist is nobody without the media to make his work known."

"I just did an interview with your daughter."

I detected a certain tension in the long pause on the other end.

"Oh, right. Little Márcia has inherited her mother's talent."

"Her father's too." I couldn't resist.

Alberto Veiga began to expound on his daring & radical conception of something or other by Nelson Rodrigues, I thought of Darlene Glória as Sister Helena wailing, *Herculano, this is a dead woman speaking to you!*, I jotted down the address and hung up. I didn't think he'd be able to shed any light whatsoever on Dulce Veiga's whereabouts. And if even he, her ex-husband and the director of the show that hadn't taken place, didn't know anything, then—then I was fucked. I'd become hummus in Rafic's hands.

Mother, I called.

I turned Mozart up, but that very sad adagio had already begun. While I was showering I couldn't imagine any limousine waiting for me. At best, a bus with a miraculously vacant seat.

34

Before going to the newsroom I stopped by the archives and took out the folder with the pictures of Dulce Veiga.

I wanted to see if the man holding hands with her in the club was really Rafic. The picture wasn't there anymore. But the others were, just as I had left them. Strange, I thought. And went on to the newsroom.

There were stacks of telegrams on my desk. None offered a free vacation for two to Punta del Este, Madagascar, Camboriú, or Salvador as the case might be. They were all from old Dulce Veiga fans—far more than I had imagined—praising the memoir, wanting to know more. Rafic must be gloating over the success, already duly reported by Castilhos. I cursed the hour I'd gotten involved in that crazy story.

Then I noticed the roses on Teresinha O'Connor's desk. Sort of obscene, overblown as they were, they looked fake, impossibly open in the mephitic air of that newspaper. I touched the petals with my fingertips. And gave a start, as if I had touched a thorn.

"Xangô accepted the offer," a voice said.

It was Pai Tomás. Beneath the unbuttoned shirt, I saw the green and yellow beads of a ritual necklace against his black chest.

"What did you say?"

He didn't seem to hear.

"Have you already had lunch?" he asked.

"Not yet, I just came by to drop something off for Castilhos."

"You can give it to me, I'll make sure he gets it." He took from my hands the recorder, the envelope with the interview, and a confused note requesting that a photographer be sent to Márcia's house and explaining what had happened with Rafic. "When you have lunch, eat mutton and give thanks. Xangô likes that."

I was going to ask why mutton and not fried chicken, grilled fish, or pork and beans. But he was already gone, the envelope in his hands. From the other end of the newsroom, as he arranged everything in the middle of Castilhos' chaos, he bowed and said something that sounded like:

"Okê arô!"

I stared at Teresinha's calendar, still on the previous day. I turned the page and took a peek at today's. It said, "Everything originates within me and to me it returns."

In the elevator I ran into Castilhos. Even though he smoked, he smelled of soap. Alma de Flores, I recognized it. I couldn't look him in the eye.

"The piece is on your desk. I also left you a note."

"Rafic already told me everything."

Everything what?

He flicked his cigarette in the air. The ash got in my eyes. As I blinked, rather pissed, Castilhos recited:

". . . then on the shore
Of the wide world I stand alone, and think
Till Love and Fame to nothingness do sink."

"Shelley," I ventured, and got into the elevator. "Percy Shelley."

Before the metal door closed I heard him say:

"Wrong. It's John Keats, young man. 'When I Have Fears.'"

Or maybe it was *tears*, I didn't quite catch it.

35

It was a big ramshackle building on a side street of Bexiga, almost under the overpass. I peeked through the bars of the ticket booth, there was no one behind the placard that read: "Don't ask me to give away the only thing I have to sell." The only signs of recent life in that dark hole were a TV guide with Lilian Lara on the cover, a pack of cigarettes, and a brimming ashtray.

The door was only half-closed. The waiting room, full of black and white photographs of Cacilda Becker, Glauce Rocha, Sérgio Cardoso, Margarida Rey, Jardel Filho, was also empty. Everything smelled of mold but, perhaps because of the photographs, because of the torn gilding on the burgundy velvet of the chairs and curtains, there were still remnants of nobility in the air.

This was always the saddest thing. In everything, that memory of past, more glorious times, hidden there in the theater, in the flower beds of Avenida São Luís, in the windows of the Luz railway station, in the offices of the *Diário da Cidade*, in the surviving mansions of Avenida Paulista, everywhere. Times, I thought, better times. And bumped into my own image reflected in a cracked mirror. My hair was beginning to thin out. Automatically, as I'd been doing for the past few years, I quickly looked away. I, too, had known better times.

I rubbed my palms together and pulled the curtains aside.

Only the stage was lit. Quietly, to avoid drawing attention to myself, I sat down on a chair in the back. As my eyes adjusted to the dark, I made out half a dozen silhouetted heads like a Chinese shadow play, in the first row. On a platform in the center of the stage, two men faced each other. One of them, very young and muscular, had a newspaper in his hands. The other, much older, was shaking his disheveled gray hair—and a revolver. He was shouting:

"*'No, I'm not jealous of my daughter. I'm jealous of you. Yes, I am!*

Always. I haven't spoken your name since your engagement. I swore to myself I would only speak your name to your corpse. I want you to die knowing that. My hatred is love. Why did you kiss a man on the lips? But I shall speak your name. I shall speak your name to your corpse.'"

The gray-haired man pointed the revolver at the muscular one. I shut my eyes, nothing happened. When I opened them again, he was yelling at one of the Chinese shadows.

"Stomp on the floor. Shout, darling. Make some kind of noise when I shoot."

The shadow whined:

"It's just that—it's so exciting, I completely forgot."

"Great, but make some kind of noise. Otherwise I lose the atmosphere." The man turned to the other, still immobile. "I'm going to repeat the cue. I speak, shoot, then you fall down. Here we go: *'But I shall speak your name. I shall speak your name to your corpse.'"*

He pointed the revolver. A shout came from the row of Chinese shadows. The muscular young man fell to his knees, covering his chest with the newspaper. I saw that it was the *Diário da Cidade*. The man pointed the revolver again. The shout was heard again. The youth fell flat on the floor, raising a cloud of dust and tearing the newspaper. The gray-haired man screamed, *"'Arandir!'"*

He dropped the revolver, sank to his knees and pulled the other man's body onto his lap. He caressed his hair for what seemed an outrageously long time, then cried again:

"'Arandir! Arandir!'"

I thought they'd stop there. I knew very well the end of *Kiss on the Pavement*, the father-in-law mad with jealousy, confessing his accursed love. Now the light would dim in a very slow fade-out on Arandir's corpse, until it went out completely. Frenetic applause, if there was an audience, after a certain shocked hesitation.

But they didn't stop.

The gray-haired man remained on his knees, immobile, in the same position, his arms outstretched as if embracing Arandir. Except that instead of continuing to be dead, Arandir got up and walked to a platform farther away, a little higher up. There, completely naked, lay another, even more muscular young man, his face turned to the back of the stage. Standing next to him, Arandir held out his hand dramatically.

"Kiss me," the naked guy pleaded, with a slight accent I couldn't identify. "By everything you hold sacred, kiss me. On the lips."

I thought Arandir was just going to bend down and kiss him, but no. Ever so slowly, with provocative gestures, like a striptease, he first took off his shoes, then his socks, his shirt, his jeans. I thought he'd stop at his underwear, but he took those off too, and threw the crumpled clothes on the gray-haired man's platform. As naked as the man lying on the floor, but neither as muscular nor hairy, Arandir knelt down and put his arm around him. He ran his hand over the other man's thighs, stomach, bulging pectorals.

Without moving, still frozen on the floor as if he were embracing Arandir, the gray-haired man shouted:

"Pinch his nipples a little, till they're nice and hard."

Arandir obeyed. He stopped only to raise his hand to the neck of, I figured, the accident victim. Then he took the victim's face in his hands and turned it toward the light. I recognized him instantly: the naked man lying on the floor was the Argentinean who lived in my building.

"With your tongue," he wailed. "Kiss me, for the love of God."

Arandir bent over. He gave him a lingering kiss on the lips. I thought they were going to fuck right there, but the Chinese shadows clapped. *Bravo!* someone cried. On the lower platform, the gray-haired man was sobbing, his face buried in Arandir's underwear.

I got up to leave. Maybe I really was kind of square, but this was beginning to look pathological to a guy who. The chair creaked, the gray-haired man dropped the underwear, looked in my direction and shouted:

"Who's there? This scene is secret, I don't want any of Antunes' spies around here."

"I'm the guy from the newspaper," I said. It was becoming my password of choice to placate the dramatic temperaments of the Veiga family. He came down from the stage, walked toward me. Of course it was Alberto Veiga himself. Going a thousand miles an hour:

"You arrived just in time. This is the great moment in the play, the scene Nelson Rodrigues didn't dare write. Did you notice the accident victim's lines? The syncopated punctuation following the rhythm of breathing in colloquial speech—all mine." He pointed to the stage, where the two naked men were still embracing.

"A gay pietà, that's what I want. A gay pietà desperately erotic at heart. Like an archetype of Eros and Thanatos. Ecstatic, eternal. And poor Aprigio there, collapsed in the middle of the stage, in the midst of life, of the crime he's committed, smelling Arandir's impossible youth. That's the final message: love is just a mirage. Those who haven't given up looking for it, like Aprigio, are left with the comfort of sniffing at the remains of the youth he himself has killed."

Very daring, I commented.

"At this point I draw on some passages from the pathetic diary of Roland Barthes' last days. When he renounces the love of young men, and definitively opts for the love of hustlers." He screamed, "*'Hustlers are all I'll have left!'*" And without a pause, "You've read Barthes, of course."

"The pleasure of the text," I said.

"The pleasure is all mine," Alberto shook my hand. The heads in the first row were all turned toward us. He clapped his hands. "Let's take a break, everybody. Go get coffee down at the corner, practice your lines. Marco Antonio and Arturo stay."

Marco Antonio and Arturo, I supposed, were Arandir and the Argentinean-hustler-from-my-building, that is, the accident victim. The Chinese shadows began to move. They actually looked more Peruvian than Chinese. The skinny girl with glasses, batik skirt, and Indian bag must be playing the role of the daughter Selminha.

"I don't want to take up your time."

Alberto Veiga was dragging me toward the stage.

"But my time is all yours. Were you able to decode the illusion of the *imagérie* in the final scene? The love scene between Arandir and Arturo actually only happens in poor Aprigio's eroticized mind. It's not real, but mythical. Like the phantom that eternally haunts frightened heterosexuals: the possibility of love among males. The love Aprigio is experiencing is impossible, and the love that happens between the other two an archetype of death, pure fantasy. But where is true love between men or women, if indeed it exists?"

In a closed drawer, I felt like saying. On the back of a postcard, under a bridge on the Seine: *mélancolie*.

"There's more, much more. When Marco Antonio begins to take his clothes off, in a cloud of dry ice, the kind of music you hear during strip numbers in gay clubs comes on. Donna Summer, something like that. Pure illusion, desire. Mad, perverse desire, hallucinatory desire. A desire that dares not violate the established boundaries. A desire that's never sated, except in solitary fantasy or death itself. This is the essence of Nelson Rodrigues, of contemporary society, of Brazil, and the kind of theater I want to make."

"*Very* daring indeed," I repeated. "It never occurred to me."

"Are you the guy who called this morning?" Arandir asked.

"Yeah." Alberto Veiga's theory and those sweaty hunks standing naked in front of me were making me dizzy.

"I know you," the Argentinean guy said. Among the curly hairs, darker toward his belly button, his rosy nipples were still hard.

"I'm sorry," Arandir continued. "I thought it was for the audition."

Alberto Veiga butted in:

"It's true. I was auditioning for Arandir. I wanted a completely new face. A real man, a hunk of beef. I had over fifty candidates, Arturo here placed second. Perfect physique, too bad about the accent. It was only when I wondered how to take advantage of a talent like his that I got the idea of the gay pietà."

Arturo's talent, as anyone could see, was truly huge.

He asked:

"Don't you *leeve* in my *beelding*?"

"On the top floor."

Alberto was circling around the three of us. Me and the two naked guys.

"Small world, things are always kind of magical. Then you already know each other? Not in the biblical meaning, I imagine."

"We've never spoken," I said.

"You're *muy* close," the Argentinean said.

"You like Carlos Gardel."

"And you, Nara *León*."

That was enough, I thought, perhaps it was enough, yes. One ambiguous, complicitous, sly gesture or word and Alberto would immediately interrupt the rehearsal and the four of us—me, Arandir, Arturo, and Alberto, too many *a*'s for my head—would end up at his apartment. I recklessly imagined some very sick things. But I was a straight-shooting guy, I wasn't a homosexual, so I said I needed to talk about Dulce Veiga. In private, I stressed. Arandir picked up the crumpled clothes and headed down to the main floor. Arturo disappeared behind the curtains, humming *si crucé por los caminos como un paria que el destino se empeñó en deshacer.*

He had such a gorgeous ass that, for a moment I, too, doubted that Arandir had never seen him before that kiss.

36

When Dulce Veiga disappeared, she and Alberto had been separated for almost two years, practically since Márcia's birth. They had been married for ten years, which he referred to as "the happiest of my life." He didn't reveal the reasons for the separation, but it was apparent that, while Alberto increasingly embraced his homosexuality, Dulce had started drinking, doing drugs, taking bizarre lovers. Following a phase of recriminations and accusations—"that space of inevitable rancor," he said, "when love is over and hasn't had the time to turn into something else, also good"—the show was a way of publicly sealing their friendship. And beginning, perhaps, another kind of marriage. Less passionate, more artistic.

The last time Alberto had seen Dulce Veiga was in the early morning hours the day the show was to open. He held the door of the apartment for her to enter, with Márcia in her arms, but declined to go in himself, have a drink—it was always cognac—talk. He regretted not having done so to this day. Perhaps that night, a few hours before disappearing, all Dulce needed was to vent her feelings with somebody. But he was exhausted, the past few weeks they'd been rehearsing until two or three in the morning. Working with her was becoming increasingly difficult, she showed up late all the time, couldn't memorize the new lyrics, felt persecuted. At times she cried a lot, without apparent reason, repeating that she wanted something else, something else. Everyone was patient and affectionate with her: they were sure that the show would be a great success because Dulce, in spite of her feelings of insecurity, was singing better than ever.

Early that morning, in the hallway of the building on Avenida São João, Alberto kissed her forehead and turned to leave. Before entering the elevator he looked back once more and found her very thin, very pale, very sad. Leaning against the door, a little hunched over, Dulce Veiga held the sleeping baby in one arm, a cigarette in the other hand. She'd been smoking nonstop lately. Alberto even thought about going back, having that cognac with her after all, listening to Billie Holiday or Bessie Smith, "Me and My Gin," which she listened to all the time. But the elevator came, he left. That was the last image he had of her. Standing at the apartment door, holding her daughter, a cigarette between her fingers, Dulce seemed afraid to go inside. And find—what?

The following night, the theater packed, he first called her apartment, nobody answered. Then he called Lilian Lara, with whom Dulce left Márcia at times, when she didn't take her to the rehearsal. "This child loves music," she used to say. Márcia was at Lilian's, but not Dulce. She'd left the baby, Lilian told him, saying that she was going to the hairdresser's to have a manicure and a facial, something like that, women's stuff. And that she sounded good, positive about the show, her daughter, even life. Then Alberto went to her apartment, he had a key, and nobody was there.

Pinned to that green velvet armchair she liked so much was a hasty note to him. Dulce said that she was tired of everything, she couldn't take it any longer, she didn't want to hurt the people who loved her, she was disappearing forever, no use looking for her. She also asked Alberto to take good care of Márcia, do what he could to send her to school in England, as they had agreed. It was a short, scrawled, desperate note. Just the thought of it, Alberto said, and he seemed sincere, "Just the thought of it makes me feel like crying."

He still had it. In a box, with other small things. A bottle of perfume, a glove, an earring, a box of powder, like mementos of someone already dead. I could see the note, if I cared, I could see everything. All I had to do was go to his apartment, he'd take advantage of the opportunity to invite Marco Antonio and Arturo, show me some photos, some videos, talk more about his work. To which, he said, "I devoted all of my wounded soul after Dulce chose the shadows." But, he assured me, there was no clue in that note. Or in the apartment, the day she disappeared, in any other place or with anybody else. If I wanted to, I could also talk to Lilian Lara, who had been her closest friend. Alberto was sure it wouldn't do any good. He himself, and many others—"she was very, very, very much loved," he said—had done their utmost to find her, over the past twenty years.

To no avail. Nobody knew anything about Dulce Veiga.

37

The air so clear outside. Not a cloud in the February sky. Standing in front of the theater, in the slightly less intense heat, almost five in the afternoon, I heard a kind of silence, which perhaps was inside me—a little gloomy from the moldy theater, a little dazed from listening to Alberto Veiga, a little drained, like the afternoon.

I leaned against the wall, lit a cigarette, stood there gazing at the overpasses. On the opposite sidewalk, dragging a bag of old newspapers in slow motion, was a beggar woman, her body covered with flour sacks. She looked like the image of Death in a medieval print, only without the scythe.

What about Saul, I had asked, who's Saul. But Alberto, like Márcia, didn't remember anyone by that name. He needed to go on with the rehearsal, he called Marco Antonio and Arturo, told them to take off their clothes, to repeat the gay pietà, this time with fury, as if they were dying to fuck each other, while saying that Pepito was a frustrated, wretched drunk who confused names, times, stories, and I decided to believe him.

The sun was shining on my white face. It felt good, after those hours buried in the dark theater, among dark memories. Maybe I should look for Pepito again, maybe go to Rio de Janeiro and talk to Lilian Lara. Maybe a number of dynamic & exciting things & etc., if I planned to keep playing Philip Marlowe. At the moment, what I really wanted was to consider the whole case closed. And stay there, leaning against the wall, doing absolutely nothing.

I put out my cigarette. I walked into the bar next door and ordered water. The low sun was shining on the image of St. Francis of Assisi, the bird perched on his shoulder, in a niche high up on the wall, surrounded by faded roses.

"Not much business today," I said.

The Portuguese bartender with light-colored eyes sighed, leaning over the counter:

"It's the goddamned summer, man. This time of year everybody goes to the beach."

"Those who can afford it," I said, and remembered Rafic, cabanas in Guarujá. He smiled, scratched his hairy arms. He had sweet eyes, and being stuck in the city made us brothers in misfortune, albeit on opposite sides of the counter. I've gotta see Portugal, I thought.

And once again, closing my eyes, I saw that sea of green waters, full of floating seaweed. I drifted beyond the surf to some point from where, looking back toward the beach, all I could see was a coconut palm and maybe a blonde in an antiquated two-piece, shouting in scratchy German, *Ist es nicht aufregend dieses Leben?* How long had I forgotten the meaning of this word which, as a child, had the taste of the sun on your face and bare feet? Holidays, I repeated, *férias, vacaciones, urlaube*.

"Are you in theater?" the Portuguese guy was asking. He must have thought I looked like a faggot.

"Yes," I lied. And felt a mad urge to start recounting my glorious descent down the steps, crying, *citizens of Thebes!* and ordering the soldiers to tear Antigone away from the body of her beloved brother Polynices.

"We're rehearsing a play right across the street."

Not even during that time of censorship, persecutions, prohibitions, and torture, Alberto assured me, had Dulce gotten involved with communists. She liked to stay home memorizing lyrics by Dalva de Oliveira, Edith Piaf, Patachou, Marlene Dietrich, and didn't have the faintest idea what was happening beyond the walls of her apartment. Somebody was lying. But I was the one who would have to account for those lies to Rafic. Maybe at one of those real artistic *soirees*, drinking Jack Daniel's with Melinha Marchiotti.

"Must be a wild life," the Portuguese guy was saying.

"More or less," I sighed.

Across from the bar, the beggar woman stopped at the corner, as if she were trying to decide which way to go. She could keep going straight, I thought, walk under the overpass and down to the streets of Bexiga, where there were always plenty of leftovers outside the restaurants. But she could also turn right, toward downtown, there must be lots of paper on the corners of Avenida Ipiranga. Or turn left and take one of those streets that end up in Liberdade, sushi in the garbage. I took the water bottle and stood in the doorway, looking at the undecided beggar. I'd feel great if I had the courage to call her over and buy her a grilled ham and cheese sandwich and a Guaraná. She crossed the street but instead of walking directly beneath the overpass she went around and up on top of it, where only cars were allowed.

"Lots of parties, lots of women, lots of booze," the Portuguese guy was repeating.

On the overpass, the beggar put down the bag of paper. Then, with both hands free, and a gesture that was too elegant for her, she took off her hood. She had blond, straight hair parted in the middle and cut at chin level. She held her arm up, her forefinger pointing to the sky, and turned her face toward me. Even filthy and with a scabby nose, her face still showed traces of its past beauty.

I cried:

"Dulce, wait for me, Dulce Veiga!"

I started running with the bottle in my hand. The Portuguese guy shouted something I didn't catch. I lost sight of her for a moment, until I managed to cross the street, go around the concrete island under the overpass, and run up toward her. Ah, I'd take her home, give her a bath, get her to tell me all the obscure details of that crazy story, then we'd go to the opening of Márcia's show together. Happy ending: in the back, Dulce would sing "Nothing More" beneath a deluge of roses and applause. In the forefront, Márcia and I holding hands, gazing into each other's eyes. Credits rolling over the freeze-frame.

But we weren't there yet, it wasn't like that yet.

When I reached the top of the overpass, she had crossed to the other side. As if she were running from me, without knowing that I was her savior, the singer of her praise, her creator. I stood beside the passing cars, waiting for the first break to cross. I caught a glimpse of her through the cars as she began to take the newspapers out of the bag and toss them up in the air. The crumpled sheets hovered for a moment, then fell under the cars' wheels, over her grimy cloak, on the other side of the street. Then, as I waited, she climbed onto the low wall of the overpass and stood there, swaying back and forth, as if she were on a horse or a seesaw. Like an amazon, a child. A madwoman—she was looking at me, laughing a toothless laugh. I shouted, look out, Dulce Veiga, you'll get hurt, something like that, but I knew she couldn't hear me over the noise of the constant stream of cars.

Before I could make a move, she jumped off the overpass.

No one screamed, the cars didn't stop.

I wondered whether it would be faster to go back the way I had come, and cross the street, or cross right there, among the cars. Right at that moment a light at an intersection somewhere changed and the overpass was suddenly empty. I ran across, leaned over the edge, looked down at the cement sidewalk where she must be lying smashed, seventy feet below.

There was no one in the street. No trace of blood or body. Dead or alive, real or imaginary.

The wind continued to blow the newspapers everywhere. Wrapping itself around my legs, a page of the *Diário da Cidade* showed Dulce Veiga's face. Smiling, far from everything, full of light. At that moment, maybe because I felt lost and everything seemed so crazy, I remembered the mystery, I remembered the shell divination ritual.

38

Across the table, covered with an immaculate tablecloth, Jandira first lit an incense stick and waved it between us. Then she closed her eyes and prayed:

"Blessed and praised be all the universal powers, all the cosmic powers. Blessed and praised be all the *oduns* of peace, happiness, and prosperity. Bless me Ifá, bless me Lodumaré."

A motorcycle roared by outside, but not even that managed to dispel the fascination with which I stared at the objects around us, on the outside of the circle formed by the colorful beads of the ritual necklaces. Crystals, crucifixes, a lit candle, a glass full of water and chunks of sea salt, a doll dressed in yellow, a card with the image of a strong man in red and white with an ax in his hands. Everything in perfect order, without a speck of dust. Behind all that, she didn't look like the Jandira I knew. Solemn, she shook the shells in her closed hands, reciting something that sounded like:

"Aroboboi Oxumaré aroboboi, Obá nixé kaô kabiesile, ogunhê patacorê Ogum, jace jace, ora iê iê fiderô mã, iê iê oh my Oxum, epa rei e kide rei Iansã, Oiá misolorum, eu eu Osanha asa, odê kokô ma iô, okê arô Olodomin ofá, lelú Iemanjá odô iá. Bless me Obá, bless me Ená, bless me Iná, bless me Jessu. Kobalaroê Exu kobá, bless me all of you gods."

She cast the shells between us, in the middle of the circles formed by the ritual necklaces. She watched without saying anything, with the knowing face of someone who'd seen something I couldn't see. I took the opportunity to glance around. The apartment was the size of mine, I couldn't figure out how she and Jacyr managed to live in that space. But, like the table, everything was clean and tidy, poor but decent. The waxed floor gleamed. The maidenhairs and other ferns hanging in the windows filled the dark precipice of the inner courtyard with green. They had improvised a partition in the middle of the living room with an armoire. On the side facing us there was a collage of African *orixás* and Catholic saints with Buddha, Mother Theresa of Calcutta, Chico Xavier, the Pope, and movie and TV stars. I tried to decide whether the bare-chested guy—I needed glasses—was Arnold Schwarzenegger or Sam Shepard, and I was thinking that Shepard would be too intellectual for Jacyr's taste, when Jandira said:

"Axeturá."

I looked at the table. Some shells were scattered in small piles but, in the center of the circle, four or five of them formed a more or less straight line. Jandira's eyes were completely crossed.

"The paths are much more open than you think, son. Only, they look crooked. But it's along the crooked paths that you must walk, and things will come your way. All you have to do is listen to the paths and follow them."

But will I, I started to ask. I think I wanted to know if in the end I'd be able to hear those paths, if they really were that crooked, maybe silent too.

Jandira cast the shells again. I lowered my head, peeked between my lashes. This time they all landed in the corner on my right. Except for two, alone in the opposite corner.

She asked:

"Do you know Logunedé's story?"

I said no, and began to feel like smoking. Her eyes fixed beyond me, on something or someone that wasn't there, Jandira began.

"Logunedé is a prince, almost a child. The son of Oxum, queen of the waters, and Oxóssi, king of the forests. For six months, Logunedé turns into a charmed princess and sleeps lying at the bottom of a boat in the middle of the river. In the meantime he also turns into a star. He leaves the princess there sleeping at the bottom of the boat, all alone, and goes wandering through the forest. Like a star, in search of his father Ilê."

But wasn't his father Oxóssi, I wanted to ask.

She took her eyes off that uncomfortable invisible thing behind me and fixed them on my face. So crossed that, at best, they might see the point where my eyebrows came together, at the bridge of my nose. The free territory preferred by nine out of ten blackheads and zits.

"Leave the sleeping princess, son. Turn into a star and go into the forest, Ilê is waiting for you."

The oracle of Delphi has nothing on her, I thought. With the disadvantage that Apollo wasn't anywhere around. Except for Schwarzenegger, or was it Sam Shepard? I needed glasses, besides needing to let go of the princess; and perhaps Jacyr, in addition to housecleaning, could rake in some cash decodifying oracles at the exit. Aside from the fact that, as far as forests were concerned, here there were only the sorry trees of Praça da República, Trianon, or Ibirapuera Park, and I kind of felt like a worm for thinking those things.

Celtic, druidic, shamanic, Jandira picked up the shells and cast them between us again. This time I looked quickly and counted, half were facing down, half up.

She said:

"Ejionilê."

Huh, I said.

"When three white hairs grow on your chest, son, Oxaguiã heralds and brings peace."

Just one more, then. Until yesterday morning, I remembered, although I would rather have forgotten, there were at least two. Visible, because hair is the kind of thing that never stops growing on a guy's body. My concern wasn't those two, or the three she announced, but rather the ten, the hundred future, uncontrollable white hairs. And besides them, the gray and hairy-chested guy I was slowly turning into, while life passed me by and nothing, nothing happened. Not even gold chains to show off among that gray forest.

She said:

"Time is such a powerful *orixá* there's no horse, no spirit medium able to withstand its weight. That's why it doesn't incarnate, it just hovers around."

Enigmas, that was all I encountered on my path. Insoluble enigmas, impenetrable sphinxes, insanity. Dulce Veiga falling off the overpass, a gay pietà, Virginia Woolf's reincarnation, stuff like that. A phone rang in the distance, it must have been mine, could it be Pedro? I began to feel distressed by that Afro-Brazilian hermetism. I resolved to be more rational, even though out of step with the *orixás'* time, which perhaps was like Lacan's time.

"I need to find somebody. A person who disappeared many years ago."

Jandira adjusted her turban, this one wasn't silver or gold, like the others I had seen, but green and yellow. A green and yellow that made me think of the forests through which I should be wandering, transformed into a star, in search of Ilê. She shook the shells and cast them in the space between the ritual necklaces. One of them bounced out, toward me. I moved my chair back, afraid it would fall in my lap. I didn't want it to touch me, that shell on the edge of the table.

"Don't worry, you will find this person. She's a friend of Ossanha, Oxum is watching over her. And you will find many other things, son, things you can't even imagine. One day the star returns, enters the body of the princess, and the princess awakens. Listen to what your mother says, and follow the star without fear."

. . . but what if the star suddenly disappeared from the horizon, if it had already died while its light still reached us, what if it wasn't a star, but a pulsar, quasar, black hole, if it was Nemesis, the wandering killer planet beyond Pluto, what if it was out of reach like Vega, Canopus, Aldebaran, what if . . .

"Where's Jacyr?" I asked distractedly.

"Out there, living, his saint is watching over him."

Uh-huh, I said. I didn't want to think about the Kenya Bar, one leg on the toilet, the other spread wide, and ten inches up the kazoo. Abruptly, I asked:

"How much is it?"

Jandira seemed uneasy.

"Whatever you can afford, son. I never charge anything for what I have learned for free. But I need to make an offering, the saint calls for one. Do you have any money?"

Black hen on the corner of Rua Caio Prado, white dove flapping around Praça Roosevelt, popcorn at the edge of the Minhocão expressway.

"Not with me. I'll run next door and get it."

"You can give it to me later. I already know what to do."

I stuck a bill under the doll's yellow lace skirt, from which other bills and checks poked out. I got up to leave. No great love, no letter, inheritance, or party.

Confusion, no connection, I thought. It sounded like a line out of a movie, and when I thought about movies, I also thought that taking a shower, calling up an old friend—there were still a few left—and going to the movies was perhaps the best way of closing that meaningless day. Perhaps I'd find a rerun of some old Fellini film around town if I looked hard enough.

Jandira placed her hands on my shoulders. She smelled of cinnamon, basil, rue. She was no longer cross-eyed when she looked me in the eyes.

"Before you go to sleep, put a glass of sugar water at the head of your bed, son. To call the fairies, they get thirsty and come to drink next to your head in the early morning hours. And tomorrow dress in white and don't eat any meat, to avoid driving away your father Oxalá, may he protect you."

39

Out in the hallway, I bumped into a woman dressed all in black. It was Teresinha O'Connor.

"You, here?"

"I *live* here, next door."

She kissed me three times.

"I've heard she's great, I don't know what to do any more. He treated me really bad today, like I was I don't know what."

"Good luck," I said. Without understanding any of it.

40

I turned on the radio. I wanted other noises in my brain besides my own thoughts. More profane, less confused. A very excited falsetto voice cried *flaaaaash-baaaaack!* and it didn't seem like such a bad idea after all to take a shower listening to *help I need somebody help I need someone,* even though I couldn't sing, I think I still knew all the lyrics by heart. Unexpectedly, as if emerging from the depths of time, the time I had met her, Dulce Veiga began to sing "Nothing More."

I turned off the radio. The silence I had felt on the way out of the theater returned. And me, inside of it. Me, me alone, alone.

Old friends then, take a shower, call, go to the movies, dinner afterwards. There weren't many people left from that long period of silence and pain. Maybe Nelson, I began to count them off, railing against his wife and three daughters, all I do is work to feed those females; maybe Maria do Carmo, each time looking a little more like a typical member of the Wretched Army of the Victims of Feminism: a son, no husband or lover, flesh and dreams hanging around aerobics gyms and women's magazine newsrooms; maybe Fernando, eyes of cold fire, chasing after coke until his teeth gnashed, then a hooker—or a transvestite, would I be capable of that?—at the first street corner, pay and go limp. Otherwise, there was also the Lively Legion of Those Who Had Made It, all paired off, come over on Saturday, we'll do dinner, you have to see the videos we brought back from Tokyo, the computers from New York, the wines from Paris.

No, I didn't want to see any of them. I didn't want anything, I didn't want anyone. Like Dulce Veiga, what I wanted was to find—something else. I preferred being by myself to bitterness, explicit or softened by fondues, slide shows, and imported Armagnacs. It was cleaner. At most an old Bergman film, replete with traumas. Then the doorbell rang, and everything started happening very fast.

It was Patrícia, pale, disheveled, helmet in hand. She walked in without waiting to be invited.

"Sorry for barging in on you like this. I asked for your address at the paper, a girl gave it to me. I've been calling you all day, nobody answered, I thought your phone was out. You have to help me."

"What happened, *Virginia*?"

"It's Márcia, do you understand?"

I didn't understand anything.

"She's disappeared."

Repeating the question I'd asked dozens of times the past few days was inevitable.

"What do you mean, *disappeared*?"

"Since two in the afternoon. She didn't come to the rehearsal, left hanging some people who wanted to tape something for TV. Lots of things, lots of people. She didn't call, she didn't say anything."

I noticed something furry just below her neck. It was Vita, the cat, tucked in her jacket, with only her head sticking out. Patrícia was wearing the same heavy glasses she had on the previous day, the stems held together with scotch tape. She'd been crying, and now kept repeating:

"Like her mother, just like her mother. The very day the show opens."

Without meaning to look cynical, I reminisced:

"When I was younger, show people used to do this kind of thing, it was called a *publicity stunt*. Singers were assaulted, actresses busted their bra straps at carnival balls, stuff like that. Nowadays I think it would be called a *media coup*."

Vita meowed politely as she took a good look at the surroundings. Patrícia slammed her helmet down on the table. There was nothing left on it or anywhere else in that apartment that wasn't already half broken. She was serious.

"Don't talk like that, this is for real. Márcia's been acting crazy, snorting too much coke, she hasn't slept for three days. She only smokes and snorts. Then all of a sudden this story on her mother's disappearance. Maybe she decided to do the same thing, I don't know."

Electra, Alcestes, Iphigenia: which complex was this?

"Did you call the police?"

"No way. There's drugs involved, all kinds of shit."

"Did you talk to anyone else?"

"A few people, friends. Nobody knows anything."

"So why did you look for me?"

Very tall and thin, unsteady as if she might fall any minute, she paced back and forth, squeezing Vita inside her jacket.

"You seem alright. And a journalist must know what people do at a time like this."

"I think they call the police."

"No!" she cried. Vita meowed again, underscoring the cry. "Not the police."

Heavy drugs, death squads, elimination of witnesses, Medellín cartel. Márcia floating in the Pinheiros River, the white foam of pollution in her hair, almost as white, a toad sitting on the tattooed butterfly between her breasts. At the wake, a wreath in the shape of an electric guitar, the Toothed Vaginas singing the backup vocals on "My Heroes Died from an Overdose." I looked for a clear space on the table, knocked on the wood. And began to worry.

"I don't know what I could possibly do. All I can think of is stuff like that—police, hospital, morgue."

Patrícia sat on the couch under the window, unzipped her jacket, Vita jumped out. Her tail in the air, she began to investigate the apartment. Patrícia crossed her legs, put her face in her hands. Her distress was real, but I didn't want to believe that story. Strategy, I repeated, stratagem. Suddenly I thought of Jayne Mansfield's scandalous display at the Copacabana Palace carnival ball, I really was old. Or else stars like those of the past no longer existed.

Patrícia raised her head:

"Give me a cigarette."

"You don't smoke."

"How do you know?"

"I'm a very observant guy."

She grabbed my hand, her fingers were cold. Vita was sniffing through some papers on the table.

"That's why I looked for you. Please help me. Did Márcia say anything strange during yesterday's interview?"

I pulled my hand away. I lit her a cigarette, then another for myself. Behind her, the night was falling.

"She said a bunch of things. All strange, but nothing—" Nothing but, I thought, a beautiful illusion. I felt like turning on the radio again. But Dulce Veiga's song must be over by now.

Patrícia got up, pulled Vita away from the table, sat down again. She looked at her watch, one of those digital things for divers. Huge, full of buttons.

"Almost seven. She should have been at the Hiroshima by now. We need to check the lights, the sound, a bunch of things. Do you really think she'd repeat Dulce Veiga's story?"

Ismene, Clytemnestra, Jocasta: my Greek repertoire wasn't that broad. I knelt before her Cyd Charisse legs, sheathed in torn jeans and boots, Maria Schneider-style. But I wasn't too impressed with that script, delivered with wild eyes and quivering voice à la Meryl Streep. And why didn't she get on the phone and call this Hiroshima place, Alberto Veiga, or a thousand other places, anyway?

We just sat there smoking in silence, for a moment so long that, if it hadn't been for that electric field around her body, I might have rested my head on her knees and told or listened to some spicy story from Bloomsbury while she stroked my hair. As if reading my thoughts, Vita jumped down to the floor and rubbed against my legs. We might have even looked for Jandira, who would have said something like, "The small flame of the Apocalypse went out before the fire began," or told the story of some *orixá* who, when the stage is set up, turns into a laser beam and flies off through the buildings.

It was almost dark, Patrícia began to cry. The neon sign from the funeral home came on outside, Vita looked up, her eyes flashed like two headlights. The green neon shone on Patrícia's tousled hair, and she no longer looked like Virginia Woolf, but an androgynous adolescent, lost and in love. And I liked her, shit, I always ended up liking all these goddamned people and their craziness. Perhaps because of that, because I liked her and wanted to help her, I suddenly understood what anyone not as dumb as me would have understood from the very beginning.

Patrícia was in love with Márcia. Madly in love.

The minute I realized it, maybe because we both looked fragile and unreal in that light, in that situation, I had the absolute certainty that she was hiding something. I held out my hand, touched her pointed chin lightly.

"Listen, Patrícia."

She sniffed. I put on my deepest voice of the Mature & Understanding Man, Although Tired of Youth's Folly:

"If you really trust me, you'd better tell me everything now. Otherwise we're going to sit here, staring at each other's faces until the day after tomorrow. And nothing's going to happen. The most I can do is order a pizza and some beer, and put on some music."

"Right," she said.

"Right what?"

"I trust you."

"Then tell me everything."

She tossed the cigarette butt out the window. For the first time since she'd come in she looked into my eyes. She took off her fogged-up glasses, leaned her arm on Vita's back and rubbed her eyes. They became even redder, more frightened.

"I think I know where she is."

For one crazy second, one hand holding Patrícia's chin, the other on Vita's back, my mind racing, I thought—Dulce, she knows where Dulce is, and she was going to tell me everything, and then I'd tell Rafic, Castilhos, everybody, we'd do a big piece for the front page, I'd take Dulce on all the TV shows like "This is Your Life," Rafic would make loads of money, heaps of prestige, he'd be elected representative, senator, whatever, maybe he'd get me an appointment abroad, maybe in Tirana, Albania, where in the winter, in the cold of the Balkans, I'd finally write poems again, good ones this time, maybe epics, like a rhapsodist, and maybe one day I'd get a letter from Pedro, setting up a tryst in Ibiza, Alexandria, or Volterra, and.

"Where?"

"I can't tell, I promised. If I tell, Márcia will send me away." She sobbed loudly, then wailed, "I can't live without her, don't you understand?"

I shook her chin gently, it was wet with tears. She stuck her chewed nails in the cat's fur. This time Vita's meow was almost a howl. Her hair was bristling.

"The full moon makes her nervous."

"Tell me what you know right now. Or else get out and leave me alone."

In a whisper, as if she were afraid somebody else, besides me, might hear her, Patrícia said:

"It's a house, a very old house in Bom Retiro. I think it's a boarding house, a tenement. Márcia's been going there almost every day since we moved in together, since Ícaro died and I came to São Paulo. She always takes food, medicine, at times clothes. Women's clothes. One time I followed her."

"Who lives there?" I was almost shouting. "Who lives there, Patrícia?"

"I don't know, I didn't see, I didn't go in. I just stayed out in the street, watching. Márcia found out, I don't know how. She made me promise I'd never do it again. I'd never tell anyone. It was a secret, she said, a horrible secret."

I sprang up. Almost at the same time, Vita jumped out of Patrícia's lap, her fur bristling, ran across the apartment and began pacing in front of the door, scratching at the wood as if she wanted to go out immediately. Patrícia got up too.

"Do you think," she stammered, "do you think that—"

"It's got to be," I said, my heart pounding, "it's got to be her."

Neither I nor Patrícia had to utter that name. And when we went out, even without having said it, I had the impression that it continued to reverberate alone in the apartment, pulsating like a living thing in the funeral home's green light.

41

The tires screeched around the curve by the church, near the Tiradentes subway station. Vita let out a piercing meow. Ignoring the traffic lights Patrícia cut in between the buses. A couple of neanderthals yelled from a bar, I had to hold tight to keep from falling off. For a long time she wound through narrow, dirty alleys lined with shops and finally pulled up in front of an old rusty gate.

"It's here," she said. "This is the house Márcia entered that day."

I jumped off the bike, glanced inside. Weeds grew between the cracks of the moisture-stained concrete walk that led to the crumbling steps. Through the half-closed door, painted dark green—deep green, I thought, moss green like Dulce Veiga's armchair—you could see an orange plastic couch with a picture of Iemanjá behind it. I went up the walk, climbed the steps, stood in front of Iemanjá. Arms outstretched, hands opened toward me, she was walking barefoot over waters that looked muddy beneath the layer of dirt coating the picture. From inside the house, through a narrow hallway, came a smell of fried onions and boiled cabbage. There was nobody in sight. I wanted to go down that hallway, then I remembered Patrícia.

She was still standing next to the bike, with Vita's face poking out of the open collar of her leather jacket.

"You're not coming?"

She was banging her helmet against her knees, undecided.

"You go ahead, I don't have the guts."

All right, I said. I was ready to solve the mystery all by myself when, suddenly, I heard a strident meow and a furry streak shot between my legs.

"Vita," Patrícia cried, "Vita Sackville-West, come back here, now."

Running after the cat, Patrícia crashed into me, nearly knocking us down on the torn orange couch bursting with tufts of straw. Patrícia chased Vita down the hall. In the corridor with numbers painted in white on the closed doors, the smell of fried food, spoiled food, dirty clothes, poverty got stronger. A bulb hung from the wooden ceiling, but the yellow light wasn't enough to illuminate the entire hallway. We couldn't see the cat.

Patrícia squeezed my arm. From behind one of the doors, a baby began to cry.

Vita sat in front of a door near the end of the hallway, very quiet. It was number eight I noticed, as Patrícia knelt down to pick up the cat. Music came from inside, a voice singing a familiar tune, even though it was mixed up with the baby's crying, the unmuffled exhaust pipes of the cars in the street, Patrícia's panting, and my own heart beating. I put my ear to the door, trying to hear better. When I recognized the song I felt an almost uncontrollable urge to turn, retrace my steps down the hall, turn my back on Iemanjá's image, take a cab, go home, throw a few things in the backpack, and go some place very far from there. In the middle of the flight

I didn't dare put into practice, it was already too late, I recognized the voice and the song.

It was Dulce Veiga. Behind the closed door of that sordid tenement was Dulce Veiga's voice singing "Nothing More."

In Patrícia's arms, Vita's eyes gleamed in the shadows, violet like Liz Taylor's. The two of them were staring at me, immobile. Because of all the movies I'd seen, and they were thousands, all the books I'd read, all I'd been taught about the way a man should act in these situations and all that—and, in short, because of many other things, I couldn't simply turn my back and run, leaving the two of them standing there, alone, female, defenseless.

My God, I thought. I hadn't thought about God in a long time.

I put my hand on the latch. An old latch, made of metal. It felt warm, sticky. Maybe it was my sweaty palm. I mentally counted to three. I pulled the latch down and noiselessly opened the door.

In the center of the room was a green velvet armchair with its back to us. And fallen against the top of the armchair, hanging over one of those wings level with the person sitting, was a woman's blond head. Her hair was straight, disarrayed, parted in the middle, cut at chin level. We couldn't see her face, just her head, part of her shoulders, and one arm. In the yellow light the skin of the arm flopped over the green velvet had a sickly hue, almost yellow as well. Scarlet nails dug into the mount of Venus in the upturned palm. In the crook of her elbow, just above the scarlet nails and thin wrist, a vein throbbed.

It was that vein Márcia was massaging, kneeling at the feet of the woman, holding a syringe. She was repeating things I couldn't make out, gentle things, probably, as if she were speaking to a baby. Loving, soothing, hypnotic. The woman writhed in the chair, opening and closing her hand to make the battered vein stick out more.

Down the hallway, the baby cried louder.

Márcia didn't look up. She slowly bent over the woman's arm and, absorbed in her task, dressed in black like the negative of a nurse, a nurse of darkness, she stuck the needle in the vein. The woman stopped writhing. Márcia pushed in the syringe, injecting the liquid. The blond hair fell back over the green velvet.

At that moment I decided to go in, interrupt that horrible scene. Patrícia grabbed my shirt. I glanced around, standing in the doorway. The walls were almost entirely plastered with magazine covers and articles with pictures of Dulce Veiga from twenty, thirty years before. Besides the green chair, the room also contained an old iron bed with filthy, crumpled sheets and an open armoire full of old-fashioned dresses, tattered scarves, shoes, hats. Next to the closed window, on top of the vanity, among apples, cream jars, and perfume bottles, an old 78 RPM was spinning on the turntable of a portable record player. Cracked and scratchy, Dulce Veiga's voice was singing her last hit.

Márcia pulled out the syringe. A drop of blood spurted in the air. She began to disinfect the woman's arm with cotton. The cotton turned red with blood. Márcia took another ball and pressed it against the vein. Another smell, more penetrating than fried food and dirt, wafted in the air, cloying, like crushed almonds. The woman's blond hair swayed, brushing her bare arm. Márcia sighed, raised her eyes. It was then that Patrícia let go of my shirt, Vita jumped inside meowing, Márcia dropped the syringe and looked up at us, terror-stricken.

Before she could cry or make a movement, I entered the room. Stepping on the shards of the syringe, I went around the armchair to see the woman's face.

42

The second time I saw Dulce Veiga, and it was the last one, she wasn't alone. Besides the baby, who not until twenty years later would I discover was Márcia, there was a man in that apartment with the curtains always drawn on Avenida São João. Everything was so fast, so confused, I can barely sort out the recollections in my memory, I don't know what came before, during, or after.

I'd gone back to get some pictures, song lyrics, perhaps to talk to her a little more, I don't remember for sure. For some reason the editor of the magazine wasn't satisfied, it was my first celebrity profile, and it wasn't up to snuff. I rang the bell, a man opened the door, a tall man with light-colored eyes wearing a very sweaty undershirt. He was moving back and forth, throwing clothes and books, mainly books, lots of books, into an open suitcase in the middle of the living room, his hair plastered to his face with sweat. I remember he opened the door just a crack, looked at me, scared, over the chain of the lock, as if he were afraid I was someone else. Only when I told him who I was and what I wanted did he remove the chain, open the door and let me in. Then I saw her, for the last time I saw Dulce Veiga, but not her face.

There was an archway without curtains dividing the room in two. Standing next to the man who was tossing clothes and books, I saw Dulce Veiga's chair in the other room, with its back turned toward us. From where I stood I could only see her blond hair hanging in disarray, part of her right shoulder, and a bare arm stretched across the green velvet. An empty syringe hung from her hand, a fine thread of blood gleamed on the skin of her arm. Darling, the man said, as if it didn't bother him, it's the guy from the magazine, but she didn't answer, you need to think of your career, he said, especially now that I'm leaving, but she didn't move, tell me where it is and I'll give it to him, but she still didn't answer, immobile in the green chair.

While the man spoke, continuing to throw things into the suitcase, I looked over there, where Dulce Veiga sat, and I could see the baby's cradle, with an Indian cloth suspended over it like a tent, and the little table with the marble top, and on it, among packs of cigarettes and some papers, several phials, gauze, cotton, a bottle of alcohol. The man kept talking. Dulce didn't move. Then, gently but firmly, he began to push me toward the door, telling me to come back later, some other day, that he was in a hurry, he was going to travel, that Dulce wasn't feeling well, that there was no time, not even a minute, and he needed to leave, flee, urgently. When he opened the door for me to leave, the baby began to cry. Over his shoulder—he was very tall, he was very strong—I saw Dulce ineffectually try to get up from the chair, and before I went out into the hall she called to him in a voice that seemed to come from far away. Much farther than the other end of the room, from the other side of the world. From another world, she called to him.

Saul, she said, she asked feebly. Saul, see about the baby. The man left me standing at the door, went to the cradle, rocked it gently until the baby began to calm down, and when she finally stopped crying he tenderly caressed Dulce's hair, then took the syringe from her hand, carefully, as if it were a loaded gun ready to go off. He placed it on the marble table, where it couldn't harm her. Then he returned to me, repeating that I had to go, that he had to go too, before the men came, and he drew nearer, he was sweating heavily, he was shaking, I could smell his clean sweat, and see his eyes up close, they weren't exactly green, but very light brown, they must turn green when the sun shone on them, but there was no sun there, the curtains were always drawn. They were eyes of fear, eyes of horror, the eyes of the man very close to me, gleaming in the dark. He put his hands on my shoulders, told me to be careful, that I was very young, not to tell anyone he was there, to publish the interview and write for everybody to read that Dulce Veiga was a great singer, the best of all, in the entire world. The man ran his hand over my face, his eyes filled with urgency and panic, repeating those things with a shadow of sadness, or despair, or leave-taking in his voice, and he came very close, each time closer to my face, then suddenly he leaned toward me, grabbed me, and kissed me on the lips.

The baby began to cry again in the cradle, Saul, Dulce called again, Saul, the child. He pushed me out into the hallway, slammed the door. I pressed the elevator button. I must have run my hand over my mouth, tasting the sweaty salty taste of the man's mouth, I must have run my hand over my mouth many times, not as if I felt disgust, but just touching, investigating what had been taken and what had been left there, without understanding any of it, I was very young, I didn't know anything. I don't remember if it was when the elevator got down to the ground floor or when the door opened on the floor where I waited, I no longer know the exact moment when out of the old caged elevator burst four or five men in suits, one of them with a gun in his hand, and they pushed me against the wall. The singer's apartment, they demanded, the guerrilla, where does Dulce Veiga live, the terrorist, where's the apartment of that whore, of that communist, and without quite knowing what that meant, everything was going too fast, it wasn't my fault, I told them the number, without meaning to, I think it was seventy, I said: they live over there. The men rushed past, I left.

I barely remember anything after that. In the elevator, or on the way out of the building, I heard the men kicking and banging on the apartment door. In the street people whispered, hurried by with their eyes on the ground, pretending not to see the secret police car parked on the sidewalk, with armed men all around it. Down there, on Avenida São João, right in front of that building where, twenty years ago, before being swallowed by the world, Dulce Veiga once lived.

43

In spite of the blue silk dress, the high heels, the scarlet fingernails, the pearl necklace, and the blond hair exactly like Dulce Veiga used to wear—the person sitting in the green chair wasn't her. Through the black stubble and the layer of makeup highlighting the cheekbones and the proud, almost hard line of the jaw that made the false face even more like hers, I recognized without too much trouble the brown skin and the eyes filled with panic from twenty years before. The dilated pupils were fixed on me.

In a low voice, I called his name.

"Saul."

But even though he was looking straight at me, I realized he didn't see me. Neither me, nor anything or anyone outside himself. He was living in another world, maybe the same one from which Dulce Veiga had called to him once, while he was preparing his escape, to look after the baby, the same one who was looking after him now. He was smiling a pinched smile, a thread of drool running from the corner of his mouth, his legs spread, the arms with bruised veins abandoned on the green velvet. As if he were traveling in space, as if he were piloting a spaceship. Lost in galaxies, his head thrown back, the blue eyelids half-closed, far from us and everything else, alone at the wheel of his madness.

Márcia went to the dressing table and turned off the music. She looked perfectly calm in the middle of that uncomfortable silence. Or too exhausted to be scared.

"Do you know him?"

"I could lie and say no, like you did," I said, and she lowered her eyes. "But I saw him once. Many years ago, in your mother's apartment."

Patrícia was picking up the blood-stained pieces of the syringe. Vita was gently rubbing against the legs of the man dressed as Dulce Veiga as if she wanted to caress him. The baby had stopped crying. The rancid smell from the hallway wafted in through the open door.

"They were very good—" Márcia began. Then she hesitated, ran her hand over her head, spiking up her bleached hair. And repeated, more firmly, "They were very good *friends*, Saul and mother. He doesn't have anyone else left in the world except me."

"And why you, exactly?"

"That's my business."

"You could be arrested for drug trafficking, you know that?"

I immediately regretted having said it. As if by magic, Márcia's calm or fatigue suddenly vanished. A spark went through her body, and she became her old raving self again. Hands planted on her hips, she screamed:

"Go ahead, turn me in. There must be a police station around here, why don't you go and turn me in as a dealer. A thief, a murderer. Whatever you like, go ahead, what are you waiting for?"

Maybe the same way, I thought bitterly, maybe the same way, without meaning to, I turned in Saul twenty years ago, and you don't even know it. It was a horrible thought. And it wasn't my fault, I wanted to throw myself at Saul's feet, scream like a madman, crazier than him, rolling on the floor, gnashing my teeth, that I was so young, I didn't know what I was doing.

Vita meowed, frightened, looking at us. Patrícia put her hand on Márcia's arm, explaining in a low voice:

"I was the one who called him. I didn't know what to do, you disappeared, the rest of the band is in a panic."

Márcia pulled away with such violence that the shards of the syringe in Patrícia's hand fell back to the floor.

"You're an idiot, you just had to blab my whole life to a complete stranger, didn't you? I warned you that if you did that you could pack up and get the fuck out."

"Our show, the opening night," Patrícia wailed. In Márcia's presence she turned whiny and imploring like a little beggar. "I thought it was important, I was just trying to help you."

"You've been trying to help me for years, and you always fuck everything up. Wasn't it you who told Alberto that I'd lost my mind in New York? Do me a favor—don't try to help me ever again. I want to fuck myself up on my own, honey. Like I did when Ícaro died."

Suddenly, without anyone expecting it, Márcia threw herself on the bed and burst into tears, her face buried in the filthy sheets. Before that living-dead man disguised as another living-dead person, Patrícia and I stared at each other, like actors who haven't learned the lines or the stage directions of a film or play, or maybe a book, of dubious quality. She glanced at her diver's watch.

"We should already be at the Hiroshima."

But we are there, I thought. In the center of the atomic mushroom, at the second of the explosion, blind and dumb with the ghastly light. Stuck in the mirror of the dressing table was a picture of the real Dulce Veiga. The black tulle of a veil covered her face almost completely. Except for her thin-lipped mouth, which was smiling at us. Vita had jumped on the bed and was purring in Márcia's hair.

"Maybe it would be better if you two went to the theater," I said. "We'll talk later."

Then a woman appeared at the door. She was fat and placid, very brown, the straight hair of an Indian, a thick mustache. She looked like a Bolivian, a Yanomami. She was rocking a snotty baby in her arms, probably the same one who'd been crying. She glanced inside.

"What's going on, dona Márcia? I heard cries, is your Saul sick again?" From the chair, Saul let out a moan. The woman laughed, went near him and said, "He's funny, he doesn't like people to call him *Mr. Saul*. He turns into a regular tiger, only he doesn't bite. He wants you to say *Dulce Veiga*, who knows why."

"It was nothing," Márcia mumbled.

"The opening, the show," Patrícia said.

Saul groaned again. The woman repeated rhythmically, like a song, until he quieted down:

"Dulce, Dulce Veiga. Everything's okay, Dulce Veiga, everything's all right. You're looking so pretty today, dona Dulce."

Márcia got up.

"Let's go. I have to sing."

And the show must go on, I thought. Not telling them the apartment number wouldn't have helped, the police always knew everything in those days. Márcia was walking to the door. I grabbed her arm.

"You're gonna have some explaining to do."

"I don't have to explain anything, goddammit. Stay out of my life."

"But I need to know."

Suddenly, she relented.

"All right," she said, and pulled her arm away, so meekly I could hardly believe it. She had violet circles under her very green eyes, two deep lines on the sides of her mouth. Her skin looked worn, dry. I tried to hug her, say again that it wasn't my fault, but she pushed me away without anger. "Later, after the show. Look for me at the Hiroshima, we'll talk."

In my ear, Patrícia asked in a whisper:

"Who is this guy?"

I didn't answer, I couldn't. In a way, I didn't know either. Márcia kissed Saul on the forehead and said to the woman:

"Call me if he gets sick, dona Iracema. Anytime, you know where to find me."

The woman with the Indian face was standing next to the green armchair. She was rocking the baby in one arm, while with her free hand she caressed Saul's livid forehead. You're pretty, Dulce Veiga, she was saying, I've never seen you looking so pretty in my entire life. Like the silvery track of a snail, the drool continued to ooze out of Saul's mouth onto the blue silk of his dress.

44

I stood in the shower for nearly an hour. When I finally came out, feeling just as dirty as before, I remembered they used to run off the arts section of the following day's paper around ten o'clock. I could go by before the show and take Márcia the published interview. Or, I had always dreamed of this, burst into the printer's crying, "Stop the press! Stop the press!" But there would be nothing new to print. Other than perhaps a picture of Saul dressed as Dulce Veiga. And me at his feet, my head on his knees, like a bisexual pietà: "Twenty years later, reporter bemoans consequences of his tip to police." Not tip: *denunciation* or *betrayal* were more the *Diário da Cidade*'s style.

I slapped myself, cool it, it wasn't your fault, everything was already set up. On the way out, I took some money, put it in an envelope, and slipped it under Jandira's door, as if I were trying to buy the sympathy of the *orixás*. I went down the stairs pursued by a swarm of raging Exus.

The full moon was rising behind the overpasses of Bela Vista. Huge, round, yellow. I walked down Rua Augusta, staring at shop windows, magazines, people, kicking empty cans, pebbles, mentally adding up the numbers of the cars' license plates. I could lose my mind if I wanted to, I knew so many terrible stories. It would be just as easy to walk into the first bar, drink myself to sleep, and wake up with a throbbing head and vague memories of some nightmare.

When I saw the paper I felt better. Above the color photograph of Márcia, Castilhos had put a full page headline—*Márcia F.: Everything More*. You could see the colors of one of the butterfly's wings between her breasts beneath the unbuttoned blouse. It was nice, provocative. The text seemed pretty good too, despite the typos. Slowly, my shoulders began to relax, and I felt like a good person, I felt decent again. I decided to buy roses for Márcia. White roses, roses of peace. It took me so long to get to Largo do Arouche that by the time I arrived at the Hiroshima it was almost midnight. There were a lot of people in front of the lilac neon atomic mushroom.

I ran my fingers over my parched lips. In a way, that kiss was still burning. As if a piece of my mouth had been missing all those years, still clinging to Saul's mouth.

V

FRIDAY

The Mercury Maze

45

That was Armageddon right there, no doubt about it. Punks, People In Black, skinheads, Goths, junkies, crowding together in the final battle. A legion of replicants, mass-produced clones, all in black or purple, chains, crucifixes, eye patches, tattoos, shaved, bleached heads bristling like geometric, asymmetric crests, dyed green, red, violet.

Dressed all in white, the white roses in my hand, I was the weirdest of them all. An android hunter, disguised as an angel. I pushed my way to the bar. Two or three whiskeys would knock off that strangeness in a matter of minutes. Above the mutants' heads, the video screens reproduced Márcia's image and, as I tried to get the attention of the Japanese bartender, I heard her voice. Husky, angry, the piercing wails of the guitar in the background.

"It's fallen, the Great Babylon has fallen! It's turned into a lair of demons, prison of every impure spirit and every impure and repulsive bird, because all nations have drunk the bitter wine of its lust, the kings of the world have prostituted themselves to it and its unbridled luxury has made the thieves of the earth rich!"

In the background, between the words, the Toothed Vaginas were rhythmically shouting in chorus *yeah, yeah, it's fallen*
the great Babylon has fallen!

I drank the whiskey in one gulp. It tasted bitter, like boldo tea, rectified alcohol, without sugar. Márcia seemed in great form even though, truth be told, I came from the times when Maria Bethânia shook her bracelets in the air, reciting Fernando Pessoa, "The man I love lives with me in my house." Was it really him? I couldn't remember, it might be Bivar, Fauzi Arap, Luiz Carlos Lacerda, but it might be him too, he wasn't too discreet, the uncle, all those hairy sailors in the "Maritime Ode," I remembered, some boy in London, *when I die, Daisy,* that whiskey was deadly, it was all making me think of Pedro, I was getting drunk faster than I had planned. I put the roses down on the counter, the replicants looked at them as if they were a bouquet of worms, God how time passes, and when you realize it, suddenly, one day, Newton's binomial has finally and actually become more beautiful than the Venus de Milo.

I ordered another whiskey and stood there watching Márcia's

performance. It was sensational. The white makeup underscored the atmosphere of urban decay, the dark circles under her eyes had been accentuated with black shadow. She ended the apocalyptic speech with her closed fist raised in the air—whatever happened to Angela Davis, I thought—the spiked leather bracelet gleamed beneath the spotlights. Then she picked up her guitar and, without a break, launched into one of those rock songs that spoke of cesium, bubonic plague, mercury, nuclear disaster, atomic waste, cyclamate, and ozone. Holes, of course. The audience was clapping and dancing frenetically: Márcia Fellatio and the Toothed Vaginas were a hit.

And I thought: wherever she is, dead or alive, this must be good for Dulce Veiga's soul. That made me feel sad, I wasn't in the habit of thinking about souls, from this or the other world. I was beginning to feel very lonely, and old, and out of place, and square, in need of at least twenty hours of sleep, when someone touched my shoulder. It must be Patrícia, I figured.

No, it was Filemon. A can of beer in his hand, perfectly in tune with the surroundings. He seemed happy to see me.

"I never thought I'd see you here."

"Me neither."

"Castilhos asked me to write a review. But he said he's only going to print it if it's favorable."

Perfect: from behind the scenes, Rafic was already beginning to move. For the mother's triumphant comeback, of course, it would be strategic to pave the daughter's way real well first. I could almost picture their harrowing encounter on some TV show or magazine cover. Rafic between the two of them, the rising star, the supernova, next to the extinguished star.

"What do you call extinguished stars?"

"Huh?"

"Never mind. I don't think you'll like it. This is Satan's den."

Filemon shook his head, he was looking a little drunk too. The crucifix earring swung.

"On the contrary. I know Márcia well, she's very religious. All this is to glorify the name of Jesus. In the clinic all we read was the Bible."

Ah, I thought. And I remembered the dedication on the record cover, something about paths of light, side trails of darkness. Another enigma, I sighed with exhaustion, blessed are the raving mad. On the counter, among the roses, Filemon's hand was trying to brush mine. I withdrew my fingers, he noticed. I tried to dissemble.

"Filemon, Filemon. What a strange name you have."

"My father's idea, he's a Jungian therapist."

"It must be great to a have a shrink for a father. You can lose your mind free of charge, anytime of day or night." I felt like asking him for a Lexotan prescription, Lidia's inheritance had been squandered.

"Listen," he said, very close to my ear, the red mouth in the middle of the pale face almost touching my skin. I felt an almost uncontrollable impulse to kiss him again. That was a compulsive kind of business. Or magnetic, I don't know which. Fluids, imperceptible scents, vibrations. What was it that, independent of reason, attracted or repulsed people? "We need to talk. I've been thinking about what happened."

I drew back.

"Not now, I need to watch the show."

"It's down there, I'll take you."

He dragged me down to the basement where the stage was. Staring at the shaved back of his head, among angels of the apocalypse, crazy monks, radioactive sirens, dethroned kings, infected prophets, wounded beasts, apathetic mountebanks, I thought, he wants to know why I kissed him. In the twilight, after the rain, before Dulce Veiga disappeared inside the Itália building. A strange impulse, I could explain. The name of a movie, Walter Hugo Khoury, a perfume, some vulgar and erotic dime store romance. A strange, strange impulse since, aside from Pedro, I wasn't a homosexual. But I could also tell him—if I had the courage, if there was time, if it was worth it—Saul's story. The story of that other kiss, the kiss Saul had given me. As I had given one to Filemon, suddenly, without explanation. A sort of curse, passed down from mouth to mouth. At that time Saul must have been the same age I was now. Twenty years from now, after all kinds of crazy ups and downs, perhaps one day Filemon would find me dressed as Márcia F., frozen in time, in frustration, doing lines of coke. It was grotesque, but I couldn't laugh. Like a strange curse, I mentally repeated to the beat of the music, passed down from mouth to mouth.

The second whiskey was having a bad effect. It felt like I had drunk five, smoked three joints, snorted seven lines. The descent down the iron spiral staircase to the basement, without air conditioning, among the cries of *yeah, yeah, the Great Babylon has fallen* interspersing every song, literally seemed like a descent into the underworld.

Suddenly I stumbled, and bumped into Jacyr. He was dressed like a guy, black leather pants, skin-tight. He let out a little cry and pointed at Filemon.

"Keeping good company, eh, breeder?"

A colleague from the paper, I tried to explain. My white clothes soaked with sweat, the white roses stained with the paper's black ink. Filemon was weaving his way through the androids, pre- and post—the only *during* was me—trying to get close to the stage. I followed him.

Jacyr yelled, behind him I saw the black Rasta.

"I'm blowing the dough you paid me," he adjusted the invisible shawl on his shoulders, pointed to the stage. "In homage to the goddess. She's a woman, but she's well worth it."

By the time I managed to get near the stage the show was over. The audience was asking for an encore, the lights went out, they were clapping their hands shouting en-core-en-core-en-core, Filemon passed me his beer can—I had finished my whiskey—I took a swig, the stage lights came on again. Filemon drew nearer, I really like you, he said in the dark, I pretended not to hear, Márcia came out again and, among the cries and applause, when I thought she was going to call out the Toothed Vaginas to play "Nothing More" or some contaminated rock song, she picked up the acoustic guitar, sat on a stool, pulled the microphone close to her and said:

"My mother, Dulce Veiga, was a great singer. No one knows where she's been for the last twenty years. She left some poems, this among them, which I set to music. I dedicate this song to her, wherever she is. It's called 'Green Armchair.'"

Sitting on the stool, her legs crossed, round knees below the leather miniskirt, she looked like Nara Leão. In a bossa nova beat, very close to the microphone, just one spotlight on her, Márcia sang in a soft voice:

"Here I sit, abandoned,
contemplating this squalid world,
everything and nothing.
Lost, hallucinating
on the green velvet
of this chair, enamored
with everything and nothing,
I sail among silks, lose myself at sea,
I, so far from the sea of life,
weary of loves, tired of bars.
Here I sit, my body burning,
contemplating the world turning,
nothing and everything.
Wounded veins, paralyzed,
drowning in the green mire
silent velvet, armchair life,
only friend on the long road,
that embraced me, then escaped me:
Here I sit, enlightened.
Contemplating the world,
the good, the bad,
everything and nothing
and beyond."

Let me take care of you, Filemon whispered in my ear. I didn't answer. At least half the legion of replicants was climbing the stairs, booing, nonplussed by the heavy metal betrayal. Very self-assured, Márcia walked to the edge of the stage smiling, held out her hand to me and called:

"Come on, let's talk."

46

Menacing, screaming, the Toothed Vaginas surrounded Márcia. In their midst I saw Patrícia, very pale. The Japanese chick was brandishing the electric bass in the air like a samurai sword.

"You traitor. You should have called the entire group on stage. You want all the glory for yourself, you snake?"

As if she hadn't heard, Márcia walked to her dressing room, pulled me in, slammed the door, locked it, took off her blouse and wrapped herself in a towel before I could get another glimpse of the butterfly between her breasts. They began to pound on the door. Among cries and knocking, a woman's voice began to sing in the distance. It sounded like Madonna. I held out the half faded roses, stained with ink, and the paper with her interview. They looked even more ridiculous in the crowded dressing room, barely bigger than an elevator. She glanced at them and smiled, almost imperceptibly.

"Everything more, that's good. Everything more than what?"

She drank water straight from the bottle. Then she lit a cigarette, sat in front of the mirror and looked at me. Her very green eyes in the middle of the black makeup reminded me a little of Vita's. I sat across from her.

"Why did you lie and say you didn't know Saul?"

She poured the rest of the water over her head.

"You saw him, didn't you? In that state, it's better if nobody knows he's alive. What's the point, man?"

"Your father also lied and said he didn't know him."

"My father," she lowered her eyes in search of an ashtray. There weren't any. She dropped the ash on the floor and with a sort of irony, contempt, she repeated, "*My father* prefers to believe Saul never existed. You have to understand, he's a very vain man. It must be difficult to admit that mother had other men. Many others."

Somebody kicked the door. Márcia balanced the cigarette butt on the edge of the table, among other burn marks. She grabbed a towel and began to wipe her face with it. Mixed with sweat and black eye shadow, the white makeup was gradually coming off, washed away by the water, letting the skin show through the streaks, like the mask of a clown.

"How did you find out about him?"

"It was when I came back from London. Some friends of my mother's were taking care of him."

"What friends?"

"Friends, that's all. People you don't know. No one could stand him anymore. I liked him, I understood his madness. I've been crazy too, after all."

And you still are, I thought, because then, as if she had gone away, as if she'd left her body sitting there, drenched with sweat, water, makeup, while a part of her went somewhere else, she twisted her head slightly, then raised one of her hands to her neck and began to caress it with the tips of her fingers. Abruptly, as if I wanted to bring her back to that grungy dressing room, I said:

"I liked the encore, it's your best song."

Distant, she continued to caress her neck, squeezing gently from time to time, as if she were feeling something. Round, small, imperceptible.

"Mother left some poems, some journals, too. They were never found. I'm putting what's left of them to music, maybe one day I'll make a record just with these songs." Her voice became so low I barely heard her when she added, "But I don't know if there's gonna be enough time."

"Sure there is, why not?"

"You don't understand. I lied about other things, too."

As if I were talking to the child she'd been once, in the apartment on São João, I asked:

"And what did you lie about, Márcia?"

She didn't answer. She took my fingers in her cold fingers, the stubby nails painted black and, lowering her head, placed them on the back of her neck, making me feel the same place she'd just been feeling. I stretched my fingers over her skin. Under it, beneath the streaks of makeup, the drops of sweat and water, like seeds, rolling at the slightest touch, were small lumps. My hand began to tremble, but I didn't withdraw it. I felt around them, touching them lightly. She closed her eyes. They were oval, fugitive. Exactly like the ones that had appeared a few months before on the back of my own neck. Not just on my neck—in my groin, in my armpits.

"In other places too," she said. "They're all over my body. I'm afraid of seeing a doctor, doing the test." Suddenly she opened her eyes, almost glued to mine, and asked, "Are you gay?"

I remembered Pedro. I withdrew my fingers.

"I don't know."

Márcia straightened her head.

"I don't really know either, at times I, Patrícia, you know. But it's strange not to know. I don't think anyone knows. It must be more comfortable to pretend you are or aren't, to *define*. But I think those who think they're gay understand these things better. I saw you with Filemon, he likes you."

Without getting up, she began rummaging in the purse hanging from the chair. She took out a little package of wax paper and emptied the contents on top of the table. Among the burn marks of countless cigarettes, with a razor blade, she began to break up the white grains. And said:

"Ícaro died of AIDS. I think I have it too."

Outside someone knocked again, yelled louder. I leaned against the door, as if I wanted to protect her from the people pounding on the door. I could feel the vibrations through the wood, like punches in my back.

"They're going to knock the door down."

"So let them. I know very well how to deal with those people."

"Do you want me to open it?"

Leaning over the table, with the fine point of a tiny sword-shaped blade, she was drawing something with the lines of white powder. At the base of the sword, in profile, was the golden head of an eagle. Just like Rafic's eagles, I thought vaguely. The ring, the lighter, the wallet. It must be a coincidence.

"If you want, all you need to open a door is turn the key. Or do you want to know something else?"

"The chair. That green velvet armchair of Saul's, is it the same as Dulce Veiga's?"

She finished drawing, leaned back to see better. I couldn't see anything from where I was. Just her wet, bleached hair. She touched up something with the tip of the sword, then turned her surprised, innocent eyes toward me.

"Chair, what chair? It's just an old armchair, falling apart. I don't know who it belonged to. What importance does it have?"

None, I thought. Or decided to think, I needed to get out of there immediately. As a detective I was definitely a failure.

I opened the door. Madonna's voice burst into the dressing room with "Material Girl." And the three Toothed Vaginas with it, plus a crowd of people, all talking at the same time. Patrícia pretended not to see me, somebody popped a champagne bottle. Sovereign in the midst of it all, Márcia smiled, imperturbable, holding out the rolled bill to her subjects. Before crossing the stage to the crowded floor and trying to reach the street without running into Filemon, as I stood by the door, I managed to catch a glimpse of the drawing Márcia had made on the tabletop with the coke.

The fine, elongated lines, irregular and wavering like those of a Chinese or Japanese ideogram traced with a brush and India ink, had more or less this shape: 兑

47

Torii.

Someone had told me once that was what the red arches of Liberdade, on Rua Galvão Bueno, were called. Standing under them, far from the commotion of the Hiroshima, I touched the back of my own neck, the way I'd touched my lips before. The ganglia were still there. Elusive, rounded, exactly the same as Márcia's.

Then I remembered the night I'd found a postcard under my door, a few weeks after Pedro had disappeared. All golden, like him, it must be fall in Paris, but the postcard had no stamp, it didn't come from there. By a riverbank, beneath a tree, a man sat alone, his head hanging. On the back, right under the caption *Pont Neuf sur la Seine: Mélancolie*, in his slanted, sort of childish handwriting, Pedro had written:

"Don't try to find me. Forget me, forgive me. I think I've been infected and I don't want to kill you with my love."

But you already have, I thought that day.

And now again, under the red arches of Liberdade, as I'd thought every day since the day he disappeared, and the following months, without daring to go to the doctor or do the test that might confirm my suspicions, touching my entire body in search of the accursed signs, night sweats, spots on my skin, I thought again—but you've already killed me.

But I was still alive. At my feet, under the overpass and all around it, the city glowed beneath the full moon. I felt like raising my head and howling at it.

48

From above and far off, on top of a building, at the edge of an overpass, on board a plane, nothing is clear, I look down, into the center of something that looks like a labyrinth, an ellipse. Shifting, devouring, concentric circles. Somebody pushes me from behind, I make a futile attempt to grab on to something. The edge of the wall, the open door of the airplane. It's safer to stay here. From above and far off. They push me again, harder. I fall into space, spinning.

I woke up before touching the ground. The words still spun in my head, like my body during the fall. From above and far off. Past noon, the words weren't going away. I need to travel, I thought, I need to look at all those people, all those things, like that. From above and far off. I remembered Rafic's offer, "tickets, from the airport, at a moment's notice," and decided to go to Rio to talk to Lilian Lara. It would almost certainly be pointless, but, after all, she was the last person who'd seen Dulce Veiga.

49

A mulatto woman in a pale blue uniform and white starched cap opened the door.

"Are you the nurse?"

"No, I'm the journalist who called."

"From São Paulo?"

"Right."

"I can tell from your color."

I didn't say anything. She told me to wait in the living room, dona Lilian was coming, and disappeared inside the apartment. It was a penthouse in Copacabana, overlooking the ocean. There were two living areas with sofas, many paintings, not as bad as Rafic's, and a profusion of decorative objects like copper deer, porcelain dalmatians, marble elephants, stuff like that. From the windows that opened onto the ocean the summer air came in, a light so bright and tropical that, looking at the palm leaves below, standing out against the green of the water, the curve of Copacabana flowing into the point of Leme, I had the same feeling I had every time I arrived in Rio de Janeiro. In the background, on a soundtrack I alone could hear, Gal Costa was eternally singing "Aquarela do Brasil."

"O meu Brasil brasileiro—my Brazilian Brazil," I sang in my head, *"terra de samba e pandeiro—land of the samba and the tambourine."*

I looked at my hands, and the other feeling I always had in Rio also returned. In that excessive light, my skin looked too white, my nails dirty, grimy, the cuticles all ragged, fingers yellowed by cigarettes and other stains, veins and bones and hair too visible. I crossed my arms, closed my hands, and pressed them against my shirt, damp with perspiration. On a corner of the coffee table was a strange object, like a flat box.

It was a game. American, Japanese, there was no indication. A maze in the shape of a hexagon, against a black background, with a silver drop of mercury on the outside of the maze, all encased in clear hard plastic. I turned it in my hands, the drop of mercury hit against one of the walls and split in three. I turned it again, more slowly. One of the split drops entered the maze. With increasingly gentler movements, I managed to make it slide along the corridors, toward the center. Of the two drops that had remained on the outside, one split into two more, another also entered the maze, slid toward the one that was already inside and fused with it.

"You like the game, darling?" the voice of a woman, a familiar voice, asked.

Lilian Lara was a tall, thin woman, a flowered scarf over her head, the ends crossing under her chin and tied behind her neck. The scarf covered her ears, part of her cheeks, and forehead. As if this weren't enough, she was wearing huge sunglasses that hid most of her nose, turned up like a girl's. Funny that you'd want to be incognito in your own home, I thought. Then I remembered an item by Teresinha O'Connor about the plastic surgery.

I got up, the maze in my hands. Without realizing it, I had been kneeling next to the table.

"Fascinating," I said. I jiggled the box, one of the drops on the outside of the maze split into at least ten more. They gleamed against the black bottom. Metallic, so tiny they were nearly invisible.

"But it isn't easy at all, darling. You have to put the whole drop right in the center, without letting it split. I've never managed, I have no patience or talent for that kind of thing."

Her hands were shaking slightly, much older than her face. Or, at least, than the visible *inches* of her face between the scarf and the sunglasses. Bored, Lilian plopped down on the sofa, arranged the colorful sarong over her legs, took a cigarette from a silver box and waited for me to light it. When she thanked me, I recognized her voice—it was the same as Leda's, which I heard on the little old ladies' TV, in my building's hallway.

"Of course you want to know the end of *Walls of Blood,*" she was blowing the smoke through her stiff nostrils, practically without moving her red mouth, and inevitably I remembered Nelson Rodrigues' rich-bitch-with-corpse-like-nostrils. "That's what all of Brazil wants to know, darling. It's already been taped, but I can't talk about it. I'm very sorry, it's in the contract. I can't even reveal whether Leda goes back to Rogério or elopes with Mário Sérgio. I'm only authorized to say that Eleonora turns in the letter that absolves her, and I'm not going to allow photographs."

"I didn't come to talk to you about the soap, Miss Lara."

"You didn't?" She looked surprised. "Call me *Lilian*, please."

"It's about someone you knew once, *Lilian*."

"Go on, darling."

"Dulce Veiga," I said.

Lilian's nostrils quivered a little. Then, without naming too many names or giving too many details, I tried to explain the whole story, which I myself no longer understood. As I spoke, the mulatto woman set a pitcher with a yellow liquid and ice cubes in the center of the table. Lilian served, raised her glass in a toast, I tasted it—vodka with orange juice, very sweet. I began to talk again. When I said Saul's name, she filled her glass again, and with the utmost naturalness, as if everybody knew about it, she lamented:

"He was the one who suffered the most, poor guy. After all, he's Márcia's father."

I almost jumped up from the sofa.

"You mean that Alberto—"

"Just imagine, darling. I followed all this very closely, we got pregnant at the same time. Of course Alberto and Márcia, that little punk, took it upon themselves to spread a different story. They must be dying of shame. Alberto of being a cuckold. And Márcia a bastard. What happened was very sad, darling. Dulce left Alberto to live with Saul, who was involved in a thousand political complications. You know, it was tough back then. Not like today, when communists have all turned into wimps. Saul was put in jail, tortured, and when he came out of jail, half crazy, Dulce had disappeared and Alberto had sent Márcia far away. So he ended up in an asylum, for years."

Márcia's innocent eyes, I remembered, Alberto Veiga's theatrical speech: all lies. It made me so mad I had the impulse to get up and leave, return to São Paulo, go straight to Márcia's house and punch her in the face. I barely listened to what Lilian Lara was saying, totally crazy people, people with no class, cheap scum, darling, I'm not surprised poor Dulce decided to disappear forever, and she had talent, she was a real artist, like me. More and more excited, Lilian got up and took a box out of a closet.

"When Dulce disappeared," she said, "we were making a movie together. I took some clips and had this video put together. These are her last images."

Lilian put the film in the VCR. Then she closed the curtains, took a bottle of vodka and poured it in the pitcher, the ice cubes half-melted in the yellow water of the orange juice. She sat down next to me, filled her glass again, the remote in her old hands. The scarf, a little crooked, showed the gray roots of her hair and a vertical scar next to her ear. The sarong slipped, she didn't bother to put it back. She still had nice legs, firm and tanned.

The film, in black and white, had no sound. Dulce Veiga was sitting in an armchair, in front of a man with his back to the camera. She was moving her lips, you couldn't hear anything she was saying. She shook a little bell in the air. A door opened and Lilian Lara came in, almost unrecognizable, twenty years ago. Lilian was carrying a tray and wore a uniform similar to the mulatto woman's who opened the door for me. She put the tray on the table, between Dulce and the man, bowed and left. Dulce served two long-stemmed glasses of liqueur. Handed one to the man and held the other to her lips, with a vague smile. The image froze on the close-up of that face. Beautiful, impenetrable, the green eyes semi-closed by the slightly cynical, slightly cruel smile, the glass full of liqueur almost touching her thin lips.

Neat, I said.

Lilian was busy refilling her glass. She filled mine as well, but I didn't drink.

"She's poisoning him. Dulce was an idiot to leave the movie. She was very reserved, you never knew what she was thinking. And she dropped that child in my lap, good thing Alberto took her right away. But that film, ah what a great film. And it was a super role, the main one. We won a barrel of prizes. *Diabolical Vertigo*—isn't it a beautiful title, darling?"

She wasn't watching the video. She began to list the prizes, the tape kept playing. After a few seconds of blank film, another image came on. At first it looked exactly like the previous clip. But when the woman shook the little bell in the air and the camera came closer, I realized that this time she was no longer Dulce Veiga, but Lilian Lara herself. And the maid a completely unknown young woman.

Suddenly Lilian sat up on the sofa, pressed a button on the remote and the image disappeared.

"Wait," I said.

"That's all."

"I wanted to see the continuation, the change of actresses."

"Oh, you noticed? Well, when Dulce disappeared, the movie had to go on no matter what. The director offered me her role. I didn't want to accept, I don't know. But I was just starting out, it was a great opportunity. A golden opportunity, darling."

I was going to insist on seeing it again, when a tall girl walked into the room. She was wearing a bikini, she must be coming from the beach. With the curtain drawn, I couldn't see her face well. Lilian got up, went to the window and pulled open the curtains. The bright light, not as harsh in the late afternoon, flooded the room again. On the table, the drop of mercury gleamed in the maze.

"Honey, I've asked you a *thousand* times to use the service elevator when you come back from the beach. I don't want that disgusting wormy sand on my Persian rugs."

"Buzz off," the girl said.

Lilian introduced her:

"This is my daughter. She arrived from São Paulo today, she spends her life on the São Paulo-Rio air shuttle. She has some secrets there, which she's not telling me."

I looked at Lilian Lara's daughter: It was Patrícia.

"Nice to meet you," she said, holding out her hand as if she'd never seen me in her entire life.

"Nice to meet you," I repeated. It was so absurd that, for a few seconds, I doubted it was really Patrícia. But there was no doubt. Even without the heavy metal getup and the glasses, her hair matted with salt and sand, it was the same person. The long-legged bird, Virginia Woolf in a bikini, tanned by the February sun.

Patrícia disappeared inside the apartment. Lilian sat down again, took off her sunglasses. Between purplish swollen lids, her eyes were red, bloodshot.

"We have such a difficult relationship," she complained. "She's very rebellious, it seems as though she hates me. At times I think Dulce was right to disappear and abandon her daughter. God knows what I've been through with this girl."

A racket of screams, slamming doors was coming from within. Lilian got up, went to see what was going on. Beyond the white foam of the waves on the beach, the ocean water was now a more intense blue, almost black. Blown by the breeze, the palm leaves were swaying gently. *"Onde amarro a minha rede—where I hang my hammock,"* I silently hummed, *"Onde a lua vem brilhar—where the moon comes to shine." Brilhar* or *brincar,* shine or play, I couldn't remember. *Lindo e trigueiro,* beautiful and brown like wheat, *trigueiro* was nice: my Brazil. Alone in the room, without expecting it myself, I suddenly grabbed the maze and stuck it in my pocket.

When Lilian came back, asking if I wanted another drink, stay for dinner, maybe I'll send for a little caviar, darling, I was already up, ready to leave. She filled her glass again. This time straight from the bottle.

50

The vodka hit me on my way out of the building. I leaned against the wall taking deep breaths of the sea breeze until the vertigo passed. Which wasn't diabolical, but sugary, nauseous. I hadn't been to Rio for over a year, since the time I'd met Pedro in the subway. I pushed the thought of Pedro away and stretched, thinking of going up to São Conrado to see Vicente, maybe, or down to Laranjeiras to visit Jacqueline.

I began to walk, looking for a cab or bus. Salt and sex floated in the blue afternoon air, so many available bodies. If I didn't look at the trash and beggars scattered on the street and kept my eyes above all the heads, toward the ocean, the horizon where the islands lay sunk in the mist, it would be easy to imagine I was in Hawaii. *Seja aqui*, let it be here, I intoned, but I lowered my eyes more than I should have.

Across the street, dressed once again in the Toothed Vagina uniform, Patrícia was drinking coconut milk, one leg resting on a cement bench. Out of place like a punk collage over a south seas landscape.

I crossed the street to meet her.

"What are you doing here?"

"That's what I want to know—what are *you* doing here?"

Her hair was thick with salt, parted in the middle and pinned up. Absurdly, I'd never seen her look so much like Virginia Woolf. She raised the coconut toward the windows of Lilian's apartment.

"I came to recharge. I had a horrible fight with Márcia yesterday." She threw the coconut away and, imitating Lilian, she pulled her face back with her hands, "*That bastard, the daughter of a madman and a loony* . . . She hates Márcia, she doesn't know I live with her. She thinks I'm staying at a hotel, that I study literature. She doesn't care about me."

"Nobody cares about anyone, darling."

"But she's my mother. You didn't tell her anything, did you?"

"Nothing, I didn't say a thing—" I was going to say something else when a big commotion broke out. A police car stopped, the siren turned up full blast, another car pulled out at high speed, tires screeching on the asphalt, some people ran, children screamed.

In the blue afternoon air, a shot rang out.

"Run," Patrícia cried, and took off running too. From far away, among people running in all directions, she shouted again, "If I die, tell Márcia no woman was ever loved as much as her."

I ran. Kidnapping, they were screaming, holdup, they got the dealers. A vendor closed his cart, green coconuts rolled down the sidewalk, I stepped on one, almost fell to the ground, kept running, the palms of my hands scraped, I heard more shots, a woman went by crying. When I became aware of my surroundings again I was in the plaza that opens onto Arpoador beach. I'd lost Patrícia, as well as the desire to go to São Conrado, Laranjeiras, Botafogo, or anywhere else in that Beirut. All I wanted was to go straight back to São Paulo. There at least, I thought. But didn't know what came next.

The plaza was calmer. Half dazed by the vodka and the running, I began to walk toward the green metal fence that separates the plaza from the ocean. And on the rocks of Arpoador, all dressed in white, her blond hair and dress billowing in the late afternoon breeze, silhouetted against the night drifting in from the other side of the ocean, was Dulce Veiga. I grabbed the bars, like a prisoner. She raised her right arm in the air, her hand half closed. When her arm was completely outstretched, she opened her hand and released a white dove. For a second the dove's wings reflected the sun's rays, filtered by the buildings on the other side of the street. Then it disappeared in the blue, among the seagulls. Blown by the wind, Dulce Veiga's hair covered her face. She shook her head until her face was free again. Through the fence, even though she was far away, beyond the street on the other side of the plaza, on the cliffs still hot from the sun, I distinctly heard her cry something like:

"Epa, epa, epa babá!"

I could have climbed the fence, jumped over it. But the police were patrolling the plaza and the streets around it, and that would have been very suspicious. The last thing I wanted was to end up at the police station. I turned back, looking for the entrance or exit to the plaza. Once again, I got lost among the flower beds, dogs, and nannies, and when I finally managed to find it, the entrance, the exit, to go back by the side path that led to the beach, Dulce Veiga was no longer there.

Some surfers were floating in the water, the sunlight filtered through the buildings on Vieira Souto.

Maybe right now, I thought, on the other side of the rocks, on the other side of the Fort, she is walking in the sand, barefoot, singing something like *Copacabana, little princess of the sea, in the morn-*

ing you are life's song, accompanied only by the sound of the waves breaking on the beach. Very white, her feet sink in the damp sand at the exact point where the waves break. The wind blows through her white clothes, drops of sea and salt spatter her face, everything smells of the sea. She doesn't feel, see, or hear anything but the song she's singing, dedicated to something that no longer exists, is no longer there. Like a requiem.

I heard more shots in the distance.

I knew looking for her was pointless. So I walked down to the beach, took off my tennis shoes, my socks, rolled up the bottoms of my pants, walked into the ocean, and washed my face seven times, in the seventh wave, with the cold salty water of Guanabara Bay.

51

From afar, in the waiting line at Santos Dumont Airport, I saw Patrícia take her boarding pass and disappear through the gate. I breathed a sigh of relief, all I needed was for her to have died in the gunfire. At least half of Rio de Janeiro seemed to have decided to spend the weekend in São Paulo. After what I'd seen, I thought it was a great idea. And, leaning against a column, I tried to make the drop of mercury go inside the maze until my number was called. I kept trying on the plane, but the light turbulence made the drop bump against the sides of the box and break into countless new drops.

I tried in the cab—impossible. Getting the whole drop inside the maze without it breaking into many others required absolute concentration and almost complete immobility. I waited until I got home, suddenly succeeding in doing that had become a matter of life or death. Life or death was an exaggeration, but sanity or madness, no.

To reach the center, without breaking up in a thousand fragments on the way. Complete, total. Without leaving any pieces behind.

There were ways, tricks. Even if the drop split before entering the maze, it was possible to make a part of it wait, in there, for its lost parts, which came little by little and merged with it. At that point join them into one, then make the single drop slide, with the utmost gentleness and precision, between the walls of the maze, toward the exact geometric center. I don't know how long that went on. My eyes and shoulders ached.

Then, suddenly, it was there. Right in the center, I had succeeded. Sitting there, whole, the mercury drop had a strange shape. Like a capital P typed over a capital L, like this: ♇. I had seen that mark before, I thought, and it took me a while to remember Vita Sackville-West's tail on the astrological chart made by Patrícia. There was a symbol like that on it. It wasn't Neptune, which I remembered. Neptune was the trident, the red lines. Maybe Uranus, I thought, or perhaps Pluto, I was almost sure. Pluto, Hades, lord of the underworld, a coin beneath the dead person's tongue to pay Charon for the crossing of the river Styx toward Persephone.

I crossed myself. I was getting weird.

Even though filthy, sweaty, my hair thick with the salt air, I was still dressed in white. I left the maze right in the center of the table, exactly on top of the *g* of *Armageddon*, Márcia's album. It was past eleven when I finally left home.

52

It was raining hard when I got to Liberdade. Rainwater and steam clouded the lilac neon of the atomic mushroom in front of the Hiroshima. From the half-open cab window I heard the heavy sound of the Toothed Vaginas pouring out the *Great Babylon* refrain. I was undecided between getting out in the rain to face another drugs and rock 'n' roll scene, without the sex, or go back home, forget about it all, and look for the last Lexotan and the record of Chet Baker singing "My Funny Valentine."

Then Márcia ran out to the sidewalk, with Patrícia behind her. Crouched in the Volkswagen Bug's back seat, I pricked up my ears.

"You've got to come back, don't be crazy. The show's almost over."

Márcia was still dressed in her stage clothes. The rain was beginning to wash off the white makeup on her face.

"I can't, Iracema said he's very sick. Wrecking everything, calling for me like a lunatic."

"Just half an hour longer. I'll take you there."

Márcia started looking for a cab. She was completely out of control.

"Don't you understand? There's no time, I need to get the smack."

A cab pulled up, splashing water over the two of them. Patrícia was shouting:

"But what do I do? You're the singer. And we need to talk, decide about our life."

Márcia got in the cab. From the window, she said:

"Let them finish the show alone. Tell them I got sick, make up something. We'll talk later."

Patrícia tried to kiss her, she rolled up the window. The cab pulled away and left. In the middle of the street, Patrícia called out her name again, then hung her head, kicked the fender of a car and went back into the Hiroshima. Then I touched the driver's shoulder and spoke, at last, the line I had dreamed of for at least thirty years:

"Follow that car."

He looked at me like I was completely crazy. I had to repeat it three times, too many for a cliché. He started, he was from the Northeast. The scene of the car chase, shot from a helicopter. Tires screeching around the curves, percussion and frenetic music, a crane slowly going up. But there was no danger in the empty streets, and the beat-up Bug I was in didn't even have a radio. I lit a cigarette, the hick told me to put it out.

Márcia's cab took Avenida Liberdade, wandered around a little, and ended up at the beginning of the nearly deserted Avenida Paulista. In the middle of the night, with the top of the TV tower invisible among the low clouds, you could only see the beams of light piercing the mist. In front of the MASP Museum of Modern Art I wished for a moment that what I was thinking wouldn't turn out to be true, that Márcia's cab would suddenly take Rua Augusta and head downtown, and maybe I'd forget about it all and go hang out in front of the Kenya Bar, drink a beer with Jacyr and the Rasta, or else that the cab would keep going, all the way down Avenida Dr. Arnaldo, as far as the Sumaré section, stop on a suspicious side street, some unknown house, or instead go on as far as Lapa, cross the Marginal riverside freeway to go up to Freguesia do Ó, where she'd pick up the dope at her own place, maybe stashed behind the poster of Janis Joplin or Jim Morrison. But, just as I feared, they went down the Bela Cintra tunnel, and among the colorful graffiti—*Alex Vallauri lives,* I suddenly read—when the cab still might have gone straight, it made a left turn and drove down Avenida Rebouças. It speeded up. When it crossed the bridge over the Pinheiros River and reached Morumbi, I was so certain I began to shake as if I had a fever.

Márcia's cab stopped exactly in front of 58 Avenida das Magnólias. Even in that rain, which was coming down harder and harder, only a blind man would have missed the pink neon 58 shining in the dark, beneath the cascade of luxuriant ferns pouring over the cement wall on which someone had written *Turk-off.* The enormous dick kept spurting dollars. Márcia got out.

It was Rafic's house.

Midnight, I saw on the car clock. I told the driver to go straight to Bom Retiro.

VI

SATURDAY

Vague Star of the North

53

The room was in a shambles. Shreds of the magazine covers and newspaper clippings from the walls were scattered all over the floor among pieces of the record player. The old dresses, scarves, hats, and shoes had been pulled out of the closet and thrown over the iron bed. Even though old, faded, and full of stains, the only thing relatively intact in that devastation was the green velvet armchair.

Collapsed among the rags, dressed in a robe of threadbare silk with a dragon on its back, Saul was sobbing. Sitting on the edge of the bed, Iracema was repeating inaudible words of comfort while caressing his head—and his head, without the blond wig like Dulce Veiga's hair, was almost completely shaved.

Like a convict, a madman, a Jew in a concentration camp, a terminal patient undergoing chemotherapy. From his right temple almost to the back of his neck, stiff gray hairs surrounded a pink scar, sinuous as a snake.

Iracema was startled.

"Ah, it's the young lady's friend. I thought it was dona Márcia."

"Dona Márcia is coming," I said, moving closer to the bed. From among the clothes, from Saul's skeletal body, from his hunched back shaken by sobs, from the green and red dragon came a smell of sweat, dirty clothes, stale piss, cheap perfume. Malodorous—it was an old-fashioned word, and it was the one I remembered.

"It's a good thing she's coming soon," Iracema said. "It's been a while since I called the club. I can't stay here all the time either. I need to take care of my own life."

I assumed a reassuring air, I was good at that.

"You can go, I'll take care of him."

"Dona Márcia said not to leave him with anyone but myself."

She hesitated, I insisted. I had a helpful, simple-minded face, maybe good, possibly idiotic. Iracema left and closed the door behind her. The rain was beating violently against the closed window. I tried to open it, to get rid of that smell, but it looked like it had never been opened before. Next to the green chair, a leak in the ceiling was slowly turning the torn papers, shards, and clothes into a gray paste. I thought about rats, cockroaches. Just at that moment, a lizard ran across a crack in the wall. Sal-a-man-ders, I enunciated, fire sprites, which was weird for me. The rain was falling, the leak was dripping, Saul was sobbing and scratching at the iron headboard with his scarlet nails, and I was shaking a little as I moved nearer and nearer.

I held out my hand, touched his shoulder. Like a bundle of loose twigs, his bones shifted beneath my fingers. He turned. In the face disfigured by madness and pain, only his eyes were still the same, very light brown. Once again, after so long, I felt certain they turned green when the sun shone on them.

Like that day, I called to him.

"Saul."

He cried out. It wasn't a cry, but a groan, a formless snarl, as if the pain couldn't find the words. Then I remembered Iracema's tactics.

"Dulce, Dulce Veiga."

He smiled. His dark teeth, cigarette-stained, eaten by decay.

"Where's Dulce Veiga?"

He cried out again, moaning without words, but he didn't seem afraid of me. I caressed his head, the very short hair pricked the raw palms of my hands. He stopped scratching the iron bed frame, twisted the edge of his robe. He looked like an unwanted mangy cat, like one I'd seen once, after it'd been hit by a car, dragging its guts along the curb, unable to die. I didn't know what language to use with him, I wasn't familiar with that kind of stuff, I'd never been on that side of things. I began to speak again in a gentle, soft, idiotic voice.

"Dulce, Dulce Veiga, do you remember her? She liked you so much, you liked her too. I like you too, I liked her too. What happened to her?"

Like an echo, Saul repeated:

"What, what happened to her?"

I continued:

"Did she die?"

He said:

"No, she didn't die."

I asked:

"Where did she go, then?"

He repeated:

"Where, where did she go?"

I suggested:
"Very far from here."
He confirmed:
"Very, very far from here."
I asked:
"Tell me where. I'll find her."
He smiled:
"You'll find her."
I promised:
"I will, I'll find her for you."
He believed me:
"For me."
I confirmed:
"For you, I promise."
He asked:
"Promise again."
I repeated:
"I promise, I do."
He demanded:
"Then kiss me."

He continued to gaze at me, scrofulous, serene, rocking in the robe with the red and green dragon. Maybe he recognized me, I thought in a panic. Beyond any memory or desire, he continued to look deep into my eyes. Like someone who's going to die the next minute might ask a stranger, someone bleeding on the pavement, that's how he asked. I have to kiss my own fear, I thought, for it to befriend me. Half-open, his mouth stunk, his lips covered with pustules, his teeth rotten. The face of a madman, the face of misery, of a curse. A curse passed on from mouth to mouth, which I could exorcise now, returning a kiss which was both compensation for the earlier one and something else altogether. Without understanding anything at all, I was beginning to understand some vague thing. It took courage to understand it, much more than courage to realize it, and no courage at all because, once accepted, it happened all on its own. I repeated that vague understanding in another way, like this: I must be able to love what disgusts me the most for it to show me how to be completely myself. Then I thought of Clarice Lispector's GH eating the cockroach, Jesus Christ kissing the lepers' wounds, I thought about the kind of kiss that isn't pleasure, but reconciliation with one's own shadow. The flipside of pity: empathy. Maybe I was crazy too. He was still waiting, his mouth open. I put my hands around his shoulders. He closed his eyes when I brought my face closer to his. And I closed my eyes too, to keep from seeing my mirror image when I finally accepted, and leaned over the bed to kiss that foul mouth.

Afterward, Saul moved away, smiling, and began to walk around the room, among the ruins. It was so unbearable I thought about grabbing him by the shoulders, slapping his face a bunch of times, shaking him until he began to scream again, until the woman with the Indian face came in and yelled at me, and Márcia came and gave him a fix, and something like that, hysterical, loud, violent, happened soon so I could get out of there and forget forever. But I remained motionless.

He approached the green chair. The rain had slowed down, you could barely hear it. He stood by the chair, I got up. Standing next to him, my hand on his madman, beggar, pariah hair, I caressed the serpent-like scar and repeated, very softly:

"Where is Dulce Veiga?"

He touched the seat of the armchair.

"Here."

It could be madness. Delirium, fantasy. Or a premonition so extraordinary that I barely realized I was down on my knees in front of the armchair. I slowly lifted the seat cushion. There was an opening underneath it. I stuck my hand inside. His arms crossed, barefoot, Saul rocked rhythmically back and forth, humming an incoherent prayer.

"Saul is the salty salt, the imprisoned night," he said. "Dulce the sweetest sweet, the light of day, bright and free, amen."

I spread my fingers inside the chair, they didn't meet anything. At most a spider, I thought, small rosy mice, newly born, with their wormlike tails. I didn't feel any fear. Kneeling the way I was, my hand couldn't touch the bottom. I straightened up, reached deeper inside. And then, down there, at the bottom, my fingers finally felt something. I closed them around it and pulled it out.

It was a notebook. Torn, covered with moisture stains, one of those old school notebooks with a group of Boy Scouts walking in the middle of a forest on the cover and a Brazilian flag unfurling: *Onward!* Some papers fell out.

"In the north," Saul said. "Right in the center of the star."

I picked up the papers, they looked like letters, put them back inside the notebook, then I carefully replaced the cushion on the seat of the armchair, covering the hole. Nobody would suspect anything, there were no traces. I was opening the notebook when I heard an ambulance siren in the distance, coming closer and closer.

"The wires," Saul moaned. "The sparks."

Suddenly, like a vampire out of some cheap horror flick, he screamed again and threw himself on top of me, trying to stick his scarlet nails in my eyes. But we've already forgiven each other, I thought without fear. I dodged, he banged against the dressing table. The broken mirror fell to the floor in pieces, seven years bad luck, I thought again, but not for me, I didn't do it. Dulce Veiga's picture hovered in midair, still attached at one corner to a shard of glass. Saul was throwing cream jars, perfume bottles, apples, and old records all over the place.

"No, not the wires," he was shouting. "Not the sparks!"

Something inside told me there was no more time. I opened the door, went out to the hallway. Iracema was watching me, the snotty child in her arms. I passed her without answering her questions, the notebook in my hand, quickly walked across the room with the torn plastic couch, the painting of Iemanjá—*Odô iá!* a voice I didn't know saluted inside me—walking over the muddy waters, the route that led out to the street.

I hid under the awning of the shop next door, holding the notebook against my chest. The first thing I saw was the ambulance turning the corner and pulling over right in front of me. Two male nurses got out, with a straitjacket. Some neighbors were watching from the windows of the buildings nearby. Only a few, they must have been used to it. Behind the ambulance, a cab pulled up and Márcia got out. Even at that distance, I could see the shine in her eyes, her bleached hair, greenish beneath the streetlight. She talked to the nurses for a moment, then they went in together through the iron gate. The cab left. The ambulance driver turned off the siren, the lights, the engine. The neighbors closed the windows. The colored vibrations of a television continued to flicker through the blinds of a seventh floor apartment. In the back of the house, Saul's cries gradually ceased.

When the street was completely silent, I walked out into the cold rain. It had become very fine, you hardly noticed it. To be sure it was falling you had to look up, there where the yellow glow of the streetlights made it more visible, drawn slantwise against the dirty violet sky. I stuck the notebook under my shirt so the rain wouldn't dissolve and confuse even more the words kept inside it, letting them slide down my white clothes soaked with sweat and rain, to my feet, where they'd sink in the mud on the sidewalks, the dirty stream flowing down the gutters, and carry them diluted by the muddy water, forever illegible, to the gaping manholes, the filthy sewers, full of rats and shit, and then maybe to the polluted rivers, and finally to the sea filled with trash where all the words written at one time or another and then lost end up, useless, cast off.

I wanted to take care of the words.

Even though I didn't know who they belonged to. As if they were mine, as if they were beautiful, I wanted to so much.

54

It was Dulce Veiga's journal, written the year she disappeared. Some pages were missing, some incomplete. In others, it was impossible to make out her handwriting or the meaning of the deliriums transformed into words. In others still, time and mildew had eaten the meaning away. I also found two letters and a map of Brazil, with a six-pointed star drawn over it. In the exact center of the six points, marked with a green circle, was a town called Estrela do Norte, Northern Star. The letters, signed by a certain Deodato, also came from there.

55

"R. can't accept the fact that I've left him. I said there was no one else, he didn't believe me. He slapped me, accused me of having other men."

"Alberto and Lilian say getting involved with Saul is dangerous, that he's mixed up in things I don't understand. Ah, old loves. I don't want

to listen to them. When Saul kisses me, and takes my breasts in his hands, and enters me, I forget everything. I've never met a man like him."

"R. found out I've been seeing Saul. He said he's going to have him investigated."

"I can't break up with R. completely. Saul doesn't understand. There are things, I said. I've always worn long sleeves."

"R. said he's going to unleash the entire press. They'll throw tomatoes and rotten eggs at me at the opening, the critics will call me ridiculous."

"I received another letter from Deodato, he says the community is open whenever I'm ready. He sent a little, I tried it. It's too bitter. I felt like I wanted to be something else."

"R. says he's paid people to throw rocks at me on my way out of the theater. I can't stand it anymore. I can't say anything, The only thing I can do is run away."

"I only want to sing. I don't want any of the things I see around me, I want to find something else."

"I'm going to help prepare for the New Era. And forget about myself."

56

By dawn that Saturday, I was sure I knew where Dulce Veiga was. Then I slept a deep, dreamless sleep. When I awoke around noon I called Rafic and, with the utmost innocence, said I needed another plane ticket, I had a crazy clue, something like that. He insisted I tell him more, but I didn't give anything away. He said he trusted me, told me to look for a certain Julia at Guarulhos Airport. I called the airport, I was lucky—there was a flight that afternoon, with lots of stopovers, that would take me very close to Estrela do Norte. I was hardly thinking, didn't feel anything. I only knew I had to pass through all those stages one by one, like tests.

I showered, put on clean clothes, threw a few things in the backpack, and went to the airport.

57

After the green of the forest down below—interrupted only by the clearings left from deforestation, patches of oil in the sea, wounds on the skin—the heat on the ground felt like a blow to the back of my head. My lids, my limbs weighed tons. Huge trees outside the windows and those short people, with straight hair and small eyes, moving in slow motion in that humidity, gave me the strange feeling that I was in another country. But the real one, as if the false country was the one I had left behind.

I felt scared. I was an alien coming from the tiny neurotic court at the center of the nation. I could go back the same night if I wanted, there was another flight soon, all I needed to do was to buy some magazines and—absurdly—I thought of *i-D, The Face*: to run away from all that, to the soon-to-be-twenty-first century—it'd be easy to while away the time.

But I wanted to find her.

Even more, I felt ready for it. Like a timorous foreigner, I asked around and found out that during the last twenty years the town had grown so much that Estrela do Norte was now just an out-of-the-way neighborhood. The periphery of the periphery in the periphery of Brazil, I forged ahead.

58

The Estrela Boarding House, read a sign with faded floral decorations right above the street name and the number, the same as in Deodato's letters.

The two-story house on the corner was very old, whitewashed, with dark green doors and windows. In the living room with windows opened wide onto the banana trees in the backyard, an old parrot was flapping around a television tuned to a talent show. A transvestite lip-synched to Carmen Miranda singing "South American Way." There was nobody watching. I clapped my hands, three times, almost called out, *Hello, anyone home?* as was once the custom in Passo da Guanxuma. I don't know what it's like there today, I left for good.

Shuffling in her flipflops, a gourd-colored woman appeared, straight graying black hair parted in the middle falling around her broad face, a thick down on her upper lip. She must have been about fifty. Before I could say anything, she saw my backpack.

"If you're looking for a room, we're full."

Her face, her drawl, reminded me of someone.

"I'm just looking for someone who used to live here. Have you worked here long?"

She looked insulted. She leaned one arm against the door, rested her right foot on the other knee. The parrot swooped down and alighted on her shoulder.

"I was born here. I'm the owner of the boarding house. Who are you looking for?"

"Deodato," I said.

She scratched the parrot's head with a familiar Indian gesture. I was exhausted. It must be the heat, the time zone. The parrot covered its eyes with the whitish film of its lids.

"Mr. Deodato died a few years ago. May God keep him in his eternal glory, he was a holy man."

"Amen," I said, beginning to feel anxious. "But his wife, children, a relative."

"Mr. Deodato didn't have anyone, except for the people from the church. He was a very solitary man, very decent."

"Perhaps then you also knew a friend of his. A young woman who came from São Paulo, a young blond woman." I pressed my hands together forcefully. "Dulce Veiga, have you ever heard of her?"

The woman frowned and brushed the parrot away. It squawked a nasal curse word, three feathers came off in the air. The woman reached out to close the door.

"No, I've never heard of her, Mister. And now, if you'll excuse me, I've got to fix dinner, take care of my life."

At that very moment, just before she slammed the door, at that sentence, I remembered: she looked just like Iracema, the woman who took care of Saul. Maybe they all had the same face, but I ventured:

"You look just like someone I know."

She was eyeing me with growing distrust.

"Are you from São Paulo?"

"Yes, I am."

"I have a sister who's lived there for about ten years."

I asked:

"Is her name Iracema, by any chance?"

The woman's face darkened and she spoke angrily.

"Look, young man, there are lots of Iracemas in God's world. There are lots of people with nothing to do and plenty of time to stick their noses where they don't belong. We're peace-loving folks here, I think it would be a good idea if you left now. I don't know anything."

I took a step forward. The door slammed in my face. Inside, the parrot cried another profanity—sonofabitch, go fuck yourself, up your ass, something like that. Some barefoot children stopped and stared. I must have looked strange standing at the door. Strange, exhausted, covered with sweat, crazy with hunger and thirst, unable to breathe right in that infernal heat.

Then I gave up.

At that very moment, before the closed door of the white house, I gave up on everything. This isn't fun any more, I thought, forget about getting a room, shit. I'd already gone too far. The best thing to do was to go back to São Paulo, bury it once and for all, look for another job, maybe go back to Passo da Guanxuma, which I should have never left. Unless I got caught up once again in that maze of vague clues, mysterious names, false leads, equivocal signals, madness and damnation. I wanted something else: a simple life. My energy, if I'd ever had any, had died there, at that door. And it was with relief that I said aloud:

"That's it, it's over."

I asked the children where I could find a café, diner, McDonald's, barbecue joint, anything. They directed me to a place a couple of blocks away. I started walking down the beaten, dusty, red dirt street, the old houses surrounded by a monstrous nature that constantly threatened to invade the plots of land and destroy everything.

Ah, let the lianas come, I cursed, the parasites, the leeches from the riverbanks, the poisonous snakes, the tall, uncontrollable grass, let all the mosquitoes and fevers come, let all the dengues and malarias invade Estrela do Norte and turn that infernal place to mud, solitude, and ruin forever.

59

It was getting late, birds screeched in the forest.

The saddest man in the world—he, who was me, walked with

his head down, dragging his backpack on the ground. The mosquitoes were beginning to come out, invisible, red welts itched on my arms. I was about to sit down on one of those uneven sidewalks, among the skinny stray dogs, put my head in my hands and cry over the lost time, the lack of meaning, my defeat.

Then I heard the voice of a woman.

Not very far off, probably coming from the same place I was headed, accompanied only by a piano, the woman was singing an old Vinícius de Moraes song, and speaking of nostalgia, where are you, something like that, I didn't know the lyrics well, a song of absence, nostalgia, and loss, that much I knew, and I raised my head to listen more closely, trying to catch the snatches of verse fading in the air, carried by the warm breeze, where are those eyes of yours I can't see, I followed the parts I still remembered, it was so old, without singing along, I didn't know how, I slung the backpack over my shoulder and started walking faster in search of that voice, and speaking of you, my reason for living, what if you came to me, and I'd always been certain, from the very beginning, even though it all may still have been just madness, desire to fly, that I had nothing to lose in following a song, my reason for living.

The voice became clearer outside the barbecue joint. It was still early, there was hardly anyone. A couple, half a dozen people at the Formica tables covered with checkered tablecloths, the cool tile floor, the blades of the fan turning on the ceiling, the waiter waving the flies away. I stopped at the door, waiting for my eyes to adjust to the dimmer light inside.

In the back, between the pianist and the kitchen, was Dulce Veiga. She didn't run away, or raise her arm to the sky. This time, without interrupting her song, she looked at me as if she recognized me and nodded to the closest table. I sat down, I was dead tired, so close to her there was no need to raise my voice.

"I want to talk to you."

Dulce Veiga smiled, brushing the blond hair sprinkled with white from her forehead. She had changed, I realized. Not just the wrinkles around her green eyes, or the deeper lines at the sides of her mouth. Her jaw had lost the hardness, the pride, and that cynical, ironic, somewhat cruel expression had disappeared from her thin-lipped smile. A woman a little over fifty, wearing no makeup, a light yellow cotton dress, sandals on her small feet, with unpainted toenails. She was no longer beautiful, she'd become something else, more than that—maybe real.

Between two lines, she said:

"Wait until I'm done singing."

And she continued singing old and new songs, some unfamiliar. Her voice created a sort of bell jar that seemed to protect those around her. I waited, forgetting my hunger, thirst, as the barbecue joint slowly filled until it was almost completely packed. It was unusual to sing at that time, too early, but everybody seemed to be there to see her. Every time she finished a song they clapped, called her name, asked for more, even though there wasn't even a microphone and the piano needed tuning.

"*Ora iê iê ô!*" someone cried.

She thanked them and sat down in front of me.

"Do you remember me?" I asked.

"Of course I do. You came to my apartment in São Paulo, many years ago."

"I've changed a lot, how do you remember?"

"I've changed too, maybe that's why."

I said:

"Twenty years."

She agreed, without any sadness.

"Twenty years."

It was hard to talk. I began, but she interrupted me, saying it would be better to talk at her place. Out on the street, one of the kids from the boarding house tugged at her skirt and whispered something, pointing at me.

"He's my friend," Dulce said. "Tell your mother it's okay."

I looked up, a bit dazed. The night, the sky too huge, the equator. Vertigo, I repeated, and, who knows why, the word from the park came back to mind—*pentimento*, that was it. The full moon was rising behind a palm tree, its golden light sprinkling a phosphorescent mist on the treetops. Strange sounds came from the forest. They no longer seemed sinister, just unknown. Alive—and I stopped hating Estrela do Norte.

At the curb, Dulce was taking off her sandals.

"I always do this when I'm done singing. I walk home barefoot in the dirt. Don't you want to do the same?"

I sat down next to her, undid my shoe laces. They were leather boots with rubber soles, in the best Toothed Vagina style, which weighed a ton and hurt like hell. I tied the laces together, stuck my socks inside, and slung them over my shoulder. Except for the past Friday, on the sands of Arpoador, I couldn't remember the last time I had walked barefoot in the dirt.

I lit a cigarette and began talking about everything and everybody, hatching paranoid doubts, revealing terrifying suspicions, asking delirious questions. She didn't answer. She hardly seemed to listen, walking by my side, sandals in her hands, singing softly. At times she smiled while continuing to sing, as if she found what I said funny. It wasn't indifference, or cynicism or coldness, but something else I couldn't identify because I hadn't learned its name yet. I kept talking, stressing the sordid details, the most dramatic ones, as if I were a desperate storyteller trying to win the attention of his audience at all costs. In a soft voice, she sang unfamiliar songs that spoke of moons, stars, rivers, birds, and forests.

After a twenty-minute walk, we left the main streets and took the little road that led to her house, on top of a low hill. I had smoked five cigarettes, was exhausted, completely hoarse.

60

Dulce Veiga opened the window overlooking the garden, a white cat jumped up on the sill. She caressed it while she gazed at the night, breathing the scent that came from outside. Moonflower, manaca, jasmine.

She turned, motioned me to sit down. Everything was clear and linear. There weren't many places to sit besides the table with four chairs, a few mats and cushions on the floor. There were no pictures on the walls either, or knickknacks, or any decoration. Just a white cloth at the center of the table, some yellow flowers, a fruit basket in a corner.

One by one, all the muscles in my body ached, in detail. As if I had exercised for hours, or caught the flu.

Dulce Veiga walked into the kitchen and opened the door facing the patio. A dog charged into the living room, stopped in front of me and began to lick my hands. It was large, meek, and clumsy. I heard her voice, laughing:

"That's Dick Farney, don't be scared if he gets a little needy." She glanced in from the kitchen door, something in her hands. "I like to give them singers' names. You should have known Elizeth, she was such a cute kitty, she was like a person. She died in childbirth the last full moon, left four kittens. I named them Elis, Raul, Nara, and Cazuza."

Give me Cazuza, I wanted to say. But I could barely speak, I lay back against the cushions. Dick Farney ran out through the front door. Outside, he howled at the moon. Dulce knelt before me and handed me an agate mug.

"Drink, it'll do you good."

I saw a yellow liquid, cold, thick, sort of golden. Its smell reminded me of tangerine, almonds, wet dirt. The exact word that came to mind was: pungent. It hurt, somehow.

"What is it?"

"Tea, just tea. Drink it, it'll do you good."

I took the mug from her hands, tasted it, and grimaced. It was certainly the bitterest thing I had tasted in my entire life.

"It's too bitter."

"But it's good for you. Close your eyes and drink it."

For some crazy reason, or absolute lack of reason, I not only felt I had to do it, but I trusted her. Maybe because of her patient, maternal voice. I thought of Jandira de Xangô, a glass of warm milk at the apartment door, my mother, bread on the checkered tablecloth. She had the same tone, the same ways. Maybe I needed to quit playing the tough guy once and for all and start learning to: accept caring gestures.

I drank. As if it had glue or birdlime in it, the liquid went down with difficulty. I closed my eyes and felt Dulce Veiga's fingers drawing a cross on my forehead. Not as if I were dying, but like a blessing, a baptism. The bitter taste lingered in my mouth.

I opened my eyes. She was touching my feet.

"You're very tense. Stretch out, I'm going to give you a massage."

She touched the soles of my bare feet, the tips of my toes. So firm, her fingers, that I glanced over to see if she was using some wooden or metal instrument. She wasn't using anything, just her fingers. Wherever they pressed, it hurt terribly.

The worst taste in the world, the worst pain in the world.

Her fingers moved up to my ankles, pressed the anklebones. I vaguely thought that I didn't want her to see my feet like this, so close up, frail, ugly, I hardly knew how they could support me, but I forgot as she moved the pressure to my sore calves, she touched that remote spot behind the knees, hours were going by and I was fading, she had poisoned me, nobody knew I was there, nobody knew me, I'd be thrown into the river, it was probably full of piranhas, it was all over, I tried to laugh, dynamic reporter disappears mysteriously, I couldn't. To keep from succumbing to those thoughts, repeating to myself that it was only tea, a massage, I tried to speak again, I needed to know why, in the end, she had disappeared, and a lot of other things too, ugly perhaps, dirty, crazy, I needed to know, although I don't know whether I actually asked or only thought about it in order to interrupt those other thoughts that wouldn't go away, as if I was going to be murdered the next second, and I was, but in a different way, only in a sense, sweetly, I thought, deliciously Dulce. Before I sank into some kind of slumber, because in a way I was still awake, more awake than ever, I heard her voice, growing softer and softer, and when her fingers began to move up my aching spine, applying pressure to the vertebrae one by one, I no longer felt my legs, and wasn't sure if it was really her voice, that kind of husky voice, thick like the green velvet of that armchair that now seemed so remote, lost in a filthy room in a city in the south, the voice of my mother maybe, or the mix of sounds coming from the road at the foot of the hill, from the forest beyond the house, from the river in the distance, from the night enveloping all things, or maybe my own, my own voice, coming from within and from the pit of my exhausted brain, serene and assured, even though what it said seemed silly, almost childish, that voice I no longer knew to whom it belonged, repeated:

"They're all stories, my child. Each of us turns the story being told into another, into the story we want. Choose, among all of them, the one your heart likes best, and follow it to the end of the world. Even if no one understands, as if it were a fight. A good fight, the best of all, the only one that's worth it. The rest is a mistake, son, it's perdition."

VII

SUNDAY

Nothing More

61

It was after midnight. It was my birthday, I remembered.

I wanted to tell Dulce Veiga, but the room was empty. My body didn't ache any more, neither did my head. I got up and began looking around the house. In her room, next to the twin bed, was a letter. The handwriting on the envelope was exactly the same as Márcia's in the dedication she had written for me on the album *Armageddon*. I opened the drawer of the night stand. It was filled with more letters in the same handwriting, some, near the bottom of the pile, in envelopes with red and white borders from abroad. I closed the drawer, had no desire at all to read them, Márcia F.'s letters.

I looked out the window, the moon had climbed to the part of sky above the house, you couldn't see it any more. Just its light, faint and golden, over the forest. *Oh moon,* someone was singing in the distance. The door to the garden was open, I started to go out but, in the middle of the living room, I realized my body was entangled in gray threads, I could barely walk. I touched them. Sticky, disgusting, they left a silver slime on my hands.

I stumbled out to the garden, I needed to tear off those threads, one by one. They were cobwebs, webs so tangled it took me a long time to remove them all. My hands were sticky with their remnants.

Like coming out of a cocoon, it seemed.

62

I washed my hands, my face, my feet at a faucet in a corner of the garden. There was nowhere to dry them, so I began to shake them until I felt completely dizzy.

Then came the nausea.

A feeling of loathing, a bitter revolt at the pit of my stomach, a churning. I leaned against the wooden wall of the house, alone in the world, in the middle of the wilderness far from everything, closed my eyes, and threw up. I had barely eaten that day, or the day before. A bitter spout born at the bottom of some dark thing, in the center of something tortured, poured out of my throat, transformed into a silver snake, a comet, that hit the ground and splattered everywhere. The earth drank the poison.

I washed my face again, filled my mouth with water and spat.

I unbuttoned my shirt. And in the moonlight, in the light that came from inside, I saw there were three white hairs on my chest.

Everything glowed around me.

63

Sitting on a stone down below, near the road, Dulce Veiga was playing the guitar and singing. It was strange, but she had put in her hair a kind of tiara, diadem, a small crown of shiny stones. She had changed her clothes and was wearing a green pleated apron over the long white dress.

I sat next to her. The moon, it was possible to see it from there, was on the other side of the house, coming down behind the forest. And suddenly, in a way I hadn't been able to see it since I was a child, as much as I tried, but I had lost those eyes, I unexpectedly managed to see again St. George with his spear, killing the dragon on the surface of the moon.

I just sat there, listening. Dulce was singing those unfamiliar songs again. Besides the moon, the stars, and stuff like that, the space over our heads, I realized they also talked about creatures of the earth, hidden among the trees, in the depths of caves, within the curves of the road.

She said:

"Strength and faith, repeat with me: give me strength and give me faith, give me light."

I repeated:

"Strength and faith. Give me strength, give me faith, give me light."

Dulce asked me if I wanted to sing with her. I said no, I'd rather listen. I can't sing, I explained. At the same time, without hearing what she was saying, and perhaps she wasn't saying anything, just singing, a shooting star crossed the sky. I thought of making a wish, it was my birthday. But I had nothing to ask for.

Living things, I thought, living things don't need to ask.

64

They looked like diamonds, the stones surrounding the path from the front door to the gate and the road down below. I knelt next to them. Tiny crystals, topazes, amethysts, rubies.

Beneath them, the earth was purring like a satisfied cat. I bent over to listen to it, but I stood up again, frightened by a huge living form in front of me. A man, an animal, I thought—it was a tree.

I pressed against it. First my back, then the front. I encircled it with my arms. It was trembling, and so was I. I spread my legs, pressed my hard sex against its rough bark, then my stomach, my chest, my arched shoulders, to better mold it against me. I placed my face against it too, the top of my head where the hair was beginning to recede.

The body of the tree was receiving my body the way the body of a person receives the body of another when they make love. Beneath its rough bark there was a soft center I was penetrating.

I trembled more violently against it, and felt myself getting all wet.

65

The way I'd always heard it happens to drowning people—I was afraid of the sea—my entire life passed before my eyes in a matter of seconds. I'm going to die, I thought, any second now, in a few more seconds, I don't know how many.

Linked, chronological, like slides or film frames, some in color, others in black and white, living tableaux—my life was rolling before my eyes, day after day, one by one, all the scenes from the past week. All logical, natural, one scene engendered another and together they led me right to the place where I was.

I was there, where I should have been. Whole. Like a drop of mercury.

66

Overhead, the sky wasn't a lid closed over the earth, as I almost always saw it, buried alive. It was open and without end and full of worlds, and unspeakable except in this banal way, because there weren't any words for it, the Much Greater Than Everything.

Galaxies, black holes, supernovas, white dwarf stars, pulsars, quasars, constellations, asteroids, comets, planets, satellites, rings, points of shade and light. My head was turning, following the determined movement of the stars above my shoulders, which supported the world.

For a second I was afraid my body would continue turning as I looked up, and suddenly something inside me, or all of me, would escape without any destination, or else return to the sky, so populated that any dark spot I stared at a moment too long immediately filled with stars too.

To keep from getting lost, I opened my mouth and eyes and filled myself with stars, like the sky.

67

Between my eyebrows and my hairline, in the center of my forehead, there was a spot, like the lens at the end of a telescope I was pointing toward the people I loved who were far away.

Almost all of them were sleeping, except Saul, lying in a hospital bed, with Márcia smoking next to him, Patrícia sitting on the floor with her head against Márcia's knees, and Vita Sackville-West in her lap. I wished for Márcia to touch Patrícia. Then she put her cigarette out, spread her fingers, and sunk them into Patrícia's hair, still thick from the sea air.

Next to Castilhos, Teresinha O'Connor was also sleeping. And Filemon, completely naked, lying on his stomach. And Jacyr, in a pair of rather ridiculous short pajamas, with Garfield's face printed on them. And Jandira de Xangô, without her turban. And Lilian Lara, the scarf still on her head, all tensed up as if she were awake. And Alberto Veiga, between Arturo and Marco Antonio in a round motel bed, and Pepito Moraes leaning over the piano in the empty bar, and all the others, and Lidia in her house with sea-blue windows, among unfinished paintings, and the others before them, those from much earlier times.

The only ones I couldn't see were Rafic and Silvinha, a cloud was obscuring the lens.

Then I turned it toward Pedro, but it was still foggy.

68

I asked:

"Don't you want to go back?"

She said:

"Never, I'm happy here."

I asked:

"What is it that you want, anyway?"

She smiled:

"Besides singing?"

"Besides that."

"Nothing more: I want to find something else."

But you've already found it, I thought.

69

A rooster crowed in the distance.

I asked:

"Is that Frank Sinatra?"

Dulce laughed, handed me a cup of freshly brewed coffee.

"That one's not mine, he doesn't have a name yet."

When I had finished putting on my shoes, she gave me something that at first looked like a skein, a ball of wool, of hot snow. It was a white kitten, with eyes the same green as hers, and a pink nose.

"For you, it's your birthday. This is Cazuza, take good care of this young prince."

But I didn't even say anything, I thought.

"I'm not sure I know how," I said, the kitten in my hands.

"Sure you do, it's not hard."

She kissed me on both cheeks, then on my forehead.

"You know the way, come back when you need to."

"What shall I tell them?"

She walked me to the door, I began to descend the wooden steps.

"Tell them what you want, do what you want. Don't say anything, if you think it's better. Lie, it won't be a sin. But if you tell everything, don't forget to say that I'm happy here. Far from everything, close to my singing."

70

I began walking down the path lined with stones. The pack on my back, Cazuza in my hands. He was sleeping, he seemed to have faith in our future. I didn't have much. In the dawn light the stones weren't crystals or diamonds, sapphires or emeralds, topazes or amethysts. Common, riverbed pebbles, polished by the water. I put a green one in my pocket.

Across the river the sun was rising. All you could see was a red semicircle above the horizon, slowly climbing as it began its journey through the multi-colored sky.

When I got to the gate, at the edge of the road that curved and then disappeared toward Estrela do Norte, the airport, the south of Brazil, before leaving, as I always liked to do, I looked back once more.

71

All in white, Dulce Veiga was standing in the door of her house, next to the dog. A macaw alighted on the tree next to her. The first rays of the sun made that strange crown—tiara, diadem—she wore in her blond hair shine.

I blinked, dazzled. She raised her right arm toward the sky, her hand closed, just her forefinger pointed up, like an arrow.

Then she cried something that unraveled in the morning air.

It sounded like my name.

It was nice, my name.

And I began to sing.

São Paulo, 1985–1990

"Oh, Force of all that Exists,
help me,
you whom they call the God."

Clarice Lispector, *Agua viva/The Stream of Life*

Afterword

Of Cabbages and Kings*

per il Blepo

Caio Fernando Abreu (1948–1996) has been defined as an "urban author." His writings deal with a contemporary, urban Brazil stripped of folklore and postcard images; recurring themes are (homo)sexuality and the narrator's ontological anguish, presented in an ironic, often self-conscious narrative filled with references to high and pop culture alike. The characters of Caio's novels and stories inhabit enclosed spaces—cities, apartments, streets, bars—but their concerns and their B-class status situate them at the periphery of the power structure that has created the image of the city and the myth of welfare and progress such an image embodies. They are often disillusioned and cynical; yet, in spite of the failure of the utopias and ideologies they embraced in a not too distant past, they still want to have faith and hope.

Born in 1948 in the state of Rio Grande do Sul, in the south of Brazil, Caio belongs to the generation who witnessed the 1964 military coup with the consequent repression and opposition movement, the political activism and experimentation of the sixties and seventies, the reflux and cocooning of the eighties, and the onslaught of AIDS. As he once put it:

> I'm actually a very cliché person. In the fifties, I rode motorbikes and danced a lot of rock 'n' roll. In the sixties, I was beaten and arrested as a communist. Then I turned into a hippie and experimented with every drug. I went through a punk and a disco phase. There is no cliché experience of my generation I haven't lived. Consequently, HIV for me is simply the face of my death.

Hence the disclosure of his HIV-positive condition in his *Estado de São Paulo* column and his resolutely public stand on AIDS, rooted in the belief that it's necessary to speak out in order to desacralize the virus.

A journalist, novelist, short story writer, and playwright, Caio Fernando Abreu is the author of eleven books and one of the most interesting and innovative Brazilian writers today. *Whatever Happened to Dulce Veiga?*, first published in Brazil in 1990, has all the trappings of a hard-boiled detective novel—a down-and-out, cynical protagonist, a missing singer, slow-building tension, and unexpected revelations. It's also a book that deals with fundamental human issues, such as self-discovery and coming to terms with one's innermost fears and needs, without ever losing the rhythm of a good detective story. It's serious and funny, simple, yet ironically sophisticated and very postmodern in its often campy and wide-ranging cultural references. In this context the theme of (homo)-sexuality takes on the role of catalyzer of a number of other elements in the novel, from the construction of the story and the narrative voice to the protagonist's ontological preoccupation, which express themselves and come into being through the issue of sexual identity.

A central idea through which the author brings into question the writing process, the notion of a centered, whole being/voice and the issue of sexuality is that of pentimento, "an underlying image in a painting, as an earlier painting, a part of a painting or an original draft that shows through, usually when the top layer of paint has become transparent with age."[1] On the plot level, it applies to the memories of Dulce Veiga and Pedro that the protagonist has removed or suppressed; structurally, it points to the three storylines, three narrative voices, and three time dimensions that gradually emerge and come together; stylistically, the notion of pentimento describes the intertextuality and multiplicity of references and quotations of one kind or another, including the ironic recycling of B-culture elements and conventional formulas; while thematically it applies to the multiple versions of sexuality present in the novel and the rejection of fixed notions based on the opposition homosexuality-heterosexuality. The same complex and elusive layering is repeated on many other levels, from the protagonist's eclectic and quintessentially Brazilian reconciliation to the spiritual sphere, to the multiplicity of clues, lies, masks, story versions.

The novel's protagonist, lost, disillusioned, and appropriately nameless, is an empty shell, a signifier to be filled and given meaning. He is confused and longs for some sort of identity, yet terrified by the stigma attached to most society-imposed labels ("faggot," for one); at the same time, he rejects totalizing definitions aimed at constricting the whole individual into a known category. Given these premises, a variation on the classic quest story becomes an almost inescapable course: a quest for Dulce Veiga, and ultimately for the protagonist-narrator's identity—literary, sexual, and otherwise—as an individual and as a narrative voice in search of ways to shape its story.

The backdrop for this quest reflects the same escape from a fixed norm that characterizes the protagonist in spite of his insecurities: a cast of characters marginalized by social class, race, gender, and sexuality, including fortune tellers, transvestites, hustlers, junkies, and revolutionaries; the decadent and contaminated atmosphere of a contemporary megalopolis filled with dilapidated buildings, trash, disease, and assorted freaks, standing in clear opposition to a dominant society's fiction of family, order, and progress. The story unravels over a week, its pace set by a barely visible but all-encompassing web of signs and messages linked to Afro-Brazilian cults and their *orixás*, or gods, who preside over each day of the week.[2]

Indeed, the presence of the numinous plays an important role in *Dulce Veiga*, not only thematically but also structurally: the novel is divided into seven sections, each corresponding to a day of the week over which the action develops, in turn connected to one or more presiding *orixás*. A few examples will clarify the way Caio Fernando uses the references to Afro-Brazilian cults. The story begins on a Monday, the day consecrated to Exu and Iansã. On his first day at the *Diário da Cidade*, the disillusioned and cynical protagonist meets Pai Tomás, whose appearances are marked from the very beginning by a certain uncanniness. Reminiscent of a *Preto Velho*, an Old Black Spirit of the Umbanda religion (Pai Tomé is actually the name of a Preto Velho connected with Yorimá, one of the seven *orixás* of Umbanda), Pai Tomás is the newspaper's gofer or factotum, an appropriate occupation for one of the messengers and mediators between the world of the *orixás* and the protagonist. On this first encounter he wears Exu's colors, red and black, and the only words he utters are the traditional salutation to Exu, "*Laroiê!*" (Hail!). Exu is the messenger between men and *orixás*, the most effusive and dynamic spiritual element, indispensable to the realization of any ritual; by invoking him, Pai Tomás opens up for the protagonist the spiritual connection that will eventually lead to the final epiphany.

Later on, in the moments preceding a storm, the protagonist witnesses the first in a series of apparitions of Dulce Veiga and hears her cry out, "*Eparrê, eparrê-i, Iansã!*" The salutation to Iansã, *orixá* of tempests and winds and the first female entity to open Afro-Brazilian rituals, is spoken to enter into harmony with the energy of the storm. Dulce's association with Iansã and the storm surrounds her with a supernatural halo and establishes her connection with unearthly powers. This connection is continuously underscored by an abundance of symbolic details, such as the color of Dulce's clothes and accessories (red and white on this occasion, the colors of Iansã), her gestures, and the place, time, and conditions of her apparitions. As the week proceeds, Dulce will pay homage to several other *orixás* and preside over the protagonist's reluctant move toward the spiritual sphere.

The novel's polymorphic nature resonates the most in the figures of two *orixás*. The first, Oxumaré, reprises and develops the theme of multiplicity and coexisting contradictions. Six months of the year female and the other six male, he/she links earth and sky and thus is often associated with the rainbow and the snake, which symbolize change and the unity of opposites—female and male, good and evil, cause and effect. Unlike the negatively charged snake of the Christian tradition, Oxumaré is a positive symbol of the coexistence of opposites, a celebration of the ambiguity and shiftiness that pervade the novel and its characters. In his increasingly frantic search for Dulce Veiga, the protagonist comes up against a wall of lies, masks, false clues—things look one way and turn out to be the opposite, without the second hypothesis necessarily invalidating the first. Examples of such ambiguity are Jacyr, the teenage transvestite "son" of Oxumaré whose name (a combination of his parents' names, Jandira and Moacyr) betrays his dual nature;[3] the androgynous Márcia, a character neither the protagonist nor the reader can ever entirely decipher or fit into any one category; Saul, a human wreck in drag enacting a tragic and grotesque impersonation of Dulce Veiga; and the elusive Dulce herself, Madonna and fifties femme fatale, junkie and healer. A further touch of ironic ambiguity is contained in the dream sequence with which the "Thursday" section opens, a pastiche of Afro-Brazilian and Christian symbols, often of opposite meaning, that plays on the protagonist's (sexual, spiritual, cultural, etc.) ambivalence and fears.

The possibility of the coexistence and free circulation of opposites becomes an explicit model of behavior for the novel's main character when the fortune-teller Jandira urges him to be like Logunedé, the other *orixá* endowed with a dual identity—six months of the year a young hunter, the remaining six a river nymph—and appropriately represented by a seahorse, yet another in a long series of hybrid figures. The association with Logunedé prompts the protagonist to go hunting for his true self and frees him to accept his duality not as disruption but as continuity, preparing for the final catharsis and spiritual rebirth.

Another typically postmodern trait of *Whatever Happened to Dulce Veiga?* is the almost incessant dialogue it maintains with other texts.[4] Its intertextuality functions on multiple levels—from songs and films to literature—and in varying degrees—from quotations to references, from homage to cannibalization. The tone of the novel is set right at the beginning by the epigraph from John Fante's *Dreams of Bunker Hill*. The passage draws attention to the process of writing and provides a frame for the novel, not only by virtue of its placement, but by ending with a colon. The colon is, in Hélène Cixous' words, "the most delicate tattoo of the text." A traditionally "open" punctuation mark, it introduces a pause but emphasizes continuity; thus, cropping the epigraph at precisely this point subverts the customary hierarchy between quote and primary text by inserting Caio Fernando Abreu's novel into its epigraph and turning *Dulce Veiga* itself into a fragment or quotation. Indeed, the subversion and mirror play go even further by muddling the issue of authorship and narrative voice with the implicit suggestion that *Dulce Veiga* is the text the Fante narrator authors.

There is one more vista the colon opens up. What follows the actual Fante passage in *Dreams of Bunker Hill*, in fact, is yet another quote, from Lewis Carroll's *Through the Looking Glass*:

> "The time has come," the Walrus said,
> "To talk of many things:
> Of shoes—and ships—and sealing wax—
> Of cabbages—and kings—"

The virtual presence of the second(ary) quote playfully adds yet another layer to the intertextual and fragmentary character of Abreu's novel, stressing even further that what is to follow will be equally hybrid and whimsically disrespectful of all hierarchies and sanctioning the free coexistence of cabbages and kings—of many mirrors and disparate texts, voices, sexual orientations, versions of reality, and culture.

The second major instance of intertextuality occurs within the novel, with the references to *Kiss on the Pavement*, the 1960 play by Nelson Rodrigues in which the ghost of homosexuality brings out and exacerbates moral conflicts. The event that sets off the mechanism of tragedy: before dying, the victim of an automobile accident begs Arandir, a stranger who comes to his aid, to kiss him on the mouth. The incident is subsequently recast in a lurid and sensationalist light by an unscrupulous, power-hungry journalist and a corrupt cop, who turn Arandir's gesture into the epilogue of a homosexual affair and set in motion a chain of rumors and false testimonies that lead to the young man's destruction. Beleaguered and increasingly isolated at home, at work, and in society at large, Arandir loses the trust and support of his wife Selminha and is eventually murdered by his father-in-law, Aprigio, ostensibly to defend his daughter's honor, in actuality because of his suppressed homosexual desire for and jealousy of the younger man. In a world dominated by prejudice, Aprigio's homosexuality is aggravated even further by the fact that the man he loves is his daughter's husband. Thus, murdering Arandir is the only way to achieve deliverance and recover a measure of inner peace; a ceremonial cleansing, not only for Aprigio, who's merely the material executor, but for all the characters in the play and for society itself, with Arandir as the ritual scapegoat, the victim sacrificed on the altar of the collective fear of transgression.

Nelson Rodrigues' representation and use of homosexuality inscribes itself in a Catholic discourse of guilt and transgression that also intersects *Dulce Veiga*. Another shared theme is the sense of isolation brought on by societal pressures and the importance of remaining faithful to one's convictions and individuality regardless of the consequences, notions dramatized by the kiss passed from Saul to the protagonist to Filemon, and then from the protagonist back to Saul. The kiss passed on from one man to the other like a torch or baton in a relay and reprised in Alberto Veiga's revisitation of the Nelson Rodrigues play is another structural element ironically reminiscent of Christian imagery and themes that links the spiritual leitmotif to the theme of homosexuality. In keeping with the rest of the book, the recurring image of the kiss is also a complex and multivalent element, a sort of mark of Cain, both a curse and a sign of distinction,[5] and ultimately a symbol of acceptance and redemption.

As for Arandir's kiss to the dying man, the protagonist's second kiss to Saul, in fact, no longer suggests initiation or pleasure, but an act that counters fear with acceptance of the (impure) other and ultimately of one's own self.

It is in this context that the reference to Clarice Lispector's novel *The Passion According to GH* is couched. The act of eating the cockroach becomes for GH an epiphany of acceptance and a way of overcoming her crisis by moving beyond the sphere of the individual. The protagonist of *Dulce Veiga* moves a step toward a new equilibrium through an analogous recuperation of the raw dimension of reality by kissing Saul: understanding and conquering his repugnance is a way to exorcise the curse by returning a kiss that is both a payback and something altogether different, a "reconciliation with one's own shadow."

These motifs form the core of a collage of references to various aspects of spirituality, ranging from religion (the Judeo-Christian tradition and the Afro-Brazilian cults) to mythology and astrology that slowly build up, often accompanied by an ironic counterpoint of sorts, to reach a crescendo that culminates in the final cathartic experience bringing together earth and sky, the spiritual and the physical.

The novel's grand finale takes place on the eve of the protagonist's birthday, when he experiences a state of near death and a spiritual rebirth. The vehicle for this experience, Dulce Veiga's bitter drink, points to one more aspect of the spiritual syncretism present in the novel. Dulce's tea, in fact, is reminiscent of ayahuasca, a drink that has been used for centuries by the native peoples of the Amazon rain forest as a means of both healing and spiritual enlightenment. More recently, ayahuasca has been used in the rituals of the Santo Daime religion, a Christian doctrine blended with native cults established in the thirties and characterized by a profound reverence for nature. The word "Daime," the name of the cult as well as the drink, comes from an invocation that recurs in the prayers of the followers of Santo Daime: *"Dai-me força, dai-me amor, dai-me luz"*—"give me strength, give me love, give me light." In the past twenty years or so the cult has spread throughout Brazil and has become well known for its work in helping people overcome alcohol and drug addictions and address physical and spiritual suffering. Although Caio Fernando Abreu purposely makes no explicit reference to Santo Daime, the novel is rife with allusions to it: Deodato and his mysterious community in the aptly named Estrela do Norte,[6] for example, are reminiscent of the cult's founder Mestre Irineu Serra and his work; Dulce, with her apparitions and final transfiguration as a sort of nature queen, is evocative of the female figure identified with the Virgin Mary, the Queen of the Forest, and Iemanjá presiding over Santo Daime; and finally, the protagonist's appeal for strength, faith, and light at the end of his journey to the north of Brazil echoes the doctrine's standard invocation, down to the repetition of the word *dai-me* (give me).

The magical, hallucinatory night in Estrela do Norte is also inscribed in the sign of Pluto and heralded by the maze game, whose mercury drop, once it finally reaches the center, has a shape resembling a capital P overlaying a capital L, ♇, the symbol for Pluto. In astrology this planet rules three important mysteries of life—sex, death, and rebirth—and links them to each other. One level of death symbolized by Pluto is the physical death of an individual, which occurs so that he can be reborn into another body to further his spiritual development on another plane; another is the metaphorical death and consequent "rebirth" of one's old self when one realizes the deeper significance of life. According to astrologers, Pluto signifies our perspective on the inner and outer worlds and, centered as it is on the deeper mysteries of life, it can show us how to attain a deeper understanding of the spiritual in our life.

This is not, however, a happy ending new-age style with a born-again hero riding into the sunrise after a night of communion with a higher power. A reality check of sorts comes from Dulce's parting gift to the protagonist of a white kitten named after Cazuza (1958–1990), a singer and composer and the first figure of renown in Brazil to publicly acknowledge having AIDS. Thus, the kitten functions as a reminder of what's to come: the new life will still be fraught with difficulties and pain; the important difference is the protagonist's newfound strength and self-awareness, his determination to go on and face what lies ahead, even though he entertains no false hopes about his future. Rather, along with his newly restored name and ability to sing, he seems to have found a new sense of self, to have come to terms with who he is.

The true end of the book, however, comes with the final epigraph from Clarice Lispector's *The Stream of Life*, which completes and closes the frame established with the Fante quote. It is not by accident that another reference to Lispector arises at this point. *The Stream of Life*, in fact, is also the story of a rebirth and of the search for "purification through putrefaction." Thus the denouement of *Dulce Veiga* and the second epigraph are the logical unfolding of the protagonist's epiphanic moment of acceptance when he kisses abject, roach-like Saul. As his quest approaches its final stages, its spiritual quality and the conscious search for the supra-individual become more apparent, until the climactic mystical experience in Estrela do Norte and the invocation of Lispector's passage, underscoring the need to acknowledge a higher power and a conscious move to the metaphysical plane.

Adria Frizzi

Notes

*I would like to thank Cristina Ferreira Pinto for introducing me to Caio Fernando Abreu's work and instigating the translation of the present novel; Jorge Schwartz for his invaluable help in practical and theoretical matters alike; Douglas Messerli, John O'Brien, Charles Perrone, and Naomi Lindstrom for reading the translation manuscript in part or its entirety and offering suggestions and corrections. I am also indebted to João J. Spinelli and Rômulo Fialdini for their generous offer of time and resources toward securing the cover for this book; to Fernando Arenas for sharing his then unpublished essay on Caio Fernando Abreu; to Leonardo Mendes for his suggestions on a number of linguistic and cultural problems; to Heather Butler and Enylton de Sá Rego for direct and indirect feedback on this essay; to the Austin Film Society, Rosenthal Alves, Talya Escogido, Richard Graham, David Jackson, Jan Kielty, Egídio Leitão, David Pardue, Rafael Ríos, Carol Todzia, and the many others who patiently answered my questions on matters ranging from film to topography, from journalese to cuisine, from pharmaceuticals to gay slang, games, and botany. Support for this translation was provided by a grant of the Fundação Biblioteca Nacional, for which I am grateful. Special thanks go to REYoung, Bebo, and Exu (*Laroiê!*) for tirelessly reading, editing, and criticizing the translation in each of its incarnations and for teaching me everything I know about the English language.

1. *American Heritage Dictionary*, third edition. The choice of the word pentimento, Italian for repentance, and the way it recurs in the protagonist's thoughts is worth noting. It resonates with Joycean echoes—Stephen Dedalus' agenbite of inwit or remorse of conscience, which signifies "the repeated bite, self-inflicted, the wound of in-looking, the hurt of self-analysis, self knowledge" (http://puniho.www.co.nz/agenbite.htm), all emotions very familiar to *Dulce Veiga*'s protagonist. Pentimento is also more spiritually/religiously charged than palimpsest, for example, thus fitting the protagonist's state of mind, one of regret, and the guilt-ridden atmosphere of a largely Catholic society.

2. For explanations of some of the names, words, and phrases related to Afro-Brazilian cults that appear in the novel, see the Glossary included at the end of this book.

3. The practice of combining the parents' names is quite common in Brazil; in Jacyr's case, however, it assumes a special significance by epitomizing the character's eminently hybrid nature.

4. This dialogue, in fact, is established from the very beginning with the title character itself, an extension of Dulce Gonçalves, the sophisticated and cynical radio diva who seduces Leniza Máier, the protagonist of Marques Rebelo's 1938 novel *A estrela sobe* (The Star Rises).

5. I'm thinking here of Hermann Hesse's rereading of the mark in *Demian* as signaling difference, a token of distinction rather than punishment, that precisely because of the bearer's otherness becomes frightening to most and consequently a curse.

6. The significance of the journey to a remote place named after the north star is apparent. Filmgoers might remember Estrela do Norte as another questing pair's final destination in the 1998 Walter Salles feature *Central Station*.

Glossary

Aroboboi! Salutation to Oxumaré, Xangô's servant. Duality is the basic concept associated with this *orixá*: male and female, good and evil, renewal and substitution. As a male he is identified with the rainbow, which links earth and sky; as a female, with the snake. In Africa the rainbow is considered the great snake of the depths that comes to drink the sky, and it is also represented as a snake biting its tail. "Good" snakes are consecrated to Oxumaré, who does not share the negative associations with sin of the Christian tradition. *Orixá* of movement, action, and eternal transformation. His day is Tuesday, his colors green and yellow.

Aroboboi Oxumaré aroboboi . . . Prayer to obtain the blessing of various *orixás*, among whom are Ifá; Oxumaré; Iansã; Exu; Oxum; Iemanjá; Obá, the least loved of Xangô's wives, associated with turbulent waters, passion, and suffering; and Ossanha, male *orixá* of medicine.

Axeturá, Ejionilê Names describing some of the positions in which the cowry divination shells can fall.

Epa, epa, epa babá! Salutation to Oxalá, father of all *orixás* and responsible for the creation of all human beings. God of whiteness (which includes all colors), of origin, creation, totality. He presides over initiation rites that have as an objective the mystical rebirth of the followers. Associated with Jesus Christ. With Iemanjá, he forms the sacred couple that engendered most *orixás*. His day is Friday.

Eparrê, eparrê-i, Iansã! Salutation to Iansã, warrior goddess of winds and storms and first female *orixá*, in order to enter in harmony with the energy of the storm. Her day is Monday and her colors are red and white.

Ifá *Orixá* of divination and destiny presiding over the shell divination ritual. According to myths, he has sixteen eyes, like the gates of the future, which is why this number is so important in the divination process. His day is Thursday.

Kaô kabiesile! Salutation to Xangô, god of thunder and lightning, also worshipped as god of justice. His day is Wednesday, his colors red and white.

Laroiê! Salutation to Exu, the messenger between men and *orixás*. Erroneously identified with the devil. His day is Monday and his colors are black, symbolizing knowledge, and red, courage.

Logunedé Male/Female *orixá*, child of Oxum and Oxóssi, from whom he/she derives his/her characteristics. He/She shares with Oxumaré a dual identity, living six months in the forest (like Oxóssi), and six months beneath the waters of a river (like Oxum). His/Her day is Thursday, colors are yellow and light blue.

Ogum iê! Salutation to Ogum, warrior and *orixá* of the streets. He favors struggles and searches of every kind. His day is Tuesday, his color dark blue. Often identified with St. George.

Okê arô! Salutation to Oxóssi, *orixá* of hunting and the woods, associated with night and the moon. He represents the constant search for knowledge and changes in lifestyle. His day is Thursday, his color green.

Odô iá! Salutation to Iemanjá, goddess of sea waters and mother of most *orixás*, identified with the Virgin Mary. Her day is Saturday, her colors are white and light blue.

Ora iê iê ô! Salutation to Oxum. One of Xangô's wives, *orixá* of sweet water and goddess of beauty, riches, and fertility. Her day is Saturday, her color golden yellow. Both Iemanjá and Oxum are mother figures, but while Oxum is the protectress of infants, Iemanjá's mother role is associated with the rest of a person's life and education.

Orixá Any of the divinities of Afro-Brazilian religions.